"A wonderful contemporary drama with great characters, a touching romance, and the beginnings of a fantastic series."
—*Romance Around the Corner*

"A sizzling good time. Kantra's story building is excellent."
—*Publishers Weekly*

"Virginia Kantra is an autobuy author who has never let me down. Her skillfully crafted, character-driven stories and knack for creating a vivid sense of time and place bring readers into the heart of her stories and the hearts of the characters who populate them. I highly recommend it."
—*The Romance Dish*

"A thoroughly wonderful read." —*BookPage*

AND FOR THE NOVELS OF VIRGINIA KANTRA

"Brilliantly sensual and hauntingly poignant."
—Alyssa Day, *New York Times* bestselling author

"A lyric, haunting, poetic voice."
—Suzanne Brockmann, *New York Times* bestselling author

"Virginia Kantra is one of my favorite authors."
—Teresa Medeiros, *New York Times* bestselling author

"A really good read."
—Karen Robards, *New York Times* bestselling author

"A sensitive writer with a warm sense of humor, a fine sense of sexual tension, and an unerring sense of place."
—*BookPage*

Carolina Girl

VIRGINIA KANTRA

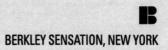

BERKLEY SENSATION, NEW YORK

THE BERKLEY PUBLISHING GROUP
Published by the Penguin Group
Penguin Group (USA) Inc.
375 Hudson Street, New York, New York 10014, USA

USA | Canada | UK | Ireland | Australia | New Zealand | India | South Africa | China

Penguin Books Ltd., Registered Offices: 80 Strand, London WC2R 0RL, England
For more information about the Penguin Group, visit penguin.com.

CAROLINA GIRL

A Berkley Sensation Book / published by arrangement with the author

Berkley Sensation Books are published by The Berkley Publishing Group.
BERKLEY SENSATION® is a registered trademark of Penguin Group (USA) Inc.
The "B" design is a trademark of Penguin Group (USA) Inc.

For information, address: The Berkley Publishing Group,
a division of Penguin Group (USA) Inc.,
375 Hudson Street, New York, New York 10014.

ISBN: 978-0-425-25122-5

PUBLISHING HISTORY
Berkley Sensation mass-market paperback edition / June 2013

PRINTED IN THE UNITED STATES OF AMERICA

10 9 8 7 6 5 4 3 2 1

Cover art by Tony Mauro.
Cover design by Rita Frangie.

ALWAYS LEARNING   PEARSON

*To mothers and daughters,
especially to my mother, Phyllis,
and to my daughter, Jean.*

You inspire me.

ACKNOWLEDGMENTS

Special thanks to Evelyn Bonano, for talking me through the stages of Tess's recovery; to Angela R. Narron, for walking me through the tangle of Taylor's custody; to Robin Rue and Beth Miller of Writers House, for their encouragement; to Cindy Hwang and the wonderful team at Berkley, for their support; to Carolyn Martin, for her sharp insights and corporate expertise; and, finally, to Mike Ritchey, for being my Sam and taking me to the Umstead.

One

At thirty-four, Megan Fletcher was determined not to turn into her mother.

She settled behind her desk on the forty-seventh floor, stowing her Louis Vuitton bag away in the bottom-right-hand drawer. Aside from her piled in-box, the gleaming surface was almost bare, every file in order, every pen in place. She rubbed absently at a fingerprint. Maybe she had inherited Tess Fletcher's compulsive tidiness, Meg admitted. But image was important. An uncluttered work space was a sign of an organized mind.

She set her BlackBerry within reach. She'd deliberately kept her schedule free to deal with the long to-do list that had accumulated in her absence.

Her mother made lists, too, stuck on the refrigerator or scrawled by the phone. But while her mother spent her days making beds and baking cookies, readying guest rooms and running errands, Meg oversaw a department of thirty people and an advertising budget of seventy-four million dollars.

She slipped off her Vera Wang snakeskin pumps, surreptitiously wiggling her toes under her desk.

It was good to be back.

She surveyed her domain with satisfaction: the tasteful artwork chosen by a design firm, the waxy green plants watered and replaced as needed by a plant service, the sliver of Manhattan skyline visible through her window. Her private conference room, accessible through glass pocket doors.

Back in charge. Back in control.

As if the past two weeks had all been a horrible dream.

She powered up her Keurig and her laptop at the same time, intending to review the latest press release about the acquisition while her coffee brewed. But when she attempted to log on to the company network, an error message popped up on-screen. INCORRECT PASSWORD.

She pursed her lips. Her password had worked fine all weekend. And earlier this morning when she'd logged on while standing at the bathroom counter, brushing her teeth. Her fingers danced over the keys again. Same result. Irritation licked like flame along the edges of her satisfaction. It just figured that on her first day back the system would go wonky.

She picked up her phone. Dead. Not the most auspicious start to her day.

Barefoot, she padded across her office and stuck her head out the door. "Kelly, can you please give IS a call? My computer and my phone are all screwed up."

"Will do," her assistant said cheerfully. "And Stan just called. He wants to see you."

Stanley Parks, the chief operating officer. Meg's boss. "What time?" she asked.

"As soon as you're free, he said. He's in the conference room now. He sounded really stressed out."

Adrenaline buzzed through Meg's blood, responding to the challenge. God, she loved her work. Another crisis brewing. Another opportunity to shine. This was what she did, what she lived for.

"On my way," she said coolly.

Full speed ahead. She slipped on her pumps and strode down the hall like a batter approaching the plate, ready to knock one out of the park. It felt good to be back in the game.

FIRED.

Meg stared blindly out the cab window at the gray blur of Manhattan rumbling by, her personal possessions in a cardboard box on the seat beside her.

Forced to let you go, Stan had said, not quite meeting her eyes. The familiar, falsely reassuring phrases had thumped into her like stones.

Until an hour ago, when she'd still held the power of hiring and firing, before she'd been escorted to the street and deposited on the curb like so much garbage, she had used the same words herself. *Eliminating redundant positions across the board*, she'd written in press releases. *Human Resources will assist you with the transition process*, she'd said kindly, passing the tissue box across her desk.

She had always prided herself on handling such situations compassionately and professionally. *I understand you feel that way*, she had murmured, secure in her job, her record, her stringent standards of performance.

Betrayal seared her throat like bile. She hadn't understood at all.

The words didn't matter. The tone didn't change a thing. She'd been dumped. Sacked. Axed.

She wanted to throw up.

Tomorrow she would make a list. Make a plan. But now she wanted to crawl off like a wounded animal, to curl into a fetal ball in the closet and suck her kneecaps. Maybe huddled in the dark beside her untouched golf clubs and unused tennis racket, she could begin to sort through the hot mess of her emotions. The ruins of her career.

She had worked for Franklin Insurance since her graduation from Harvard, earning her MBA from Columbia at night, steadily rising through the ranks, every grade, every performance review, every promotion another rung on her personal ladder of success. *Never look down, never look back.*

Until she'd walked into that conference room and saw Judi Green from HR sitting with a stone-faced Stan, Meg had never suspected that her own job could be in jeopardy.

That she could be considered replaceable. Dispensable.

This Parnassus acquisition shook things up for all of us. Stan had frowned down at the folder open in front of him. *Your absence at such a critical time for the organization was . . . noticed.*

The unfairness of it had hit her like a slap. Heat whipped her face. *Stan, my mother was in a car accident. I called you every day from the hospital. You told me to go. You told me everything would be fine.*

Derek had told her everything would be fine, too.

Derek. The smell of the cab assaulted her nostrils. Her stomach churned.

Derek Chapman, the company's tall, blond, ambitious chief financial officer, wasn't only a member of the transition team. He was the man Meg loved. She believed him when he told her this acquisition was good for the company and

4

good for them. A larger organization meant more responsibilities, more opportunities, and more money.

He must not know. He would have stopped this.

She moistened her lips, sick at heart, frightened for him. If Derek wasn't in the loop . . . What if he had been blindsided, too?

For the past six years, their corporate fortunes had been hitched together. *We make a good team*, he'd said the first time he'd asked her out at a company retreat in Arizona.

She had been flattered. Derek was perfect for her new life, intelligent, ambitious, career-focused.

After they returned to the city, it had become routine for them to spend Wednesday and Saturday nights together. With Derek, she never had to make excuses for working late or explain why she was too tired for sex. Soon she had a toothbrush at his place, closet space, a drawer. She had measured the progress of their relationship the same way she'd tracked the rise of her career. In steady, upward increments.

Two years after Derek had been named chief financial officer, three months after Meg's promotion to vice president of marketing and public relations, Derek had suggested they buy the condo together.

What would they do now, if they both lost their jobs?

She needed to know that he was all right. That *they* were all right. Instinctively, she reached for her BlackBerry.

It was gone.

She stared at the empty pocket, a pit opening in the center of her chest. Her electronic lifeline had been stripped from her along with her company laptop and corporate credit card, her ID badge and office key. She clenched her empty hand into a fist.

"Fifteen dollars and seventy cents," the taxi driver said.

She looked up. The cab was double-parked outside the discreet limestone façade of her Central Park West address.

She fumbled for a bill—a twenty—and thrust it through the plastic divider. Almost a thirty percent tip. Now that she was unemployed, she ought to curtail her expenses, she thought with the part of her brain that continued to function. Set a budget. Live within her means.

She climbed out of the cab, dragging the box across the seat. All the years of working, of scraping, of getting by, rose like a bad smell from the gutter to haunt her.

She took a deep breath, willing her stomach to settle.

She was hardly destitute. Her severance package included six months' salary and health insurance. But the down payment on the condo—an investment in her future with Derek, she'd told herself at the time—had taken most of her savings. In this economy and at her level, she could be job searching for a year.

The doorman sprang forward to take the cardboard carton from her arms.

Meg clutched the box tighter, all she had left of twelve years with the company: two framed diplomas and a photograph of her family, her makeup bag, an extra pair of shoes.

No pictures of Derek. Their relationship didn't violate company protocol. She reported to Stan, not Derek. But even though they were generally acknowledged as a couple, Derek didn't feel it was appropriate to advertise their liaison at the office.

"I've got it, thanks, Luis."

The doorman frowned, a solid, graying man in his sixties, round in the middle like a whiskey barrel. Luis had been at the building longer than she had. He might have to put up with rain and rude residents, but at least he had job security. "Let me give you a hand to your apartment."

She forced her numb lips to curve into a smile. "No, no, I'm okay."

His warm brown eyes narrowed in concern. "You sure? No offense, but you don't look so good."

A remark like that to another tenant could have gotten him in trouble. But Luis knew Meg had worked her way through college waiting tables and scrubbing toilets.

You don't need to share all the details of your personal life with the doorman, darling, Derek had chided.

But Luis had a grandson, Meg had a brother, in Afghanistan. It made a bond.

She opened her mouth and felt, to her horror, tears clog her throat.

"You sick?" Luis asked. "That why you came home early?"

"Yes." Shame flushed her face like a fever. But what else could she say? Oh, God, what would she tell her family? "Yes, I had to . . . leave work."

"I'll get the elevator for you," Luis said.

She was too exhausted to argue. She followed him down the hall to the elevators.

The third-floor, two-bedroom apartment she shared with Derek didn't provide the Central Park view he had wanted. But the space had still cost more than Meg could comfortably afford. Despite Derek's larger salary, she had insisted on their splitting expenses right down the middle.

Her parents had not approved of the condo or, she sometimes thought, of Derek. They could not understand why, after six years together, she and Derek didn't simply get married.

Meg had dismissed her family's concerns. She didn't need a ring to establish her worth or validate her relationship. The joint investment in the condo was another step, another sign that her life and career were proceeding according to plan.

She swallowed hard. Or they had been until an hour ago.

She let herself into the empty apartment. Leaning back against the door, she closed her eyes. The living room had the chilled hush of a funeral parlor. The surrounding units were quiet, everyone at work. No scraping furniture penetrated into the apartment, no footsteps, no chattering TVs, only the muted sounds of traffic drifting from the street.

What was she supposed to do with herself in the middle of the day? What was she going to do?

She took off her shoes, her jacket, her earrings, divesting herself of her corporate armor piece by piece. Without it she felt naked. Vulnerable.

She wandered through the apartment like a sleepwalker, her limbs weighted by lethargy, her body infected by an odd, internal restlessness.

She couldn't eat. Couldn't text or call or go on-line. They'd never bothered to pay for a landline or personal computer. Why should they? The company provided everything. Now, even if she'd had her BlackBerry, her phone and e-mail contacts, all her personal network, were wiped out when IS had disabled her account.

No wonder her password had failed that morning.

She stopped at the window, staring down at people flowing by like twigs caught in a current: envoys from office buildings moving purposefully along the sidewalks, mothers pushing strollers on their way to the park, tourists wandering arm in arm, stopping to point or to kiss. Everyone had somewhere to go, someone to be with, while she stood alone, apart, removed from all of them.

Where was Derek?

He didn't come at lunchtime. She was relieved. As long as he was at the office, he still had a job.

But he wasn't home at five o'clock.

Or at six.

Or at seven.

Of course he couldn't call, she told herself as the minutes and hours ticked by. She didn't have a phone. And she couldn't call him. She couldn't leave the apartment, even if she planned to buy a phone, even if she knew where to find a pay phone. What if Derek showed up while she was out? She didn't know any of their neighbors well enough to go knocking on doors. What could she say? *Hi, I've lost my job and I can't reach my boyfriend, may I use your phone?* She shuddered. That would be a hell of an introduction.

She paced the thick, mushroom-colored carpet. Her inactivity, her isolation, her helplessness drove her crazy. How could Derek do this to her? He must know she was waiting. He must have heard that she'd been . . . Her mind recoiled from the word *fired*. She'd been let go.

She didn't get it.

She'd worked hard to get to a place where she was indispensable, on top, in control. Vice president of marketing and public relations for a Fortune 500 company. No vacationing rich kid on the island for the summer, no legacy student from Harvard, no cigar-sucking, golf-club-swinging member of the Old Boys' Network was ever going to look down on her again. She flung herself onto the couch.

By eight o'clock, she was shaking with fear and a hot, defensive anger. Derek still wasn't home. What if something had happened to him? Her mother, after all, had recently been the victim of a drunk driver. Didn't he care about her feelings at all?

At nine o'clock, a key scraped in the lock.

She jumped to her feet, bubbling over with worry, relief, and resentment. "Where have you been?"

Derek stopped inside the door, his blond hair shining in the yellow light of the hall, his face shadowed. "Putting out fires."

He sounded tired.

She crossed her arms against her chest. "With what? Scotch?"

"I had to go out with the team after work. You know how it is." He stretched his neck, rolled his shoulders. "Christ, what a day."

She did know. He was under stress, too, she reminded herself. "Are you all right?"

He slid out of his jacket. Shot her a look. "What do you think?"

She didn't know what to think. He hadn't told her anything yet. "I was worried about you."

He nodded as he crossed to the dry bar, accepting her concern as his due.

She waited for him to reciprocate with questions. Sympathy. She didn't expect him to coddle her. That wasn't their way. But surely he would say something. When he didn't, she prompted, "I suppose you heard about my day."

He poured himself two fingers of Laphroaig. A calculated amount, suggesting restraint and appreciation at the same time. He would have had the same at the bar. Derek never did anything—even drink—without calculating its effect. "Hell, yes. That's all anybody wanted to talk about. I had a bitch of a time getting them to focus on the significant aspects of the acquisition."

Ice trickled down her spine. Frosted her voice. "You don't consider my firing significant?"

The bottle cracked against the rim of his glass. "Of course it's significant. I just meant I had a lot on my plate this afternoon." He set the bottle down and crossed the room, cupping her jaw in his smooth, capable hands. "It was hell for me, not being able to talk to you."

His breath was warm against her face. Meg closed her eyes. It was hell for her, too.

Derek's familiar scent enveloped her, his starched shirt,

the smokiness of Scotch, the cool, expensive tang of his cologne. "I wish you had come home," she said, hating the admission, detesting the needy, uncertain tone of her voice.

"I wanted to," he said. "I thought you'd appreciate some time to yourself."

She opened her eyes. "Twelve hours?"

He released her face. "It wasn't that long."

She wasn't going to argue over minutes. "You said we were partners, Derek. We're a team. I needed you to have my back today, and you weren't here."

His brows twitched together in annoyance. "I have your back."

"I just got fired!" With an effort, she modulated her voice. She was going to be reasonable if it killed her. "You're on the transition team. You could have fought for me. You at least could have warned me."

"You know I couldn't do that. I can't show any favoritism. I have to act in the best interests of the company."

Ouch. As if keeping her around wasn't good for the company.

"What about my interests?" she asked. "Or don't they matter anymore?"

"Of course you matter. Have you considered that this Parnassus acquisition could be the best thing that could happen to you? To us."

Meg gritted her teeth. "What the hell are you talking about?"

"Look, there was always going to be a certain awkwardness as long as we were with the same company. Now there's nothing holding us back. Personally or professionally." He smiled at her, unusually charming for a finance guy, and unease moved in her bones.

"Nothing except *I'm out of a job*."

His lips tightened. "There's no need to raise your voice,

Meg. People are losing their jobs all over. It's this economy."

"The economy didn't fire me."

"My point is, you can find another job. This could be the opportunity we need to figure out what we really want. Where we're going."

"We know where we're going. Or I thought I did." One rung, one step at a time. *Never look down, never look back.* "I thought we were getting there together."

"We are together. All the time. All we ever talk about is work. This is our chance to expand our horizons. Examine our priorities."

Easy for him to say. He had a job.

"Forgive me if I don't feel very high on your list of priorities at the moment." She sounded bitter. Well, she felt bitter. *Twelve hours.*

He examined her face. Set down his drink. "I know this is hard for you, Meg. This transition has been a strain on both of us. But I'm up to my ears right now. I can't afford to get caught up in some personal drama. I have to keep my head in the game."

She drew back, stung. "I'm not asking you to stick around and hold my hand all day. I'm just saying I could use a little emotional support."

He drew in his breath, the way he did when she was being difficult. "I understand. But you can't disappear for two weeks and then complain because I'm a little late coming home from the office."

"My *mother* was *hit* by a *fucking drunk driver.* She was in the hospital. I had to be there."

"Well, maybe you should think about going back to see her, then. Going home."

She stared at him in disbelief. She *was* home. "I just left

North Carolina three days ago. I need to stay in New York." *I need to fight.* "I need to look for another job."

"Sure," Derek said. "But it wouldn't hurt for you to step back and get a little perspective first."

Her face felt stiff. She had to work to keep her voice even. "Are you saying you don't want me around?"

"Of course not." His breath escaped in a long-suffering sigh. "Don't you think I could use your support right now? My job's on the line, too, you know. You can't get upset because I don't have the luxury of giving you the attention you deserve."

Her jaw ached. Probably because she was clenching her teeth so hard. "Fine."

She would not cling. She refused to whine. Even at sixteen, she'd had too much pride to beg.

She squared her shoulders. "My mother gets out of rehab in another week. Maybe I'll go down there for a little while to help out. That would certainly provide us with perspective," Meg added, unable to keep the bitterness from creeping back into her voice.

She waited, her blood drumming in her ears, for him to ask her to reconsider. To plead with her to stay.

He smiled, obviously relieved. "That's a great idea. It will do you good to get away. I know how close you are to your family."

It went against her nature to bite her tongue. But she was no longer the impulsive, deluded adolescent she'd been in high school. She didn't need Derek to fix her problems. She didn't want his pity. She wanted him to . . . What?

Hold her. Want her, she supposed. Fight for her.

Which was ridiculous. Of course he wanted her. They'd just bought a condo together.

So she forced herself to nod and listen as he told her about his day. As if a recitation of his schedule could somehow fill the void inside her chest.

First thing in the morning she was buying a computer to check airfares to North Carolina.

THE BAGGAGE CAROUSEL clacked in time to the headache pulsing behind Meg's eyeballs.

Her flight from LaGuardia had been delayed forty-seven minutes, making her miss her connection, stranding her in Charlotte for almost two hours.

She stood in the Jacksonville baggage claim, watching the same damn six suitcases sidle through the rubber curtain and circle the conveyor belt. *Clack, clack, clack.*

None of them was hers.

She adjusted her stance, arches aching in her three-inch heels, and dug for her new phone. With one eye on the moving belt, she checked the display screen.

Nothing.

Her stomach dropped. Maybe Matt was on his way. And maybe her brother hadn't gotten her text explaining she was late. But then wouldn't he be here, waiting for her? Wouldn't he have called?

Unless he hadn't registered the change in her phone number. Her coveted 917 number, the original cell phone code for Manhattan, was gone forever. She hadn't confided her firing to her family yet. It was too recent. Too raw. Maybe her brother was still leaving messages on her defunct office voice mail.

She winced. If Matt didn't turn up, if he didn't call back soon, she'd have to rent a car to drive the hour and a half from the airport to Dare Island.

The carousel wheezed. Bags and machinery thumped. The passengers around her pressed forward as the first bags rattled into sight and toppled onto the belt. A young mother in jeans and flip-flops retrieved an infant seat. A Marine hoisted his duffel bag. A sleek red Tumi suitcase slid through the curtain, looking as out of place in this one-runway town as Meg felt.

At last.

Meg stooped for her bag. Only to be shouldered easily aside by a large, warm, male someone at her back.

A long arm reached around her. A strong hand—tanned, long fingered—grasped the handle of her suitcase.

She recognized his hand before she saw his face.

Knew his voice in the pit of her stomach, in the telltale leap of her stupid heart, before she registered his words.

"I've got this," Sam Grady said and plucked her bag from the belt.

Two

MEG'S PULSE KICKED. Her nerves danced as if she were sixteen again. Not good. "Sam," she said flatly. "What are you doing here?"

He turned, flashing that you-know-you-want-me smile, and even though Meg told herself she was inoculated against his charm, something inside her melted. The mother with the infant seat stopped strapping in her child and sighed.

That was Sam for you, Meg thought. Women had been throwing themselves at him since puberty.

She should know. She'd been one of them.

His dark hair was a little longer and his body, in jeans and a black Polo shirt, had filled out some since his glory days in high school. But his eyes were the same, green, clear, and sharp as a broken bottle, and his smile could still sell anything to any woman foolish enough to buy. Toothpaste. Unnecessary luxury items. Sex.

"I'm here to pick you up," he said in his good ol' boy

drawl. Deeper and more resonant now, like Bourbon filtered through twilight. So different from Derek's flat, refined, New England prep school voice.

Meg smiled coolly, ignoring the liquid pull of her hormones. "Then you need to work on your lines. This is an airport, not a bar."

Sam's eyes glinted. "Matt told me you needed a ride."

Crap. It figured. Sam was her brother's best, his oldest friend. If Matt couldn't meet her at the airport, naturally he would call Sam. "Is he all right?"

Sam nodded. "Fine. He's taking a couple of lawyers out after bluefin."

Her brother Matt earned his living on the water, charter sport fishing most of the year in the sleek *Sea Lady II*, commercial fishing sometimes in winter in their grandfather's old-fashioned, wood-hulled boat. It was not the life Meg had ever wanted, but she respected her brother's choices. As a single dad, Matt hadn't had an easy time providing and caring for his son. And since their mother's accident, he'd had his hands full running his own business and keeping an eye on their parents' inn.

"And you just happened to be free," she said.

Of course. Sam never had to work. At anything.

Sam shrugged. "I was around. And . . ." He flashed another of those knee-weakening grins. "I always did have trouble saying no."

For a moment the air stuck in her lungs. But she wasn't a teenager anymore, struck breathless by his eyes, his hands, his smile. She raised her eyebrows. "I remember."

FROSTY, SAM THOUGHT, taking in her cool tone, the dismissive lift of her shoulders.

That was okay. He could work with frosty. Indifferent was harder to get around.

And he definitely wanted to get around Meggie.

He hadn't seen her except in passing since his freshman year of college. Eighteen years ago. He had plenty of reasons for avoiding the island, and Meg . . . Well, she had her own reasons for avoiding him. He'd pretty much been a dick back then. He'd always hoped he'd have a chance one day to make it up to her.

Seeing her again, he *wanted* to make it up to her.

She looked good, all black and white like some movie actress from the fifties, short dark hair, smooth pale skin, black wrap jersey dress that slid over the curves and angles of her. Her toes in skinny-heeled sandals were painted fire-engine red. To match her suitcase?

He looked up and encountered her eyes, icy blue in contrast to her hot nails and warm, pink cheeks.

Okay, so he was checking her out. Not the best way to convince her that he was a reformed character.

He grinned—*busted*—and hefted the suitcase. It weighed a ton. "This it?"

"I'm waiting for another bag."

He cocked an eyebrow. "How long are you planning on staying this time?"

Her flush deepened, but her voice remained cool. "That depends."

He was perversely amused by that icy tone. "On . . ."

"Things."

Unlike most women, she didn't jump at the chance to talk about herself. Or maybe she just didn't want to talk to *him*.

Not a problem. He was good at getting people to loosen up, to lighten up, to like him, a survival skill he'd picked up sometime around stepmother number two.

"I'm surprised they can spare you at work," Sam remarked. "You were just down here, what, a week ago."

Meg stiffened. Not much, but enough so he noticed. "Work isn't everything."

Another suitcase, hard and shiny as a candy apple, bumped onto the carousel. Hers, he bet. He reached for it.

"Not for me," he agreed easily. "But you . . . I thought you lived for your job."

"Family comes first."

He slid her a look as he snagged her bag off the conveyor belt. He'd expected their first real conversation in eighteen years to be awkward. He hadn't expected her to start spouting clichés. The Meggie he remembered spoke her mind and damned the consequences. "I always admired that about you."

She narrowed her eyes. "What?"

"Your family. Your priorities. The way you're there for each other."

Meg reached for her suitcase. He resisted her attempt to reclaim her bags and headed for the exit. Frosty or not, he figured she'd follow her luggage.

She did, striding with surprising speed in those skinny-heeled shoes. "It's because Dad was in the Marines. You move around so much, changing bases, changing schools, you learn to stick together."

He'd never thought of it that way. He'd always accepted her family's enviable closeness as something permanent, solid, and straightforward.

Not like his family at all.

The Fletchers had lived on Dare Island for four generations. Tom Fletcher had served twenty years in the Marines, but Sam remembered the summer Meg's father had moved his family back into the old house falling down above the bay. Sam's home life that year had sucked. Stepmom number two—pretty blond Julie, with her magazines and manicures—had moved out at Christmas, and before the school year was even over, Angela, broody, moody, and already pregnant, had been installed in her place. Once Sam might have been excited over the idea of a half sibling, but not then. He was fifteen, for Christ's sake. It was embarrassing, having a father who couldn't keep it in his pants sticking it to a woman twenty years younger.

The old man, of course, had swollen up like a bullfrog over this evidence of his mojo. *You better watch yourself, boy*, he said to Sam. *Got yourself a little brother or sister now coming up behind you. That's half your inheritance.*

It made Sam sick.

That afternoon he'd escaped on his bicycle, taking his time going home after killing a couple of hours on the beach. It wasn't like anybody would miss him. It was lame, not having a car. The old man had promised Sam a new Jeep Wrangler when he turned sixteen, but with all the fuss over the baby coming, who knew what would happen? So Sam straddled his bike at the bottom of the drive near the rental truck, watching the new family move in: a quiet boy about his own age, with big hands and shoulders; a skinny girl maybe a couple years younger; and a happy little kid who barreled in everybody's way.

The front screen slammed. The girl came out of the house and down the walk. Sam was making a study of breasts that summer, as many as he could see up close or get his hands on. This girl was too young and too thin to have much of his new favorite thing, but he liked the way she moved, quick and determined. Her hair was dark and short and shiny.

She caught him watching and looked straight at him instead of down and away like most girls. Her head cocked at a challenging angle. "What are you looking at?"

You.

He flushed. "Nothing."

Her brother came up behind her and laid a hand on her shoulder. Sam jerked his chin in a silent *what's-up*.

The boy gave him a cool look and a nod in reply. "Come on, Meggie. We've got stuff to do."

The mother approached from the house. "Matt? Who's this?"

She looked the way a mother was supposed to look, Sam thought, her dark hair slightly frizzy with humidity, smile lines at the corners of her eyes.

"Sam Grady, ma'am."

The smile lines deepened, just like he knew they would. Moms—other moms, not his own—liked being called *ma'am*. "Nice to meet you, Sam Grady. I'm Tess Fletcher. There are sodas in the cooler if you're thirsty."

"When you're done standing around jawing," barked a voice from inside the orange-and-white truck, "I could use a hand with this couch."

Sam and the boy, Matt, jumped forward at the same time.

And when the rental truck was empty and the boxes piled in every room, Tess Fletcher had invited Sam to dinner.

For the next four years, until he and Matt went away to college, Sam had hung out at the Fletchers' every chance he got, shooting hoops with Matt in the driveway, scraping paint off the old windowsills, making himself agreeable, making himself useful, doing anything so they would let him stay, so he could pretend to be one of them.

Until he fucked everything up.

Nobody knew. Meg never told. But his guilt and her silence had created a wall, an invisible barrier between them.

He had a chance to fix things now. He wasn't going to blow it.

"Matt said the island was the only place that felt like home," he said.

"Don't confuse me with my brother," Meg said. "I like change. I *liked* being a Marine brat."

"No ties," Sam said.

"No baggage. Every school year was a fresh start."

It wasn't much of an opening, but he would take what he could get. She wasn't likely to give him many chances to talk to her alone. Not until they got this out of the way.

He stopped and turned, caging her between the suitcases, trapping her between his body and the side of his truck. Her blue eyes widened.

"You like fresh starts?" Sam said. "Fine. How about one with me?"

HEAT RADIATED OFF Sam like sun off the tarmac. His dark shirt, wilted in the heat, clung to the planes and muscles of his chest. He was broader than Meg remembered, standing close enough for her to see the darker rim circling his irises and the halo around his pupils, gold against green.

Too close.

She functioned better when Sam was at a distance. Like nine hundred miles away.

Her warm flush was followed by a trickle of cold reality. They weren't intimate. He had no business acting as if they were. Served him right if she pretended not to know what he was talking about.

"There's no reason we can't be civil," she said coolly. "We're not in high school anymore. But we don't see each other often enough to make a fresh start necessary."

Or desirable, her tone implied.

Sam continued to regard her steadily, an indefinable gleam in his eyes. "We will if you stick around."

"Excuse me?"

He tossed her bags in the back of his truck, a big, shiny black pickup. Of course it would be black, she thought distractedly. Red was too obvious, silver too ubiquitous for Sam. Black was the choice of powerful men like politicians and gangsters.

"We're both staying on the island," he said. "We're bound to run into each other."

Not if she could help it.

"I thought you had your own business now." There was a bold white logo emblazoned on the door of the truck. SAM GRADY, BUILDER. "In Cary or something."

"You heard about that, huh."

The satisfaction in his voice set her teeth on edge. "Don't flatter yourself, Slick. I can't help it if people like to talk. Especially on the island."

Her *mother* liked to talk. Especially about Sam. Tess had always liked Sam, proving that even her mother wasn't an infallible judge of character.

Sam raised his brows. "I thought maybe Matt said something."

"Contrary to what you might think, I do not spend my limited family time discussing you with my brother."

Sam grinned. "Probably a good thing."

A rush of warm and guilty memories crowded in on her, all mixed up with the shadows of the deserted boathouse and the scent of musty canvas and her own voice begging, *Don't tell Matt.*

Blindly, she turned away to climb into the cab.

Sam's hand steadied her. "Watch your step."

She jerked her arm away, her chin firming in annoyance. "My brother has a truck. I know how to get into a truck."

"Yeah, but mine is bigger than your brother's."

She fought a spurt of laughter. "Very funny." She twisted

on the seat, tugging her skirt down her thighs. The cab still had that just-detailed, new truck smell. At least she didn't have to worry about tangling her feet in fast-food wrappers. Or women's underwear. "I'm not impressed by size."

Sam's eyes met hers. "I remember."

Her breath went. *Oh, God.*

Sam had been her first. Her first love, her first lover. She had been terrified of appearing ignorant, overwhelmed by the seeming impossibility of fitting—*that*—inside her. *The musty canvas, the smooth hot muscles of his back, the pinch and draw between her thighs* . . . It seemed to take him forever to come.

By the time Meg graduated from college, she'd learned to attribute Sam's amazing staying power to the fact that he was drunk. She'd even learned to appreciate a guy who lasted longer than ten minutes. But eighteen years ago . . .

"I didn't think you were in any condition to notice," she said.

Sam's gaze darkened. His voice lowered. "I noticed, all right. Listen, about that night . . ."

To her horror, she felt her throat tighten. "Don't apologize." *Not again.*

"I wasn't going to."

Right.

She yanked on her shoulder strap. "Anyway, it was a long time ago. Lots of sex under the bridge since then. What's past is past."

She winced. A little heavy with the clichés there, even for someone who read a lot of ad copy in the course of her job. But seeing him again unexpectedly, on top of everything else, had rattled her.

Sam slid in beside her, his knees and shoulders taking up too much room. There wasn't enough oxygen in here for both of them. "Not if you're going to spit at me every time we meet."

She stopped fussing with the seat belt. "I'm not spitting." Much. "I just don't see any point in rehashing the past. We've both moved on."

"Yeah, I heard." He shot her a glance as he shifted gears. "Derek, is it?"

She blinked. "Are you asking me about my boyfriend?"

"Just catching up," Sam said. "That's what old friends do when they haven't seen each other in a while."

Meg stared out the window at red clay and tall pines. They weren't friends. They were . . . She didn't know what they were. Right now, with her emotions raw and her carefully ordered life a mess, she didn't feel very friendly. But admitting that felt like giving Sam an advantage in whatever emotional game he was playing.

"Derek's fine," she said.

Never mind their awkward leave-taking this morning. Derek supported her. He understood her. They shared the same goals, the same values.

Thinking about Derek steadied her. Sam was her past. Derek was her future.

"We're both fine. How's . . ." Meg searched her mind for the latest name her mother had tied to Sam's. "Trina?"

"She's all right. I haven't seen her in a while."

"On to someone new?" Meg inquired sweetly.

The creases—too masculine to be called dimples, too charming to be anything else—indented in Sam's cheeks. "Nobody at the moment. I'm still looking."

"For which women everywhere give thanks, I'm sure."

The creases deepened. "Same old Meggie. You haven't changed."

The old nickname pulled something deep inside her. She

could feel herself unraveling, her nerves fraying along with her defenses. "I've changed a lot. Apparently you haven't."

"You'd be surprised." He took his hand off the steering wheel and gave hers a friendly pat. His hand was warm and callused. She stiffened, startled by the temperature of his skin and the leap of her own pulse.

"I've settled down," he said.

She slid her hand from under his. "And yet you're still single."

"Better single than with the wrong person."

"What is that, like, the voice of experience?"

He glanced at her, brows raised.

Too personal. She didn't want to go there with him, to presume an intimacy that didn't exist anymore. But he started it.

"You know. Because of your father," she explained.

Before Sam turned sixteen, Carl Grady had presented him with three different stepmothers. Meg had never even met Carl's first wife, Sam's mother. She lived out West somewhere, Utah maybe, or Colorado.

"I'm a little old to be blaming Daddy because I haven't found the woman I want to spend the rest of my life with," Sam said.

He wasn't offended.

She breathed in relief. "You're right. What would you prefer to blame it on? Fear of intimacy? Lack of commitment?"

He slanted another look at her. "You and Derek set the date yet?"

She straightened on the soft leather seat. "Our situation is different. Derek and I have been together six years."

"Uh-huh. What's the matter with him?"

"Nothing. He's perfect for me."

"I meant, why hasn't he manned up and asked you to marry him?"

Despite the air-conditioning blasting through the vents, warm blood surged in her cheeks. "Derek and I just bought a condo together. We don't need a contract to validate our relationship."

"A mortgage is a contract," Sam observed.

Meg frowned. She wasn't debating her life choices with Sam. "The condo is an investment."

"It's a gamble. Any time you buy property or get married, it's a risk. You pay your money and you take your chances."

"Since when did you become an expert on—"

He flashed her that sign-right-here-honey grin. "Real estate?"

He knew all about real estate. The Gradys were the biggest property managers and developers on the island. "Marriage."

He shrugged. "Like you said, I had a ringside seat to four of them. Five, counting your parents'. Enough to give me an idea of what can go wrong. And how good it can be when it's right. Your parents got it right."

His sincerity was unmistakable and completely unexpected. She swallowed, uncertain how to respond.

He turned his head and met her gaze. "That's what makes what happened to your mom so unfair," he said quietly. "I was real sorry to hear about her accident."

His sympathy ripped at her control, plunging her back into the emotional maelstrom that had followed the call from the hospital. *Meg, it's Matt.* Her brother's usually calm voice had been taut with strain. *There's been an accident.*

Shock and fear had almost swamped her. Somehow she had made the nightmare journey home, seizing on each fresh task to be done, clinging to the details of her mother's care like a lifeline, quizzing doctors, advocating with nurses, spending nights at the hospital whenever she could bully her father into snatching a couple hours' sleep at a nearby motel. Anything to stave off thinking, to put off feeling, to avoid accepting the possibility of a world without her mother in it.

"I . . . Thank you," she managed.

She pulled herself together. This was so not the conversation she wanted to be having. Not with anyone, but especially not with Sam. The present was rough enough without resurrecting the Ghost of Boyfriends Past.

"She's doing a lot better," Meg said. *If you pretended everything was fine, then everything would be fine. Eventually.* "Two weeks in the rehab center and she can come home."

"So you're just here until she's back on her feet."

Or until I find another job.

Meg cleared her throat. "That's right." She looked away, out the window, uncomfortable under his steady regard. "We haven't talked about your family yet. How's your sister?"

A pause, broken only by the rumble of the tires and the drumming of her blood in her ears.

"She's good," Sam said finally, slowly, accepting her change of subject. "You know she's getting married."

Diverted, Meg tore her attention from the flat green landscape outside. "Chelsea? She's too young."

"Twenty-one."

Meg laughed in disbelief. "She can't be. I was babysitting her yesterday. I tied her shoes."

"How do you think I feel?" Sam said, a smile in his voice. "I changed her diapers."

"Shouldn't she still be in college?"

Sam nodded. "Chapel Hill. That's where she met Ryan. Ryan Woodley, her fiancé."

Meg felt a pang she didn't want to examine too closely.

It wasn't that she was anxious to get married. Still . . .
Twenty-one. "I hope they'll be very happy."

"Thanks. They're probably going to want to talk to you."

"Me?"

Chelsea was only five when Meg left for college. She was touched the girl even remembered her.

"They're looking for a place for Ryan's family to stay when they come down for the wedding," Sam said.

So much for sentiment. "They don't need me," Meg said. "Your family's the one with all the rental properties."

"You have an inn. Ryan doesn't want his mom stuck with beds and meals and stuff."

"Well, I can certainly talk with them. But I can't promise anything. I don't want to stick my mother with too much, either. Or Matt."

"I thought you came home to help out."

When she left Dare Island, she'd been determined never to play housekeeper to a bunch of strangers again. She'd come home because she had no place else to go.

"Only for a couple of weeks."

Only for as long as it took to update her résumé. Only until Derek realized he was miserable without her. As soon as she got her life back in order, she was out of here.

"They're getting married at Christmas," Sam said.

"So soon?" she asked.

"They pushed up the wedding date."

"Oh. *Oh.*"

He slanted a look at her. "It's not what you're thinking."

Meg flushed, caught out. "I didn't say anything."

"You didn't have to. Everybody else has." There was an edge to his voice that she didn't normally associate with the King of Cool.

Ouch. Okay. Gossip was practically a recreational sport on the island, like knitting or kayaking. It was easy to imagine what people were saying about the rushed marriage; hard not to respect the family loyalty that put that bite in Sam's tone. He might be an egotistical, womanizing jerk, but he was genuinely fond of his young half sister.

She touched his arm. "It doesn't matter. In six months . . ."

"She'll be gone," Sam said. "Ryan started his medical residency at the San Diego Naval Medical Center in August. Chelsea was supposed to join him next June, after a big wedding here. She decided she didn't want to wait that long."

"That's stupid."

"Spoken like a true romantic."

She'd been romantic once. And what a disaster that had turned out to be. "You can't tell me you think this is a good idea."

"I think," Sam said finally, "Chelsea's old enough to make up her own mind."

Meg rolled her eyes. "Oh, please. She's twenty-one. If you ask me, she should at least finish college."

"She's applied to graduate in December."

"Well, that's good. But this guy she's marrying, he's, what, a lieutenant in the Navy? He must be ten years older than she is."

"Six. He just finished med school."

"That's still a huge gap in age and experience," Meg pointed out.

Sam raised his eyebrows. "Not as big as the gap between Matt and Allison."

Meg pressed her lips together. Her brother Matt had recently gotten involved with his son's high school English teacher, pretty, preppy Allison Carter. "Allison at least has accomplished something with her life," Meg said. "She's made something of herself."

"Chelsea wants to make a life for herself, too. A family."

"By running away from home?"

Sam glanced away from the road, his gaze dark, direct. "Why not? You did."

"I never ran away."

His lips curved without humor. "No, but you never came back."

Three

TESS FLETCHER DIDN'T take things lying down. But right now she was afraid to move despite the drugs the nurse had promised would take the edge off. Pain stalked her like a wolf, hungry for her bones. She closed her eyes, hoping to escape its attention.

You're a rock star, Jerome, the bald, black, very buff physical therapist had told her not twenty minutes ago. He'd eased her leg up from the plinth table, testing her range of motion. *Forty degrees. Way to go, Tess.*

Tess had appreciated both his encouragement and the compliment. She liked Jerome. A good thing, since the young man had had his hands places nobody but her husband, Tom, had touched in years. But she didn't *feel* like a rock star. Since that damn drunk driver had slammed into the front end of her car, she'd felt frighteningly frail, discouragingly old, and increasingly frustrated.

The bedside phone rang. The hospital line, Tess thought.

Meg had bought both her parents prepaid phones before she went back to New York, but cell phone reception in the rooms was lousy.

Tom cursed and lurched from his recliner to grab the receiver before the noise woke Tess.

Not that she was sleeping. The hospital buzz penetrated everywhere, nurses' voices, rolling carts, the lowered volume on patients' TVs. The adhesive around her IV itched. The bruise in her elbow from a clumsy blood draw throbbed. She was uncomfortable everywhere, in muscles she didn't know existed. And always, always, there was the faint, disturbing light behind her closed lids and the grinding ache of her healing bones.

"Meggie," Tom said low to their daughter. "No, she's fine. Just got back from PT."

Tess opened her eyes, welcoming the distraction from her pain. With her children, at least, she could be something other than a patient. There was a part of her that would always be Mommy, the woman who had answered their questions and soothed their nightmares.

"Maybe later," Tom said. "She's trying to get some sleep."

"I can talk to her," Tess said.

His gray brows drew together over his nose. "You need to rest."

Tess was tired of being told what she needed. The accident had robbed her of control over her schedule, her surroundings, her own body.

"I've done nothing but rest for two weeks," she said more sharply than she'd intended. She softened the words with a smile. "I'll talk to her, Tom. Better than lying here feeling sorry for myself."

He frowned and handed over the phone.

Tess wedged the receiver against her pillow. "Hey, baby."

"Mom. How are you?"

"Oh, you know," Tess said. "Fine."

"Mom." The exasperation in Meg's voice made her sound about fourteen.

Tess smiled. "Well, better," she amended. "A little sore."

"I'm coming home to help."

The announcement pierced the haze of drugs and pain. "What? When?"

"Now. I'm on my way from the airport."

Tess struggled to sit upright. Tom scowled at her, and she subsided against her pillows. "Sweetie, I love you, but that's not necessary. There's nothing for you to do here."

"Not at the hospital," Meg said. "I'm going to the inn."

"You just got back to New York." Tess tried to count back. "Four days ago." *Five?*

"And now I can come home."

Tess felt a blip of misgiving, like the warning beep of one of the hospital machines. In twelve years, Meg had barely taken a vacation, rarely spent more than a few days on the island. Always Christmas, never New Year's. "What does Matt say?"

"I didn't ask his opinion. I thought you'd be pleased."

"Of course I'm pleased," Tess said automatically. *Aren't I?* "But what about Derek? What about your job?"

"They'll have to get along without me," Meg said rather grimly.

Something was wrong. And her little girl wasn't telling her.

"Is Matt with you?"

"No, I'll see him tonight. He had a charter this afternoon."

"Who picked you up at the airport?"

A pause, filled with the rumble of tires or the hum of Meg's wireless connection.

"Sam Grady."

"Sam?" Such a nice boy. A little troubled, a little hungry for affection, a little eager for approval beneath those smooth manners and easy charm. But a good man.

Meg didn't like him.

"Real-ly," Tess said, two bright, interested notes.

Tom took the phone. "Your mom has to go," he said.

"Tom," Tess protested.

"They're coming with your tray in an hour. You need a nap."

She listened as he said good-bye and ended the call to Meg. "I'm not a baby," she said when he'd hung up.

His lips twitched. Tess pressed her own together. Maybe she did sound, just a little, like a cranky toddler.

But all he said was, "Nope. Jerome says you're a rock star."

"Not that, either," Tess said. "Too sore and too doped up."

He sat at her bedside and took her hands. She'd always loved his hands, workingman's hands, tanned and calloused and veined now with age. "Remember that Dead concert? Amphitheater, '74. The whole band was doped up." He paused. "So was the audience."

She remembered. Their third date in as many days. She'd been waiting tables at her family's restaurant in Chicago when Tom strolled in, a Leatherneck on leave, straight as a rifle, cocky as hell. They'd married two weeks later.

"You weren't," she said.

"Sure I was." His eyes, faded denim blue, met hers. He winked. "High on you, babe."

"Oh, Tom."

Comforted, she squeezed his hand and drifted into sleep.

SAM PARKED THE truck behind the inn beside Matt's weathered pickup and Allison's silver Mercedes. They were all back, then, to welcome Meg home.

He watched her march up the walk ahead of him with short, determined strides, her spine straight, her hips practically twitching with irritation, and allowed himself a grin.

Maybe he shouldn't have made that crack about her running away all those years ago. But the truth was, she had. They both had. Meg because she'd had better things to do, and Sam because he'd had something to prove.

He hauled her bags out of the back of the truck, catching up with her easily along the flagstone walk.

The Pirates' Rest was a two-and-a-half story Craftsman jewel from the early 1900s, like an old woman beautiful in her bones, built to withstand the island's changing tides and fortunes.

"Place is holding up all right," Sam remarked, running a builder's eye over the deck that spanned the length of the house. He'd spent six sweaty days on that deck one summer, digging holes and driving nails under Tom's eagle eye. "Have you thought about how your mom's going to manage when she gets back?"

Meg paused with one foot on the low, wide steps. "Well, obviously. That's why I came home."

"I meant, she'll have a walker. She needs a ramp to get in and out of the house."

Meg blinked, her eyes startlingly blue beneath those thick dark lashes.

Gotcha, Sam thought. He smiled at her—she looked cute, all wide-eyed and ruffled like a girl again—and said, "It's okay. I'll talk to Matt. We'll work something out."

He could almost hear Meg's teeth grind together. "I can talk to him."

"Sure you can," Sam said. "But unless you've got a building crew packed away in this bag, it won't do your mother any good."

Meg shot him a narrow look and stalked into the kitchen ahead of him.

Negotiating the screen door with her two bags, Sam missed the first warm rush of welcome. He heard Allison's pleased exclamation and Matt's deep rumble and looked up to see the two women hugging with obvious warmth.

Sam caught himself grinning at the picture they made— Allison, tall, blond, and coolly pretty; Meg, short and dark and vibrating with energy.

The screen door sprang shut behind him. As it slammed, they all turned to look at him, Meg, Matt, and Allison, and Matt's teenage son, Josh. A little girl sat at the kitchen table, a camo cap jammed over her dirty blond hair, Matt's big black shepherd mix at her feet. She looked wary and hostile, like a smaller, grungier version of Meg.

Sam winked at her and she scowled.

Yep, definitely a family resemblance there.

"Sam." Matt clapped him on the shoulder. "Appreciate your picking up Meg."

"Happy to," Sam said.

At a look from his dad, Josh came forward to grab the bags. Christ, the kid was as tall as Matt now.

"Hi, Aunt Meg." He bent down to kiss her cheek. He cocked a grin at Sam. "Hey, Mr. Grady."

"Sam," he corrected, feeling about a hundred years old. Mr. Grady was his father. "How's basketball going?"

Josh shrugged. "We're still conditioning. Coach won't let us touch a ball until November."

"You can take those bags to Mary Read," Allison said. All the rooms at the inn were named after pirates of the Carolina coast. She beamed at Meg. "I put you in your old room. I hope that's all right."

"I thought my room was booked."

"Last weekend. It's empty now."

"Great."

Only somebody who knew Meg very well would have caught that almost indefinable pause. Sam wondered if he knew her as well as he thought. Was she worried about the inn's occupancy rate? Or miffed because her brother's girlfriend was making room assignments? Remembering the warmth of their greeting, he figured it was probably the first. But you could never be sure with women.

"Does that mean Dad's staying home tonight?" Josh asked. Matt and his son lived in a two-bedroom cottage behind the inn. "Or . . ." He sent a sly glance at Allison, who flushed pink.

"Matt's been spending nights at the inn," she explained to no one in particular. "So Taylor wouldn't be alone."

Sam was willing to bet his old buddy wasn't sleeping alone, either. In his own quiet way, Matt had clearly staked his claim on the sweet-eyed schoolteacher. She was just as obviously stuck on him.

Sam felt a twinge of something like envy. Not that he was looking to get serious himself.

"We weren't expecting you so soon," Allison said to Meg.

She raised her eyebrows. At the change of subject? "Hardly soon. I'm three hours late."

"I mean, you just got back to work. To New York."

"Everything all right?" Matt asked.

"Fine," Meg said crisply.

Yeah, something there. You didn't grow up with multiple stepmothers without learning to spot when a woman was upset.

"How's Derek?" Allison asked.

"He's fine."

The Fletcher family motto, Sam thought.

The kid hunched in her chair, her eyes tracking the adults' conversation, one foot parked on the dog under the table. Apparently Sam wasn't the only one picking up on the tension in the room.

"Hi." He smiled at her. "I'm Sam."

The dog, Fezzik, thumped its tail. The kid regarded him with suspicion, like something she'd found on the bottom of her shoe.

"My niece, Taylor," Matt said, tapping a finger on the brim of her cap.

She tipped back her head to look up at him, the wariness melting in a smile.

"Luke's daughter," Meg supplied. "Hi, sweetie."

There was no big hug like she'd given Allison, Sam noted. No kiss like she'd had from Josh.

But then, Meg had only met her niece on her last visit, a week or so ago.

Luke, the youngest Fletcher sibling, was a Marine in Afghanistan. According to the island grapevine, he hadn't even known about the kid's existence until her mother died a couple months ago. Sam's stepmother Angela had filled him in on the story. The way she told it, Luke had returned home just long enough to pick up the girl and dump her on the Fletchers.

Weird to think of the skinny little kid who had tailed him and Matt around as a father. But the girl looked like Luke. She looked like a handful.

"How's it going?" Sam said.

"Fine." She surprised him by offering, "We're having corn on the cob."

"Corn and shrimp," Allison confirmed, turning from the sink with a big pot of water. "I'm cooking."

"You don't cook," Josh put in from the kitchen doorway as he returned from dumping the bags. "You boil."

She wrinkled her nose at him, clearly unoffended. "Your turn tomorrow, Iron Chef. Let's see what you come up with."

"Pizza?"

"Yeah!" said the girl.

Matt shook his head. "No more carryout. Not unless Josh is paying."

"I'll cook," Meg said. "Since we're taking turns."

Off the bench and into the game, Sam thought. He listened to the talk, amused and not a little envious of the trash talk and teasing. Even with Tess sidelined and two rookies in the mix, the Fletchers played as a team.

He thought of the way things were at home right now, no one stepping up, no one stepping in, everybody too damn afraid of the old man's displeasure to make a move, and his gut tightened.

"You staying for dinner?" Matt asked.

Sam glanced at Meg. "I don't want to horn in on your sister's first night home."

"There's plenty to go around," Allison said.

He kept his eyes on Meg.

She met his gaze. Her lips twisted in a smile. "You've never turned down a free meal before. Why start now?"

Sam grinned back. It wasn't much of a welcome, but he'd take what he could get.

He always had.

SHE SHOULD HAVE said something, Meg thought as she passed the basket of rolls across the table.

When Matt asked if everything was okay, she should have just told him. Told them. *I was fired.*

But when she opened her mouth, the words refused to come. They stayed stuck in her throat, burning in her chest like failure.

Maybe if she and Matt had been alone . . . But what could she say in front of the kids? And Allison. And Sam.

"Are you kidding me?" Josh hunched forward in his chair. "North Carolina has a better preseason ranking than Duke."

Sam grinned, leaning back. "But Duke had more wins last season."

He went to Duke, Meg remembered, along with the rest of the rich kids. But despite the schools' heated rivalry, his voice was easy. He was just arguing the way men did, to score points and for fun.

"Because the teams they play are shit," Josh said. Taylor snickered, and he winced as somebody—Matt, presumably—kicked him under the table. He shot an apologetic glance at Allison. "Sorry. Crap."

Sam picked up without missing a beat. "Duke has more players drafted by the NBA."

"Yeah, and now that Rivers is gone, they're screwed," Matt put in.

Virginia Dare Island School was too small to field a football team, but Sam and Matt had cocaptained the basketball team their senior year. Sam was more than a jock; as the only son of the biggest developer on the island, he had reigned as undisputed King of the School. Meg, two years behind, had spent that time cementing her role as Queen Geek, busting her ass, obsessing over grades, following a carefully plotted course that would take her to college, to the big world, to success.

Island kids often didn't adjust well to school on the mainland. Like little fish in the deep ocean, they were swallowed by bigger fish or carried away by the current.

But Meg's years as a military brat had given her an advantage over her peers. She was already used to proving herself. She knew how to make her way in a new school. All she'd needed was a ticket out. A scholarship.

She stared at her plate, her appetite gone. Fezzik watched

soulfully from the corner as Taylor waved her hands, telling some complicated story about a hamster.

"Then Chewy jumps on the water bottle," she said through a mouthful of corn, "and he scratches with his little claws to the top of the cage, right? And he's pushing with his head, trying to squeeze out. Only he can't, because Mrs. Webster put books on the lid. So . . ." She coughed.

Allison slid her water glass across the table. "Drink."

A thousand remembered dinner conversations, a million mealtimes, rushed in on Meg. By choice and habit, they had all left the two ends of the long oak table empty, her mother's chair, her father's place. But the food, the smells, the conversation around the table were disconcertingly familiar, like the echoes of her childhood.

Almost, Meg thought, as if she'd never left home. Never gone to Harvard, never got a job that didn't involve waiting on others, never made anything of herself.

A spurt of panic rose in her throat. She swallowed hard. She wasn't back to stay. Tomorrow she would start rebuilding her contacts list, rewriting her résumé. By the end of the week, she fully expected to have a lead on another job. No matter how stressed out and preoccupied Derek was now, he would miss her. She belonged with him, in their condo, in New York. As soon as Mom was on her feet again, Meg was out of here.

"Sam thinks we should hire his crew to build a ramp for Mom," she said abruptly.

Sam met her eyes across the table. "Not hire. My crew's tied up with insurance claims from the hurricane."

She frowned. "But you said . . ."

"Your mom needs a way in and out of the house, yeah. When does she get out of rehab?"

Matt set down his beer. "That's up to the doctors. Next week sometime."

"Good. The two of us . . . three," Sam said with a glance at Josh, "can bang out a ramp in a couple of days."

"Cool," Josh said.

"*After* school," Matt said to his son.

"Tomorrow's a half day," Allison said. "And we're off on Friday. Teacher workday."

Meg once again had the sense of things moving swiftly beyond her control. "What about our guests this weekend? They're not paying to stay in a construction zone."

"The only rooms overlooking the back are yours and Taylor's," Matt said.

"We start tomorrow, we could be done before check-in on Friday," Sam said.

"Look, we appreciate the offer," Meg began.

"It's settled, then," he said, smiling at her. "I'll see you in the morning."

Warmth spread in her stomach. It was hard not to respond to that smile. But the glint in his eye made her nervous. She didn't want to owe Sam Grady anything. The emotional cost was just too high.

"Don't you have work or something?"

Sam shrugged. "Nothing that can't wait. As long as I'm here, I might as well make myself useful."

Right. Sam had never needed to work, never held a job his father hadn't gotten for him.

"Must be nice to be boss," Meg said.

Sam's face smoothed to a pleasant mask, wiped of expression. "Yeah."

Matt shot her a look down the table.

"What?" Meg said.

"Sam's dad had another bypass surgery," Matt said. "Sam's helping out while his dad's laid up. I thought you knew."

"No, I . . ." *Crap.* "No."

A combination of guilt and concern heated her face, pinched color to her cheeks. Sam was essentially doing what she was doing, coming home to support an ailing parent. Just because he was stepping in as heir apparent to a multimillion-dollar development company while she was making beds and scrubbing toilets was no reason to resent him. Much.

"Sorry," Meg said. "So you're running two companies now?"

Sam's eyes gleamed. "No. The old man's doctors want him to avoid stress. If I really ran things, I'd give him another heart attack. I'm just overseeing day-to-day operations."

"How's the new development coming?" Matt asked.

"Dare Plantation. It's not," Sam said. "Between the hurricane and the economy, nothing's getting built. We're focusing on repairs to rental properties."

"I thought the luxury market wasn't affected by the economy," Meg said.

Those brilliant green eyes leveled on her face. "Uh-huh. How many expensive life insurance policies are you selling these days?"

She sat up straighter. "I don't sell insurance. I'm in public relations. It's my job to help people understand that no matter how bad the economy gets, they still need to pay their burial expenses. Send their kids to college. Pay off their mortgages when they die. I perform a service."

She winced internally. *Used* to perform a service. It *used* to be her job.

"Well, then, you have an advantage over me. Everybody dies. Not everybody needs to take on a second mortgage for a twelve-bedroom beach house." Sam picked up his beer bottle. "Especially not with foreclosures glutting the market."

"So you can't find buyers?"

"We can't find funding. In construction, you either build to the clients' needs or you design a project you think will make you money and try to talk the client into needing it. The old man is stuck on building another overpriced, over-blown luxury development. And that's the last thing Dare Island needs."

Meg studied him across the table. The Grady family had made a fortune building mansions on stilts, the great homes that had popped up like giant mushrooms along the coast. "That's a mighty enlightened opinion for a developer. So what does the island need?"

He grinned at her. "It's not my company. That's not my call."

"But you must have ideas."

He tipped back his chair, eyeing her over the bottle. "Not my responsibility."

She frowned, unexpectedly disappointed. She'd been drawn to his honesty, to that spark of conviction. For a moment, she'd almost thought he'd changed.

He winked at her and drank.

The conversation around the table shifted to Halloween next week. Taylor sat silent, her shoulders hunched and her eyes lowered. Maybe she considered herself too old for trick-or-treating. Or maybe she hoped no one would notice her sneaking food from her plate to her lap.

Meg smiled and turned a blind eye to Fezzik under the table.

"Lame," Josh proclaimed. Apparently the new police chief had encouraged a party at the gym for the older teens, a supervised alternative to traipsing door-to-door or drinking under the pier. "What's the point of Halloween if you can't binge until you puke?"

His father shot him a narrow look. "You better be talking about candy."

Josh flashed a smile, quick and charming. *Oh, God, he's Sam*, Meg thought. "I'm just saying, nobody will go," he said.

Allison cleared her throat. "Actually, as the newest teacher, I got drafted to chaperone. They're showing scary movies. You should come."

"You need me to hold your hand?"

Allison's gaze slid to Matt. A smile curved her lips. "Actually, I was hoping your father would do that."

Taylor made gagging noises.

Meg could sympathize. She was glad her steady, hard-working brother had found love again. But this Young Love's Dream routine was embarrassing. She and Derek didn't go around holding hands.

"I'll pass, thanks," Josh said.

Sam shook his head pityingly. "You're not thinking this through. If your dad is there, he can drag your chaperone off to a dark corner and nobody will notice what you're up to."

No, Meg thought, Sam hadn't changed.

But he *had* volunteered to build a ramp for her mother, she reminded herself later that evening as she slipped outside with the recycling. The way he'd built this deck, the way he'd labored over the house addition with her father and Matt. A hundred memories crowded in on her of Sam, sweaty, shirtless, smiling, every teenage girl's fantasy.

Including hers.

She dropped the bottles she carried into the bin and gazed out over the darkened yard. The soft night air wrapped her in humidity and darkness. A chorus of frogs rose from the trees. The whisper of the wind carried the sound and scent of water. *Home*, she thought before she had a chance to barricade her heart against the word.

The yellow kitchen light spilled across deck. She ought to go in before Matt came out or sent one of the kids after her. But she lingered, tipping back her head to stare at the evening sky. An unfamiliar yearning flooded her chest like starlight. *I wish I may, I wish I might . . .*

The points of light pulsed and blurred. The screen door opened. Heavy footsteps approached. *Matt.* She blinked hastily and spoke without turning her head. "We don't get stars like that in New York."

"There are a lot of things you don't get in New York," Sam said behind her. "Like me."

Four

SAM STUDIED THE tilt of Meg's head, outlined against the soft shadows of the yard, and the silhouette of her shoulders, braced against the night. Standing gazing at the stars, she looked oddly vulnerable and alone.

The loneliness was an illusion, of course. Her boyfriend was only a phone call away. She had an entire table full of family inside ready to laugh with, commiserate, and support her. She didn't need him. She'd made that plenty clear years ago.

But something about her pose tugged at him. The Meggie he remembered wasn't the brooding, stargazing type. She was confident, assured, and in charge.

"There are a lot of things you don't get in New York," he drawled. "Like me."

Air escaped her—a hiss? a sniff?—before she turned. Her face, sharp and fine as a pen-and-ink drawing, thumped into his chest like a fist.

She tossed her short cap of dark hair. "There are eight million people in New York City, half of them men. Even if you were one in a million, I could find four other guys just like you."

He grinned, relieved by her flash of spirit. "That's telling me," he said with approval. "Everything okay out here?"

"Fine."

The same answer she'd given her family. No reason to doubt her.

Except her eyes still swam in the light from the kitchen windows. Her long black lashes were spiky with tears. He felt that inconvenient tug again and drew in his breath.

Not his family, he told himself. Not his problem. "Okay. But I'm here if you need anything."

She narrowed those shining blue eyes. "Like what?"

He shrugged. "An ear. A shoulder."

"Thanks, but . . ."

"A full-body naked rubdown."

That choked a laugh from her. He watched, satisfied, as some of the tension drained from her shoulders. "I can do without the extraneous body parts, thanks."

"Anytime," he said sincerely. "You let me know if you change your mind."

And tried not to imagine her tight, compact body, round and responsive under his hands. Under him.

"In your dreams, Slick."

Probably. Tonight, for sure.

He shoved his hands into his pockets. "I'll see you tomorrow, then."

"Tomorrow?" She looked wary, like he was coming over to make good on that full-body naked massage.

"To work on the ramp."

"Oh. Yes. Good idea."

He cocked an eyebrow. "I'd take that as a compliment if you didn't sound so surprised."

"I meant it as one." An actual smile this time. "I appreciate you doing this for Mom."

"Not just for your mother."

"And Matt."

Matt was his best, his oldest friend. Sam shook his head. "Not only for Matt."

She pressed her full lips together. "You're not doing it for me."

He didn't answer right away. He owed the Fletchers, Tom and Tess, more than he could say. Their home had been his refuge throughout high school, an escape from his stepmother's moods and his old man's tirades. Tom had taught Sam to change the oil in his first car. Tess had taken him in and treated him as one of her own, equally quick with a cookie or a scold. He would have done a damn sight more for either of them than build a ramp.

But his feelings for Meg were mixed in there, too, a potent brew of attraction and regret.

He smiled at her with intent.

"Oh, no," she said. "You don't even know me anymore. There's nothing between us but one lousy hookup and some memories."

He took his hands out of his pockets. *Nothing between them?* "Let's see," he suggested and made his move.

MEG WASN'T STUPID. She saw the kiss coming. She could have avoided it easily enough, brushed him off with a snarky remark or a laugh.

But she stood her ground. She was no weak-willed, empty-headed coward, no longer a quivering adolescent in the throes of her first crush. If Sam needed this little demonstration to prove that she was all grown up now, fine.

It wasn't, she told herself—as his head bent over hers, as his broad shoulders blocked the kitchen light—as if she *wanted* him to kiss her.

With one hand, he tipped her chin up. He settled the other firmly at the small of her back, bringing her against him, hips, belly, thighs. Her lips parted in surprise. That was . . . He was already half aroused.

His gaze—rueful and aware—met hers. Her stomach clenched with anticipation as his breath drifted warm across her cheek, against her mouth. Her knees trembled. Maybe this wasn't such a good idea after all. But it was too late to back out now.

His hand cupped her jaw with infinite care. His lips pressed hers. He tasted of salt and faintly of beer, heady, rich, masculine flavors. She caught a graze of beard, a hint of moisture before he withdrew.

Okay. She released her pent breath. Kiss survived. Point made.

And then his hands tightened and his mouth came down hard on hers.

She jolted at his heat, his urgency. She knew better than to kiss him back. She did. But every time she tried to ease away, to end the kiss, he was there, coaxing and relentless. Pleasure rippled darkly through her. He tasted her, deep and slow, taking over her mouth, commanding her response, until her resolution eroded like a sand castle swamped by the tide and she sank into some hot, dark, liquid place. Her bones went limp, her balance crumbled as he kept on kissing her, dragging her under. Blindly, she dug her fingers into his shoulders, kissing him back, clinging to him as if she were drowning. He used his knee to push between her thighs, pressing her *there* with his hard-muscled thigh, and she moaned.

The sound shocked her back to sanity.

She pulled back, gasping. "We can't do this."

He held her close, his chest rising and falling with his breath. His mouth crooked. "Seems like we just did."

"All right, *I* can't do this." *Not again.* Her heart thudded. Was she insane?

"Sugar, you're doing fine." Desire roughened his voice. But she could still hear, beneath his deep drawl, that little undernote of laughter that was pure Sam.

She glared at him. *Didn't he get it?* "I'm with Derek."

"No, you're not," Sam contradicted, nuzzling her neck, making the nerve endings there dance with delight. "He's not here. So you can't be with him."

She hunched one shoulder, trying to ignore the tingle working its way down her body. "Stop that. Derek has to work. He can't take time off simply because my mother was in a car accident."

Sam raised his head. "You did."

She met that sharp green gaze, her mouth drying. *Because I was fired.* But she couldn't say that. Even her family didn't know that yet.

"She's not Derek's mother," she said instead. "It's not Derek's problem."

Sam regarded her without saying anything.

Right. Tess wasn't Sam's mother, either. That hadn't stopped him from offering to help. But the comparison was unfair.

"Derek doesn't really know my family," she said, driven to defend him.

"The guy bailed. He should be here to support you."

She was annoyed with Sam for pointing that out, annoyed

with herself for agreeing with him. Disappointed in Derek for not feeling the same way.

"Derek supports me. He understands me. We share the same goals. The same *condo*." Her voice was pitched too high, thin with a lack of conviction. She stuck out her chin. "Besides, there's nothing he can do here."

Sam's eyes gleamed. "Then he's either incompetent or he doesn't understand you nearly as well as you think he does." He leaned over her, teasing her with the intimate scent of his skin, the smell of sex and summer nights. His warm lips brushed her hot cheek. "Good night, Meggie. I'll see you in the morning."

She watched him stride down the flagstone path, his black shirt blending into the shadows, and pressed her lips together, trying to hold on to her annoyance. Resisting the crazy urge to call him back.

"THE TRIP WAS fine," Meg told Derek. She settled against the headboard in her old bedroom, cradling her phone to her ear. "A little delay in Charlotte, but that's to be expected."

The room had been repainted a deep blue, her old quilt swapped for the same lush white linens used in the other guest rooms. A view of the lighthouse had long ago replaced her poster of the Backstreet Boys. But her old books still crowded the bookcase in the corner. And on the wall, next to the engraving of Mary Read with her cutlass, was Meg's graduation photo with Harvard's crimson banners in the background.

Derek didn't ask how she got to the inn from the airport. He knew she was competent. He trusted her to take care of herself.

He *trusted* her. She winced.

"How's your mother?" he asked.

See? she told Sam silently in her head. *Derek cares about me. He's concerned about my family.* "She's fine. I mean, they haven't released her yet, but the more time she spends in rehab, the better off she'll be when she gets home."

"So, that's good," Derek said.

"Yes." Guilt pinched her. She should tell him about seeing Sam. About kissing Sam.

No. It wasn't like the situation would ever be repeated. Telling Derek would invest the kiss with a significance it didn't deserve. It was a momentary lapse, a onetime burst of nostalgia and hormones. She would never actually cheat on Derek. He had enough on his mind right now without her dangling some ex-boyfriend like bait, to elicit a jealous response.

Not that Sam had ever even been a boyfriend. More like a spectacular error in judgment. Like a tattoo or a winter invasion of Russia.

Meg cleared her throat. "How are things at work?"

"Busy."

She wanted more of an answer. She wanted him to confide in her, to feel a part of the office again, a part of his life. "What are people saying about my being fired?"

"Not much."

"Oh."

Derek released a breath into the phone. "No one would say anything to me anyway," he said patiently. "The higher you go in the organization, the less you hear from the ranks."

"Right."

"We had to bring in Nicole today to manage the fallout from the layoffs," he offered after a pause.

A jolt in her stomach, like a drop in an elevator. "Nicole Hayden?" Her counterpart at Parnassus, a blond, ambitious fembot in a slim dark suit.

"Stan and Gordon wanted someone to coordinate with the outside PR firm," he explained.

Meg's hands were cold. Her head buzzed like a swarm of bees. "So they called in Nicole."

"Yeah. Thank God you hired that outside team. She doesn't know a damn thing about handling reporters."

"I can't believe they kept her over me."

"Well, she's cheaper," Derek said reasonably.

"She has no experience."

"Compared to you. She'll grow into the job."

My job, Meg thought, with a stab of betrayal. She took a deep breath. "How's she getting along with you all on the transition team?"

He didn't answer right away. "All right."

She clutched the phone a little tighter in her hand, frustrated by their lack of real communication. But given the things she'd omitted from the story of her day—*Don't think about the kiss*—she could hardly complain. It would be better if she could see him.

"It would be nice if you could come down," she said. *I need you.*

"You know that's not possible."

"I know," she said, and tried to dismiss the memory of Sam's scorn. *The guy bailed. He should be here to support you.*

"I'm really busy right now," Derek said.

"I understand."

"Naturally I want to help any way I can." Another pause. "I was thinking I could assume your share of the mortgage as long as you're down there."

She felt a prickle along the backs of her upper arms. "Bribing me to stay away?" she joked.

"Of course not," he said so stiffly she realized she'd offended him.

Derek was a CPA with an MBA in finance. Naturally he thought of help in terms of money. But she didn't like feeling obliged to him, didn't want their relationship reduced to dollars and cents.

"You're sweet to offer," she said, "but it's not necessary. I have my six months' severance. Besides, I'm calling the outplacement service tomorrow."

"That's my girl," Derek said. She relaxed a little into her pillows. "Although . . ."

Another brush of cold in the pit of her stomach, on the back of her neck. "What?"

"There's no telling what a job search will turn up. Or where. You can't count on the right position opening in New York right away."

"Then I'll wait until one does."

"Who knows how long that will take?"

"What are you saying?"

"I know you. You don't like to take risks. If you'd feel better with a larger cash cushion, I'd be willing to buy you out of the condo. Obviously, you'd take a bit of a hit financially. The real estate market isn't what it was when we bought a couple years ago. But if you'd feel more secure having the cash . . ."

"No."

"I don't want you to feel pressured by your financial situation into making a decision that's wrong for you," he said earnestly.

She was confused. Afraid. *What about us?* she wanted to demand. *What about what's right for us?* But she couldn't get the words out.

"Do *you* feel pressured?" she asked instead.

"Of course not," he answered promptly. "Nothing's changed for me."

She was reassured. Wasn't she? He didn't say he loved her. Maybe it went without saying. They'd been together six years. *Nothing's changed for me.*

But too much had altered in her world for her to push him for more of a commitment right now. For the first time, she was afraid of what he might say. She'd just been fired. If she didn't have the condo—if she didn't have Derek—then everything she'd worked for, everything she'd attained in the past twelve years, was gone. What did she have left?

CARRIE UNDERWOOD WAS singing on the clock radio, almost loud enough to drown out the bugs outside and the sounds of the inn at night.

Taylor didn't even like country music anymore, not really, but Mom had. Sometimes her mother turned up the volume and the two of them would dance around the living room, waving their arms and making up stupid steps and laughing.

Taylor blinked, remembering. In the glow of the night-light, she could see the curved back of the rocking chair and the pile of schoolbooks on the desk. Fezzik sprawled on the braided rug, a large, furry lump like a bear. She missed her old stuff. She missed her cat. This room—Grandma Tess's sewing room—wasn't like Taylor's pretty blue bedroom in the house she'd shared with Mom. But it was beginning to feel . . . Not like home. It would never be home. But more like hers.

She ran her hands over the nubby quilt. Grandma Tess was going to buy her a new comforter. They'd picked it out in a catalog together, and Grandma said she would pick it up at the store. Before the accident. Taylor wondered what had happened to it. Maybe it was all bloody now.

Taylor shivered. That was a bad thought. She tried to push it away with the other bad thoughts, but her mind was going now, round and round like a hamster in a wheel, Mom and Grandma Tess, Grandma Jolene and Uncle Ernie, stupid Rachel Wilson at school, *squeak, squeak, squeak* . . .

Creak.

Taylor stopped breathing. She lay still under the covers, straining her ears, hoping she'd imagined the sound, like soft, furtive footsteps in the hall. A guest maybe. A ghost. Or . . .

Her heart pounded in her chest. *Don't be such a baby.* Uncle Matt said she would be safe. He promised.

But Uncle Matt wasn't here.

Blindly, she dropped her hand down the side of the bed, groping for Fezzik, for reassurance, willing the footsteps to go away.

If somebody opened the door, what would she do? Her stomach churned. Where would she go?

The door cracked open. A pale rectangle of light sliced through the room and over the bed. She squeezed her eyes shut tight. She could scream, she thought. She would fight. *Fezzik, Fezzik, Fezzik*, she chanted inside her head like a prayer, and the dog lurched suddenly under her hand, his nails scratching on the floor.

"Good boy," Aunt Meg murmured. "Down."

Taylor's eyes popped open. She felt sick with relief. "Aunt Meg? What are you doing?"

"Checking on you." Her face was just a blob with the hall light behind her. "I thought you'd be asleep by now."

Taylor shook her head, forgetting maybe Aunt Meg couldn't see her in the dark.

"Can I get you anything?" Her aunt's voice sounded funny, like she was upset or something. "A glass of water?"

"No. Thank you," Taylor added politely.

Aunt Meg moved out of the doorway, coming closer to the bed. "Why aren't you sleeping? Your Uncle Matt said sometimes you have nightmares. Did you have a bad dream?"

Taylor swallowed, her heart still pounding. "No."

"Because . . . Well, if there's anything bothering you . . ." Aunt Meg met her gaze and broke off. Unexpectedly, she smiled. A real smile this time, kind of crooked. "You wouldn't tell me anyway, would you?"

Taylor shook her head again.

"Okay. Well . . . I'm right across the hall if you need me," Aunt Meg said. "You going to be able to sleep now?"

Taylor scrunched deeper under the covers. She was fine. She was safe. "I think so."

"Good."

Aunt Meg hesitated, like she didn't know what to do. She stood there, rubbing the dog's head, glancing at Taylor. "Does he sleep with you?"

What should she say? Snowball used to sleep with her. But Grandma Jolene was allergic to cats. And Grandma Tess had rules about dogs in the dining room. Maybe Aunt Meg had rules against dogs on the bed.

Taylor didn't say anything.

"It's all right. I won't tell," Aunt Meg said. "He used to sleep with Josh, I think." Her hand stroked the quilt, like she wanted to straighten the covers. And then she bent and pressed her lips to the top of Taylor's head. "Good night, baby."

She smelled good, like the perfume counter at Belk's, and her hug was brief and hard.

"Aunt Meg? Are you okay?"

"I'm fine," she said firmly, straightening. "I'll see you in the morning."

Taylor watched her go, listening to her footsteps cross the hall. She didn't *seem* okay. Taylor sighed. Everybody had secrets.

Fezzik padded back from the door and dropped his big head next to her arm. His dark, doggy eyes fixed on Taylor's face.

"Do you want to come up?" she whispered.

His ears twitched, alert. His thick tail wagged back and forth.

"Up?"

He put his legs on the mattress.

She giggled and scooted over. He lurched up beside her, warm and solid against her side, taking up too much of the bed.

"Silly dog." She put her arm around him and went to sleep, comforted. Safe.

Five

SAM FOLLOWED THE smell of coffee downstairs. He usually scored his morning fix on the way to the job site, but the closest thing to a drive-through window on this side of the bridge was the line at Jane's Sweet Tea House.

He'd just grab a cup and go. *Get in, get out. No problem.*

His father and stepmother were in the breakfast room, sealed off by a wall of glass from the ocean tumbling below. For one second, Sam was tempted to keep on going, right out the front door and into his truck. But the days when he used to sneak out of the house were over. Funny, after all these years, he was just as eager to go to the Fletchers'. Maybe more.

It would be good to work up a sweat, to do something to pay back Tom and Tess for their kindness. He was looking forward to hanging out with Matt again, to spending time with Josh.

To seeing Meg.

He thought of the way she'd looked last night, on the porch and in his dreams, her cool blue eyes and her full, soft lips and that don't-mess-with-me lift of her chin.

He'd pushed things, not further, but maybe faster than he'd intended. Now that he'd made his move, though, he had no intention of backing off. Or of letting her back off, either.

"Morning," he said, reaching for the coffeepot.

"It's half caff," Angela reminded him. Even at the breakfast table, his father's fourth wife was perfectly turned out and made up, her hair in soft, loose curls around her shoulders.

"Swill," Carl growled. "She's feeding me like a fucking invalid."

There was a chill in the air that had nothing to do with the air-conditioning, set at a seasonless seventy-two degrees.

"You are an invalid, Dad. At least she's feeding you." Sam couldn't remember Angela ever actually cooking before. He glanced at his father's almost untouched plate. "That looks good."

"Egg white omelet," Angela said. "Would you like one?"

He suppressed a shudder. He wanted an egg and sausage biscuit and a cup of real coffee as much as the old man did. But he appreciated his stepmother's effort even more than her offer. Twenty years ago, he'd never expected her to stick. He'd certainly never imagined her playing nursemaid. "No, thanks. I've got to get going."

Carl grunted. "About time. I called the office ten minutes ago. Nobody answered."

"It's the off season, Dad," Sam answered patiently. "The realty office doesn't open until nine."

"Somebody should still be there to pick up the damn phone."

The coffee was weak and bitter. Sam set down his cup. "Maybe Shelley was on the other line."

"Before my surgery, I was in the office at seven every morning. Nobody was late to work then."

Sam took a deep breath, a bad taste in his mouth. The old man was supposed to be managing his stress along with his diet. Low fat, low salt, and no aggravation, the cardiologist had said.

Sam figured he aggravated his father just by breathing. But until the old man was back on his feet, they were both stuck with the situation. "Dad, relax. I'll swing by the office."

"*Relax*," Carl repeated with heavy scorn. "That's your advice? That's your plan? You have a business to run."

"Don't worry about my business. My business is fine. My crew's in Pamlico County doing flood repairs." Where Sam should be, would be if he weren't babysitting his father's company. He'd already been on the phone with his foreman, Nate, confirming the permits were in order, making sure the project was on time and within budget. "They can manage without me for a few more days."

"I wasn't talking about your little handyman operation. I meant my business. The family business. Grady Development."

It was the old argument, one Sam was never going to win. Not without giving the old man another heart attack.

"Your business has three empty houses and twenty-one lots waiting for funding," Sam said evenly. "You turned down that roofing project because the insurance settlement didn't meet your costs. And we can't move forward on repairs to the Foster property until the inspector from the mortgage company gives the okay."

"So you'll just sit on your ass all day."

"Actually, I'm giving Matt Fletcher a hand today."

Carl sneered. "Going fishing?"

There was bad blood between the Fletchers and the

Gradys, dating back eight years to when Carl had closed the commercial fish house and opened a waterfront restaurant in its place.

Sam looked his father in the eye. "Building a ramp for his mother. Tess gets out of the hospital next week."

Carl's face reddened. Bad blood or not, everyone on the island was pulling for Tess.

"Carl, don't upset yourself." Angela's brow did not furrow—thanks to Botox, her forehead no longer moved at all—but her voice was concerned. "Try your omelet."

"I don't want the damn omelet."

"Come on, Dad. Be a good boy and I'll bring you a bacon double cheeseburger for dinner."

Angela stuck out her collagen-filled lower lip. "But, Sam . . ."

"One cheeseburger isn't going to kill him, Angela." Sam bared his teeth in a grin. "And if it does, you'll be a very wealthy widow."

The old man's bark of laughter followed him to the door.

MEG TOOK A deep breath, her laptop open on the scarred oak table. The granite countertops gleamed. The dishwasher chugged in the background. The guests were gone, the kids in school, Matt had disappeared before dawn on a morning charter bottom fishing in the sound. For the next few hours, she had the kitchen and the house to herself.

She read over the first assessment question sent by the career coach at the outplacement service.

What did you like best about your previous job?

Well, that was easy. *Making money*, Meg typed. She stared at the black words on the white screen, gnawing the inside of her lip. Was that the right answer?

Be honest, the career coach had urged. *Be yourself.* But

even in grade school, Meg had prided herself on always being the first to raise her hand, on always knowing the correct answer. She was uneasily aware of having failed last night somehow with Derek and with Taylor. Of missing something, some nuance, some insight, that would set things right.

She was determined not to fail this stupid questionnaire. Her fingers hesitated over the keys.

I enjoyed developing and implementing proactive communications strategies to promote and protect the company's unique value proposition vis-à-vis clients, prospects, investors, the financial press, and the public at large.

There. That should do it.

She turned to the next question. *What would your ideal day look like?*

She frowned at her empty coffee mug. Not like this one, that was for sure. She had never wanted to live her mother's life, at the beck and call of strangers. She hadn't gone to Harvard so she could push a vacuum around.

Although it had been surprisingly pleasant to wave Taylor off this morning as she ran to join Josh on the walk to school. And the guests, an older couple from Charlotte and a writer researching her next book, had been easy to please. Meg had provided them with breakfast, bicycles, and maps before dispatching them for the day.

"The inn is lovely. We can't wait to explore the island," the older woman had said as she'd picked up her box lunch from the kitchen. "You're so lucky to live here."

Easy to say if you were on vacation. Meg had things to do.

Restless, she got up to pour herself another cup of coffee. *What would your ideal day look like?*

Maybe she'd skip that one for now.

The low rumble of a diesel motor attracted her attention. She glanced through the wide kitchen windows, her breath quickening as she recognized the big black truck.

Sam.

He parked under the crepe myrtles at the bottom of the yard. His tall, rangy figure stepped down from the cab. His soft gray T-shirt, worn with washing, clung to his broad shoulders and the planes of his chest. In faded jeans and work boots, he didn't look like a rich man's son this morning. He looked . . . good, she admitted. Cocky, comfortable. A man's man.

Her heart thumped as she waited for him to stride up the walk and knock on her door. But he didn't. He stood, thumbs in his belt loops, weight on his heels, surveying the yard before he walked around the truck and lowered the tailgate.

Fine. She certainly wasn't standing around drooling until he found time to talk to her. She had plenty of other things demanding her attention this morning.

She plopped back down at the kitchen table. *What are the setting and atmosphere of your ideal workplace?*

Oh, please. These questions were a waste of time. She could skip them. Who would know? She should be working on updating her résumé. But the career coach had stressed the importance of committing to the steps, of trusting the process.

Meg tapped her fingernails on her mug, her gaze drifting from the computer to the apples in the yellow bowl, the herbs on the windowsill, Taylor's latest test paper stuck to the refrigerator door. *Matt's doing?* Meg wondered. *Or Allison's?* Tess had always been the one to tape her children's accomplishments on display, from handprints and crayon drawings to computer-printed transcripts.

But her mother was in the hospital now.

Don't think about that. Answer the question.

Her ideal workplace. Meg closed her eyes, shutting out the sunny kitchen, deliberately summoning a vision of her

Manhattan office, the gleaming cherrywood, the blue-gray walls, the stiff and polished plants. The insulated hush, forty-seven stories above the traffic.

Thump. The sun catchers in the window rattled at the noise from the backyard. Meg opened her eyes. *Sam?*

Bump, bump. Honestly, what was he doing out there?

She yanked open the back door as Sam pushed a piece of machinery across the grass. "What on earth is that?"

His eyes gleamed. "Good morning. It's an auger."

"It looks like a lawn mower had sex with an oil drill," she said.

His laughter reverberated in the pit of her stomach. Helplessly, she smiled back. "You want some coffee?" she asked.

"Thanks. Black, one sugar."

She poured the coffee into a travel mug. The leftover grape and rosemary focaccia she'd made for breakfast sat wrapped on the counter. She cut a slice and carried both outside.

"This looks great," Sam said. "I wasn't expecting breakfast."

She hunched one shoulder dismissively. She didn't want him reading anything into a simple gesture of appreciation. Just because he'd kissed her—*she'd kissed him back*—didn't mean she was going to start serving him breakfast on a regular basis.

Although she shouldn't worry about Sam assigning too much significance to a kiss. He probably kissed women all the time, had breakfast with them, too, without it meaning anything. "You're here early. I thought you'd wait until Matt and Josh could help."

"I wanted to take some measurements, figure out what we need. Have you decided where you want the ramp to go?"

She lifted her eyebrows, reassured by his businesslike attitude. "To the door?"

His teeth flashed, white against his tan. "That would be the conventional approach, yeah. We run the ramp here, to the side of the deck apron, that gives your mom a short path to the door without blocking the steps. But you've got yourself a two-foot vertical there. With a one-twelve slope, you're going to need a twenty-four-foot ramp."

"That's awfully long."

"Your call. As a historic building, the inn isn't required to be ADA compliant. But a ramp could make life easier for your parents even after your mom is on her feet again."

She didn't want to think about her parents growing older. She wanted them to remain the parents of her childhood: her tough, taciturn Marine father; her mother, smiling and competent in the background of their lives.

But the past two weeks had shaken Meg's perceptions and cracked the foundation of her world. After the accident, Matt had had his hands full, running the inn and his own business while caring for the kids. Tess had been unconscious or dazed by drugs, a breathing tube down her throat. Tom had been frozen by frustration at his own helplessness, strangled by anger, and numb with grief. At the hospital, Meg had been the one to take the lead in conversations with her mother's doctors, caregivers, caseworker, to nail down the details of her medical coverage, to speak with the police. She'd booked a motel room and rented a car for Tom.

She was beset by decisions, terrified of making the wrong choices for her parents. For herself. She looked at Sam, tall and broad, with that dark lock of hair that always fell into his eyes, and thought what an unspeakable relief it would be to lean on somebody else for a change. To surrender control, just for a minute. To let Sam take charge.

She squared her shoulders, resisting temptation. "Twenty-four feet still takes up a lot of yard."

His sharp eyes focused on her face. "I can give you a U design. More length in a smaller space," he explained. "That takes the ramp under the master bedroom window and back to the walk. Plus, it would be out of sight from the guest patio and the guest bedrooms."

Meg narrowed her eyes, trying to visualize the layout he described. Sam knew the inn. He'd built the master addition with her father and Matt almost twenty years ago. Her parents trusted him.

"I guess a handicapped access could be a draw for guests," she acknowledged. "But we'd have to move those rosebushes."

He grinned. "Yes, ma'am. Just tell me where."

His ready acquiescence was balm to her soul. She went back into the kitchen glowing with decisiveness, once more in control. A feeling which lasted until she sat at the table again and read the next question from the career coach.

What gives you joy?

The words danced tauntingly on the screen. As if joy had anything to do with work. Or making money. Or planning her future.

Gritting her teeth, Meg typed. She was in PR, for heaven's sake. If the job required bullshit, she could write bullshit.

"SKYPING WITH THE boyfriend?" Sam drawled.

He watched Meg jump like a teenaged boy caught surfing porn sites. Her face flushed wild rose red.

He grinned and leaned a shoulder in the doorway, pleased for once to have the upper hand. "Or do you usually take off more clothes for that?"

She scowled, closing her laptop with an annoyed click. "Don't be ridiculous. I was . . ." She broke off, her color deepening.

"Working," he supplied, taking pity on her.

"Yes." She didn't meet his eyes.

Interesting.

The dishwasher was already running. He rinsed his empty mug and set it in the sink. "Thanks for the coffee and pastry."

"Focaccia. You're welcome."

"Got any more?"

"A little." Recovering, she stood, moving with brisk grace to the counter. "Are you still hungry?"

"No." He stayed where he was, enjoying the mathematical precision with which she sliced a square. Her hands were neat and quick, her fingers slim and unadorned. He wanted them on his body.

The sudden flare of lust caught him by surprise. He shifted his position against the counter. "The old man was grumbling about his breakfast this morning. I promised to bring him something tasty and artery-clogging if he behaved."

Her full lips curved. Soft, pink. Distracting. "I can wrap some for you to take home. But it's not bad for him. It's just a basic bread recipe with a little fruit, a little olive oil."

Sam winked. "I won't tell if you don't."

Her hands stilled on the knife. The memory of her whisper rose between them. *Don't tell Matt.*

She bent her head, busying herself with the plastic wrap.

"Thanks," Sam said quietly as she handed him the square of focaccia. "This is really nice of you."

"It's nice of *you*." She gave him her crooked smile. "You're a good son."

He was taken aback. Embarrassed. His family wasn't like hers. He managed not to shuffle his feet. "There are different opinions on that."

"You're here. According to *my* father, most of life is about showing up."

"Yeah? How does he feel about the absent boyfriend?"

"He doesn't . . . Derek isn't . . . Dad was talking about *family*."

So New York Guy wasn't family. After six years? Loser, Sam thought.

"Obviously he respects Derek's need to work," she added stiffly.

"Okay."

Meg glared. "Dad meant showing up for the big stuff. Weddings, funerals . . ."

"Heart attacks?"

"Yes."

Sam nodded. "Maybe. Maybe that's enough. But I've had this feeling lately that I should be . . ."

He broke off. He didn't talk about this shit. Not with anybody. Certainly not with Meg, who always knew exactly where she was going, who had her whole life mapped out and a calculated backup route.

"What?"

He shrugged. "Doing more than dropping in on life."

"Your father's life," she clarified.

Sam shook his head. "Mine."

Their eyes met. A different hunger stirred in his belly, solidifying into a hard ache. "Meg." *Meggie* . . .

Her eyes widened. Her breathing quickened. The wall phone behind him rang, and she jumped.

"Saved by the bell," Sam murmured.

She shot him a wary look as she pushed past him to answer the phone. "Pirates' Rest." Her voice was cool and pleasant.

He leaned against the counter, amused at them both.

There was too much history between them for his usual moves to work. There would be no quick drive to the basket this time, no easy score.

But there was too much heat between them to let him pick up his ball and go home.

He watched her, enjoying the rise and fall of her voice, only half listening to her side of the conversation.

". . . not here at the moment . . . happy to help you . . . I'm her aunt." Her tone sharpened, snagging his attention. "Of course I can take a message, but . . . Yes, I am living here now. With Taylor. Yes."

Her breath escaped through her teeth. She dug for a pencil. "I'm ready. Shoot."

Sam craned his neck as she jotted down notes on the pad by the phone.

"All right. Thank you. I'll make sure he does," she said and ended the call.

"Vernon Long," Sam read aloud over her shoulder. "What do you want with an Elizabeth City lawyer?"

"Do you know him?"

"Some. Decent guy. Used to play golf with my father."

"Is he any good?"

"Lousy swing. Excellent lawyer." He studied her truculent face. "What's wrong, Meg? And if you say everything's fine, so help me, I'll find the nearest pier and toss you off."

"Everything *is* fine. Will be fine," she corrected.

Uh-huh. "Who was that on the phone?"

"Kate Dolan. Taylor's lawyer."

He looked at her blankly.

Meg huffed. "The executor for Dawn's will?"

Comprehension struck. Dawn Simpson was Taylor's mother. After getting knocked up and leaving the island, Luke's high school girlfriend had made a life for herself working at a law office in Beaufort. "This Kate Dolan . . . is she the one who told Luke he was a daddy?"

"Yes." Meg's clipped tone didn't encourage conversation.

That was okay. He was good at getting people to talk to him. "I hear Dawn's parents aren't too happy about Luke getting custody."

Meg's eyes narrowed. "Matt talked to you about that?"

"Sugar, everybody's talking about it." She couldn't have forgotten how the island grapevine worked. He glanced again at the pad by the phone with the lawyer's name in firm, black script. "So, when's the court date?"

"Two weeks." Her lips pressed together. "They're claiming 'changed circumstances.' Because of Mom's accident."

He shook his head. "It doesn't matter. Luke is Taylor's father. Dawn wanted him to raise her." If Sam had a daughter—his mind stumbled briefly over the thought—he would want her raised by the Fletchers, too.

Meg's face was tense and pale. "Luke's out of the country. The Simpsons took care of Taylor right after her mom died. They're as much her grandparents as Mom and Dad are. I'm not saying the Simpsons should get custody, but they're not bad people just because they want Taylor."

"Or they want her money."

"What money? Dawn was a receptionist, not a millionaire."

He raised his brows, watched her figure it out.

"Survivor's benefits," she said slowly. Her blue eyes widened. "Life insurance."

"You would know," Sam said. "It's your business."

"That's . . . awfully cold."

"Not cold. Realistic. Not everyone in a custody dispute is invested in the child's welfare. Sometimes they'd rather have cash."

"Are you speaking from personal experience?"

"You mean, because my old man paid off my mother?" Sam drawled.

Meg blushed. "I didn't mean to insult your family."

Sam shrugged. "It's true enough. The old man's not easy to live with. Belinda stuck it out as long as she could. When she finally made a break for it, she didn't want anything tying her to her old life. Including me." When Sam was eight, his mother's choice had bewildered and devastated him. Maybe if she'd been different . . . If he'd been the kind of son she wanted . . . But he was all grown up now. He'd made his peace with it. And with her. "It all worked out. Dad got his heir, and she got the life she wanted. Everybody's happy."

"Bullshit."

Sam chuckled. "Don't hold back now. Tell me how you really feel."

"Your father had an heir whether you lived with him or not. He must have wanted *you*."

His eight-year-old self wanted to believe her. But Sam knew better. "He wanted to win," he said flatly.

Meg opened her mouth, like she was going to argue again. But all she said was, "Do you ever see her? Your mother?"

"Sure. I call once a month, go out for a visit maybe once a year." Sam smiled wryly. "That's enough for both of us. I'm not the best of sons."

"It's not you," Meg said fiercely.

His brows lifted.

"It's not your fault that she didn't fight for you," Meg said. "It's her lack. Her loss."

He regarded her with affection. She didn't understand. Meggie would always fight for those she loved. She'd always been a fighter.

Reaching out, he tugged a strand of her short, silky hair.

"Careful, sugar. You don't want to be nice to me. I might get ideas."

Her flush deepened. "Don't be ridiculous."

"I'm just saying. You, me, an inn full of empty bedrooms . . . It would be a shame to waste an opportunity."

Her lips quirked up. She primmed them together. "Go away. I'm working."

"So take a break. You need a little fun."

"And you think you can give it to me?"

He smiled at her slowly, confident now that they had moved away from discussion of his family to the more comfortable ground of sex. Maybe he'd failed to show her a good time the first, last, and only time they'd been together. But . . . "I'm sure willing to try. I've learned a lot in eighteen years."

She met his gaze, humor and a hint of challenge in her eyes. "So have I."

He grinned and heaved an exaggerated sigh. "In that case, I might as well pick up the lumber."

She straightened. "Let me get my checkbook."

"Not necessary."

Her chin went up. "You're not paying for my supplies."

"No, I'm taking them off an old job site." He stood a moment, enjoying the confusion in her face, her slim, braced body, her suspicious eyes. "Want to come?"

Six

MEG'S HEART GAVE an extra thud. She met Sam's gaze as his question hung on the air, heavy with expectation. She wanted to say yes, she realized, dismayed. *Yes*, to the building supplies. *Yes*, to going with him. *Yes*, to pretty much anything he proposed that would get her out of this kitchen and away from the career coach's stupid questions.

So take a break. You need a little fun.

No. The sooner she finished the assignment, the sooner she could begin the real work of finding a job. She wasn't abandoning her schedule to go joyriding around the island with the Boy Who Had Everything.

She dug in her heels, resisting the tug of temptation. "I'm not scavenging materials off a construction site. I'm perfectly capable of buying what we need."

"Think of it as close proximity sourcing," he suggested. Despite the gleam in his eye, he sounded almost sincere. "This isn't about money, Meggie. It's about time and energy. A trip to the mainland and back would cost me a couple of hours and half a tank of gas. This is quicker. Get in, get out. No problem."

Okay, she could accept his reasoning. To a point. *Time is money*, Derek was fond of saying. In their relationship, household chores and errands were calculated and divided as neatly as the monthly utilities. So many minutes to unload the dishwasher or carry the trash to the garbage chute, so many hours to pay the bills or wait for the super or pick up the dry cleaning . . .

Sam wasn't anything like Derek. Maybe, in this one instance, that was a good thing. "At least let me reimburse you for the cost of the materials."

"Nope."

She was forced to be blunt. "Look, I don't want to owe you any favors."

"Consider it payback."

"For what?" The instant the words escaped her mouth, she wished she could snatch them back. What did she want him to say? *For being drunk? For taking everything you offered? For not calling you the next day or for weeks afterward?* They were too old for any of that to matter now.

And if he apologized again, after all these years, she would hit him.

He smiled as if he knew what she was thinking. "For all those cookies your mom baked for me."

Her mouth jarred open. She stared at him, at once relieved and oddly disappointed. This wasn't about her. Maybe none of it was.

His eyes glinted with humor. "So, are you going to give me a hand loading the truck?"

When he put his request that way, she could almost

justify saying yes. But if she went with him, it wouldn't be because he needed her help, and they both knew it.

Her gaze dropped to the computer screen. *What gives you joy?*

Her heart thrummed in her chest. "I need to change my shoes first," she said.

He nodded. "I'll wait."

"LAST ONE," SAM said, hefting the deck board level with the truck bed. "Easy does it."

He raised his end onto the stack and then moved down the length of the board, shifting his grip, taking its weight. She tried hard—she'd always been a worker, Meggie—but she was small and female. Fun to watch, with the quick energy of her movements, the shape of her breasts under her sweat-dampened top.

Her shoulder brushed his as he nudged her aside to slide the board into place. Her arms were smooth and bare. She smelled distractingly of sweat and woman, of rosemary and Meg. He wanted to turn his face into the curve of her neck and lick her. All over.

He shoved the board hard onto the top of the pile.

He turned and caught her staring. Her cheeks were pink from embarrassment or the sun. With those big, wary, fascinated eyes, the strands of hair sticking to her forehead, she looked less like some hotshot New York executive and more like the girl he used to know. He grinned.

Her eyes narrowed. "What?"

"Your face is dirty."

She rubbed at her cheek with the back of a borrowed work glove.

"Here." He chuckled and stepped in, tugging off his own

gloves. With his thumb, he brushed at her warm cheek. She went very still. For one electric moment, he could imagine how she would feel under him, taut and trembling, silky hot. He could *remember.*

"Thanks." She broke eye contact and stepped away, leaving him half hard and wanting.

Not just wanting sex, he realized. Wanting Meg, her affection, her admiration, her trust, all the things he'd once had and taken for granted.

"It's pretty here." She looked around at the waves of sea grass capped with spiky yellow flowers. A sandy track wandered beside a makeshift fence to the deep blue water of Pamlico Sound. "I never really explored this site before."

"You never will, if the old man gets his way."

She glanced over her shoulder. "His way?"

Shit. He didn't want to talk about this now. Most of the time he avoided thinking about it. The old man hadn't beaten Sam's convictions out of him yet, but their countless battles—and Carl's illness—had persuaded him of the futility of the fight.

He jerked his chin, indicating the undeveloped acres of land, thick with vegetation and birdsong. "Dare Plantation. Gated community. No public access."

" 'An overpriced, overblown luxury development,' " she quoted back at him softly.

So she'd listened last night. She remembered.

"Multimillion-dollar houses with big lawns and private pools and piers," Sam said. Houses like the one he'd grown up in. Who was he to throw stones?

She pursed her lips, not judging so much as thoughtful. Or maybe he was kidding himself. "Are you saying that you wouldn't build here?"

"No." Her eyes rested on him, inviting him to continue. He shrugged. "I'd go with a different kind of project, that's all. Higher density, more affordable housing that would conserve the shoreline and the open space instead of chopping it up into little parcels with their own docks and septic tanks."

"I never pictured you as an environmentalist."

"I'm a builder," Sam said, trying not to hear the old man's voice in his head. *Fucking tree-hugger.* "We need jobs on the island, good jobs, construction jobs. And we need more moderate-priced housing for year-round residents," he said, warming to his topic. "People who live on the island, who work here—fishermen, firemen, teachers like Allison—are getting squeezed out of the market."

Meg nodded. "It makes sense when you explain it. Why don't you do it? You said yourself that luxury homes aren't selling now."

She was like a kid with a stick, he thought, exasperated. Stirring things up, poking things in the water to see if they moved.

Sometimes it was better to let them die.

"Maybe I don't care enough," he suggested.

She tilted her head thoughtfully, exposing the delicate curve of her neck. She had a great neck. "I don't believe you."

"Ask my old man."

"He's not here."

Exactly. Carl Grady had never been there for his family. He was too busy making a living to make a life, to make time for his wives or his son. Too busy building his fortune to see what his ambitions cost the island.

It wasn't something Sam spent a lot of time thinking about. Why focus on something that couldn't be changed?

"Look, you'd have to get a project like that approved," he said. "Dare Island is incorporated. The town board has to sign off on any new development. And then you'd have to convince investors it would pay. They only know big houses and hotels. We've never done a moderately priced development on the island."

"You can talk anyone into anything. And they'd listen to you. You're a Grady. Grady Realty and Construction."

She didn't understand. She'd always had her family's support. "You're getting me mixed up with the old man. And he doesn't want any part of it. He'd rather sit on the land and wait for the market to improve."

"Is that why you left?"

Yes. But if Sam admitted that, he'd have to admit how badly he'd failed. "What's with the questions?"

"I'm interested."

He grinned at her, deliberately misunderstanding. He hadn't brought her out here to discuss his relationship with his father. "That's promising."

She stuck her nose in the air. "Interested in the *island.*"

"Why? You don't live here anymore."

"That doesn't mean I can't have an opinion. That I don't care."

"Sugar, nobody ever said you didn't have opinions."

"Huh." But her lips twitched, like she was trying not to smile.

Encouraged, he moved closer, leaning over her. Her soft dark curls tickled his chin. "I like that you care about things." He spent too much time playing it cool, pretending not to care. "You're passionate." His mouth wandered to the edge of her jaw, found the corner of her mouth. Her lips were full and moist. "Exciting."

She inhaled, making her chest lift against his. She was so soft, so warm against him. He wanted his hands on her. He wanted . . .

She turned her head away. "I told you, I'm not doing this. I have a boyfriend."

"You have a roommate. You need more."

She flushed. "Let's not argue over semantics. The point is, I'm with somebody."

"Yeah. Me." He sniffed her hair behind her ear. She smelled really good, like sun and rosemary, warm and sharp at the same time.

"At the moment," she said breathlessly. "Not permanently."

He spread his hand across the small of her back, not really listening, nudging her against him, letting her feel how she affected him. She made a sound in her throat and hitched against him. His hand slid lower, over the smooth, firm curve of her butt. His hard-on lodged against her hip. "I'll take what I can get," he muttered.

"You always did."

The words were as effective as a slap. His fingers tightened before he dropped his hand from her bottom. "Nothing that wasn't offered."

Her cheeks went from red to white. "I suppose I deserve that."

Sam kicked himself. He was trying to seduce her, not insult her. "What you deserve is a guy who will be there for you all the time, not just when it's convenient for him."

She drew back, her blue eyes cool again. "Are you referring to yourself or Derek?"

Sam sucked in his breath. Okay, so he'd screwed up eighteen years ago. He hadn't had the control to resist her or the balls to face her the next morning. Rejection wasn't his thing. He couldn't undo what he'd done. He couldn't make things right. So he'd run, using the excuse of school to avoid confronting both her family and his own failures.

"I'm talking about you." He met her gaze steadily. "You deserve somebody who won't take advantage of you."

"Which is why Derek is perfect for me."

Sam felt a sharp, unpleasant stab. "Perfect, how?"

"He's the company's chief financial officer." Like Sam gave a crap about the guy's job description. "We're equals. Partners. We share the same goals."

"Getting married is a goal for some people." But not for her, he remembered. Never for her.

"For your stepmothers maybe. I'm not waiting around for some man to propose. Derek and I have been focused on our careers. It's important to have a solid professional and financial foundation to build on."

"Fine. But you're, what, a vice president now? How far up the ladder do you have to climb to become Mrs. Chief Financial Officer?"

The faint lines beside her mouth dug in. "You don't understand."

He hitched his thumbs in his belt loops. "So explain it to me."

She looked away. In the bright sunlight, the shadows under her eyes were dark as bruises. Like she wasn't getting enough sleep, he thought with a twist of concern. "My situation right now isn't . . . settled," she said.

He frowned. Meg was straightforward to the point of bluntness, honest to a fault. It wasn't like her to beat around the bush. "What, you get fired?" he joked.

A RUSH OF tears closed Meg's throat. She stared at him, speechless.

Sam went still. His broken bottle green eyes sharpened on her face. "Meggie?"

Oh, God. She shook her head. Blindly, she turned away, fumbling for the handle of the truck.

Sam swore. His arm came up, bracing against the top of the door, cutting off her escape. An aggressive gesture, but his voice when he spoke was deep and gentle. "Does your family know?"

His body was hard and close behind her. She fought a ridiculous urge to bury her face against his chest and bawl her eyes out. "I don't want to worry them."

Silence.

Her heart pounded in her ears. She risked a peek over her shoulder. For once, Sam's charming grin was nowhere in sight. He frowned at her thoughtfully, that lock of dark hair falling over his forehead.

She wished she knew what he was thinking. And yet it didn't really matter. A shameful, shaking relief swept over her because he'd guessed. She didn't have to pretend anymore.

Sam was family at the same time he . . . wasn't. He knew her, but he wasn't counting on her. Her success or failure ultimately meant nothing to him.

The sense of release was enormous.

"When?" he asked.

She cleared her throat. "Monday."

"Your first day back?" The incredulous edge to his voice was unexpectedly gratifying.

She nodded.

"Assholes."

His anger warmed her. Steadied her. Derek, she recalled, had not been angry.

She pushed the thought away, feeling vaguely disloyal. Derek's own career was on the line. He couldn't afford to lose his cool on her behalf. Sam had nothing at stake, nothing to lose by taking her side. But his unquestioning championship soothed her all the same.

"It was a bad time for me to be away," she said. "The company recently acquired one of our competitors. I should have been there to handle the PR."

"But you were on leave, right?" Sam said. "Family emergency. Is it even legal for them to fire you like that?"

Years of protecting the company, of putting the best possible spin on things, made her face him. "We were shedding head count anyway. Mine was a redundant position."

Sam raised his brows. "There is no 'we,' sugar. You're not playing for the team anymore. You got fucked."

Yes.

The surge of anger was thrilling. Liberating. Disturbing. Anger wouldn't get her where she needed to go.

"They wanted someone cheaper," she said.

"Younger," he guessed.

She ground her teeth together. "Yes."

"Somebody who wouldn't take ten days off because her mother got hit by a damn drunk driver."

Yes. Bitterness choked her. Three strikes, and she was out. She swallowed. "I don't know that. *Didn't* know that. Not that it would have made any difference," she added. "Mom needed me."

Sam smiled.

She narrowed her eyes. "What?"

"That's my girl," he said and kissed her, a brief, hard kiss on the mouth.

She was *not* his girl. But the kiss was nice, and the warm approval in his eyes was even nicer, and she was tired for the moment of fighting.

"We should get back," she said.

His gaze searched her face before he nodded.

She let him open her door, watching through the windshield as he walked around the truck.

He slid in beside her and started the truck. "You've got to tell them."

Them. Her family. She shuddered in rejection. "No."

"You were there for them, they'll be there for you."

Of course they would be. Years of moves and deployments had taught the Fletcher siblings to stand back to back to back. But Meg hadn't run to her brothers to defend her in twenty-five years. She stood on her own. She was the family success story, the one who'd made it.

She could not bear to be a failure in their eyes.

"Mom's in the hospital," she said. "Luke's in Afghanistan. Matt's trying to take care of the inn and Taylor on top of his charter business. They all have enough to deal with right now."

"So by keeping quiet, you're protecting them."

"Yes."

A sideways look. "Or yourself."

She straightened her spine, resisting the pull of the soft leather seat. "I don't want my family worrying about me."

"Won't they do that anyway? Sooner or later, they're going to wonder what you're doing here."

"I'm here to help out," Meg said firmly. "As long as I'm needed. As long as it takes me to find another job. Then I'll tell them the truth. That I accepted another position."

"What are you going to say if you have to relocate?"

"I won't."

I can't. She stared out her window at the pine needles and vines, at the headstones sprouting randomly along the road, *Nelson, Oates, Fletcher, Grady . . .* Family names. Dare Island names. She knew every one. And they knew her, knew the girl she used to be, smart, ambitious Meggie Fletcher, Queen of the Try Hards.

There was no going back for her.

She tightened her hands in her lap. "I belong in New York. My life is there. My condo. Derek."

"He get fired, too?"

"No." The word hung baldly in the air. "He's in the C-Suite," she added to fill the silence. "CEO, CFO, COO."

Sam slanted a look at her. "I took business classes. I know the jargon."

"Right. Anyway, they couldn't fire him. He's on the transition team."

"But he didn't protect your job."

"No, but . . ." She floundered, driven on the defensive. "The acquisition put Derek in a very difficult position. He's vulnerable, too. Any indication of partiality—"

"So which is it?" Sam interrupted. "They can't fire him, or his job's at risk?"

She glared. "Does it matter?"

"It would to me."

"You don't know him. You don't know anything about him. You can't judge."

"I don't need to meet him to recognize the type," Sam said quietly. "You're an accessory to a guy like him. Like a Rolex, something he can show off on his arm. He doesn't have your back, sugar. And somebody should. Deep down, you know that. That's why you're here."

Hot pressure burned the backs of her eyes. With the exception of her assistant, Kelly, no one from the office had been in touch with her since her firing. As if being laid off were a disease they could catch. Even though Meg told herself that her office friends didn't have her new cell phone number, she couldn't help feeling all the old insecurities of being the new kid in school. With every redeployment, it took time to establish your place, to find someone to eat lunch with, to win the liking or at least the respect of your teachers and classmates.

She'd always made good grades. It was harder to make friends.

"I'm fine," she said.

"You should tell your family. You could talk to Matt," Sam said.

Matt had given up his own chance at college when Josh was born. She didn't want her brother to know what a mess she'd made of her own opportunities. "No."

"Then I will," Sam said.

"*No.* You can't tell him. You can't tell anybody." She met Sam's eyes. Memory throbbed between them. *Don't tell Matt.*

"Meg . . ."

She didn't really believe that Sam would betray her confidence. But Sam and Matt had been best friends since high school. She'd been the one on the outside, two years younger, sharp and skinny, driven to keep up, desperate to be noticed. "Please."

He held her gaze a long moment before the corner of his mouth quirked up. "What's one more secret between friends?"

Meg exhaled. "Thank you." She risked a touch on his warm, muscled arm. "I'm grateful."

The creases in his cheeks deepened. "How grateful?"

She should have found his cockiness annoying. But she was disarmed by the understanding in his eyes, the laughter in his voice. Sam didn't take the question or himself too seriously. This once, maybe she shouldn't take herself so seriously, either.

"I'll bake you some cookies."

"Your mom's chocolate chip?" he asked hopefully.

She felt a moment's unreasonable resistance, as if committing to Tess's recipe somehow committed her to . . . What?

Flashback to fifteen-year-old Sam, hanging around her mother's kitchen, swiping raw dough off the mixer blade. *You make the best cookies, Mrs. Fletcher.*

And her mother, laughing, batting his hand away from the bowl. *Because they're made with love, Sam.*

Meg shook her head. She was not her mother, dispensing affection along with the batter. Sometimes a chocolate chip cookie was just a cookie.

"Deal," she said.

Seven

THE AUGER CHUGGED outside the kitchen windows, the grind of the drill bit punctuated by occasional pounding and the rumble of male voices. Through the glass, Meg could see the three men shirtless in the heat: her brother Matt, broad and deep-chested; Josh, still growing into his height and his hands; and Sam, long and lean-muscled, lowering a four-by-four into a post hole. His bare shoulders glistened in the sunlight. His dark hair curled damply on the back of his neck.

She could almost feel those strands, like wet silk between her fingers. Her hand clenched. Her body clenched low inside.

Meg blew out her breath. Drooling out the window at a shirtless Sam Grady was not getting her work done. She dumped the bag of chocolate chips into the bowl and turned on the mixer.

Matt and Taylor squatted beside the hole with the garden

hose. Meg watched as Matt handed the nozzle to the little girl. "Four or five inches," she heard him say. "Right there."

Taylor aimed the water into the hole, her little face screwed in concentration.

"He's so good with her," Allison murmured from behind Meg. "He must get that from your father."

"Probably. Though I can't remember Dad ever encouraging me to pick up a hammer." Meg flipped off the mixer. "That was for the boys."

Allison regarded her with warm, brown, earnest eyes. "Did you mind?"

"Not really. Dad always made me feel like I could do anything I wanted." Meg grinned. "He told the boys they had to do what he said."

Allison smiled wistfully. "Your family is so close. You must have had a wonderful childhood."

Meg hadn't met Allison's parents, a socially prominent couple from Philadelphia, during their brief stay at the inn. But from what Matt had said—and based on what he carefully didn't say—Meg suspected the Carters had stringent expectations for their only daughter. Expectations that did not include her teaching on tiny Dare Island or falling for the fisherman father of one of her students.

"Yeah, I guess we did." She pulled a face. "Although when I was fourteen, I never pictured myself twenty years later, still hanging around my parents' kitchen."

Still sneaking peeks out the window at Sam, sweating in the sun.

Josh had ripped open a bag of quick-set concrete and was shaking it into the hole under Matt's direction. Sam braced the post, holding a level against one side.

"At least you have a nice view," Allison said.

Meg started. "I was just admiring their . . ."

"Progress?" Allison suggested.

Meg met her gaze and smiled ruefully. "Something like that."

"That looks delicious," Allison said, changing the subject with the easy tact that was as much a part of her as her brown eyes or her diamond-faced watch. "Can I help?"

"I thought you had students coming over."

"Student newspaper meeting. I thought so, too. But Nia bailed, and Thalia might not want to come over by herself."

Meg set out the cookie trays. "Why not? You don't strike me as particularly intimidating."

"Thanks. I think." Allison accepted a spoon. "She's not avoiding *me*. It's . . ." She broke off, digging into the cookie dough, apparently unwilling to betray her student's confidence.

"Josh?" Meg guessed. She glanced out the window at her tall, handsome nephew, his mop of tawny hair and lazy smile, and her heart gave a little bounce of pride and anxiety. "They were dating?"

He was old enough to date, she supposed. Old enough to do all kinds of things that, as his aunt, Meg didn't particularly want to think about. She felt a sudden burst of sympathy for Matt.

"Not dating, exactly." Allison dropped a lump of dough onto the baking sheet. "It was more like a friends thing. At least on Josh's side. They were working together on a sports and nutrition piece for the paper, and Thalia . . . Well, I guess she hoped it would turn into something more."

Some of Meg's sympathy went out to this girl, whoever she was. Unrequited high school crushes were hell. Meg's gaze went back to Sam, broad-shouldered and lean-hipped in the sunlight. She pressed her lips together. *Some things never changed.*

Twelve minutes later, the timer pinged and the cookies

came out of the oven. With the last ramp post setting in concrete, the men and Taylor trooped inside.

"Something smells good," Sam said.

"Cookies." Josh reached for one.

"Hold on," Meg said. "Wash your hands."

"I did."

She narrowed her eyes.

"In the hose. Outside." He smiled at her, holding up his almost-clean palms in the universal sign of peace, and Meg's heart melted like butter on a stack of pancakes. That poor high school girl never stood a chance.

She handed him a plateful of cookies. "Careful. They're still hot."

Sam winked. "Hot is always good. Unless you're talking about beer."

"There's some in the fridge."

Josh opened the refrigerator door.

"Milk for you," Meg said.

He turned and saluted her with a gallon jug of milk. Smiling, she pulled a glass down from the cupboard.

"Must have been thirsty work," Allison said to Matt. "You're all sweaty."

"Sorry." Matt reached for his T-shirt, hanging from his back pocket.

She stopped him with a sly look and a touch on his wrist. "I like it."

Matt's rare smile broke over his face. He looked different, Meg thought. More relaxed. "Good to know," he said, and backed her up against the sink.

Allison twined her arms around his neck and drew his head down for a kiss.

Meg looked away, oddly uncomfortable, as if she'd witnessed something more intimate than a mostly clothed kitchen embrace. This was *Matt*? Her reserved, undemonstrative brother?

"Ew," Taylor said in a small pained voice.

Josh grabbed another cookie. "Get used to it, shorty," he said around a mouthful of crumbs. "It'll be worse when they get married. They'll be sucking face all the time."

When they get married . . .

Meg whirled back to her brother. *He proposed?* "You proposed? Matt!"

Matt raised his head, a faint flush staining his cheekbones. "Not in so many words."

"It was very romantic," Allison said over his shoulder. "He recited poetry."

"Matt did?"

Josh snickered. "You know, 'Roses are red, violets are blue, Allison's sweet, and—'"

"That's enough out of you," Matt said, finishing the poem.

"It was Edna Saint Vincent Millay," Allison said, her face now redder than Matt's.

"That sounds very . . . nice," Meg said, still trying to wrap her brain around the idea of her brother reciting poetry. Her brother . . . *married again*?

"And he gave me a plant," Allison said staunchly.

"A plant, huh?" Sam raised his eyebrows. "Smooth, Matt. Very smooth."

"Why a plant?" Meg asked.

Matt cleared his throat. "I thought . . . Put down roots."

Meg gaped at him, a funny catch in her chest. *To put down roots.*

It was perfect.

It was Matt.

So why did she suddenly want to cry?

She wasn't interested in putting down roots. She wanted challenge. Change. She'd embraced the bustle and rush of New York, the demanding pace and anonymity of life in the big city. Even the condo was more an investment than a home, a place to sleep and collect the mail.

But home had always been important to Matt.

Meg simply had never imagined her quiet, workingman brother would express himself in a way so deeply felt, so inherently right.

"It was a camellia," Allison said, beaming.

"Because nothing says commitment like a camellia," Sam put in.

"And you would know all about commitment," Matt shot back.

"Hey, I believe in marriage. For other people." Sam grinned and grabbed Matt in a one-armed hug. "Congratulations, you guys." He kissed Allison on the cheek. "When's the wedding?"

"Yes, congratulations," Meg echoed. She forced her lips into a smile, fighting the feeling of things moving too fast, of being somehow left behind. She was happy for her brother. She liked Allison. But they'd only known each other, what, a month? Six weeks? She and Derek had been together six *years*.

She moved jerkily forward, gave Allison a friendly squeeze and Matt a hug. There was no reason for her brother *not* to get married again, she told herself. Eventually. But . . .

"That's up to Allison," Matt said over her head to Sam. "I thought she should get done with the school year, make it through her first winter, before we set a date."

"I want Christmas," Allison said. "But I'll settle for Easter. Six months is plenty of time to find a dress and accustom my parents to the idea that we're getting married on the island." She glanced at Matt. "Of course, I'd like to have the ceremony here, in the garden, but it might be too . . ."

"Soon?" Meg suggested.

"Small," Allison said. "My parents will insist on a big wedding."

Meg dragged her hand through her hair, trying to get a grip on the situation. "Do Mom and Dad know?"

"Not yet," Matt said quietly, his gaze on her face. "I thought we'd tell them when Mom comes home."

Right. Their parents weren't here, Matt was besotted, and Allison lived in some Wonderland where anything was possible. Somebody had to inject a little reality here. "Listen, it's none of my business, but . . ."

"I want to ask you about those rosebushes," Sam said to Meg.

"In a minute. Have you considered how this could affect—"

"Now." Sam gripped her arm. "Out back. Excuse us, folks."

She let him drag her outside before she turned on him. "What is your problem?"

"Nothing. What's yours?"

Hot blood stormed her cheeks. "I don't know what you're talking about."

"Your brother's getting married. Do you have to analyze everything? Can't you just be happy for him?"

"I am," she protested. "But it's not like this is his first marriage."

Sam's face was inscrutable. "Allison isn't anything like Kimberly."

Kimberly, Matt's first wife. The two had met in college, when Matt was pursuing his dream of an engineering degree and Kimberly was, well, the rich girl slumming with the blue-collar boy from rural North Carolina. Meg suspected her brother's girlfriend had never wanted a serious relationship with Matt. Certainly she'd never expected him to knock her up. But nineteen-year-old Matt, determined as always to do the right thing, had persuaded Kimberly to marry him. Less than a year later, she'd walked out on him and their infant son. So Matt and Josh had come home to the island for good.

One more example, if Meg had needed one, that sex could seriously screw up your life. Now that Josh was older, Matt could finally begin to think about his own needs. She couldn't bear to see him throw that all away on a Kimberly clone.

"She's a trust fund blonde whose parents can't stand him," Meg said. "Are you saying you don't see a pattern?"

"I'm saying you shouldn't judge her before you get to know her better."

Meg's shoulders rose and fell. "Look, I like Allison. I do. I just don't want to see Matt hurt again."

"Then don't be such a snob."

"Me?" Her tone vibrated with genuine insult. Dare Island's Golden Grady was calling her . . . "A snob?"

"Yep. A reverse snob. What do you think, that because Allison comes from money, she's going to look down on you all? That she doesn't value what your brother has to offer?"

That was exactly what Meg thought. What she feared. Sam had never had to work for anything. He didn't know what it was like to grow up comparing yourself to others, to be ridiculed for not having the right stuff, the right clothes, the right accent. "You don't understand."

"Understand what? That somebody with Allison's background could look at your family and want what you have? That kind of loyalty. That kind of love." Sam's voice was quiet and intense. His eyes met hers. "Matt loves Allison. And she loves him."

She was shaken. Not only by his perspective of her family, but by this glimpse into Sam. The man she'd nicknamed *Slick* believed in *love*? She felt one more assumption turned on its head, one more yard of sand swept from under her feet.

"They haven't known each other very long," she said weakly.

"Not everybody takes six years to make up their minds about the person they want to spend the rest of their life with."

Ouch.

She glared. "This isn't about me."

Sam's gaze was clear and uncomfortably kind. "Isn't it?"

"No," she said firmly.

Maybe. She felt her world tilting like a deck in a storm, threatening to pitch her into a cold, dark sea. She was supposed to be the one with the great career, the one in a stable relationship, the one going forward, who had everything going for her. And now she'd been fired, and her boyfriend wanted to buy her out of their condo, and her once-divorced brother had found love with the practically-perfect-in-every-way Allison.

"It's about Matt," she said.

The familiar devil of laughter danced in Sam's eyes. "What? He isn't allowed to like any girls but you?"

Her lips twitched, but she replied stubbornly. "I'm not jealous." *Not exactly.* How could she make Sam understand how she felt? She didn't understand herself. "I'm concerned."

"I can see that," Sam said, his deep drawl unexpectedly sympathetic. Soothing. "But you have to let this one go, Meggie. Matt's going to do what Matt's going to do. You can't control his choices."

"Maybe that's what worries me," she muttered.

She wasn't in control. She hated that. She was the one who always had an answer, who always had a plan. And for the first time in her adult life, she didn't know what to do.

Sam laughed and put his arm around her shoulders. "You think too much." He gave her a friendly squeeze, tucking her against him. Was it her imagination, or did he *sniff* her *hair*? "Things will all work out."

"You can't know that," she said truculently into his naked chest.

"I know *you*. You'll make things work out. You always do." He drew back and smiled into her eyes. "Or you'll beat them into submission."

A watery chuckle escaped her. She smiled back, comforted despite herself.

SAM WAS FEELING sweaty and cheerful when he parked his truck at the end of the day. Making progress, he thought. Not just with the ramp. With Meggie.

What kind of progress—where this thing between them was headed, how far, how fast—he hadn't figured out yet. Which was okay. He'd always been more a buy-a-ticket-and-enjoy-the-ride kind of guy.

Not like Meggie. It was one of the things that attracted him to her, the way she was always so sure of where she stood, so confident of where she was going. But despite Sam's dickhead behavior in college, despite her allegiance to the so-called boyfriend in New York, she was apparently willing to give them another shot. She was talking to him again. She'd even kissed him.

Sam shook his head as he let himself into the house. Pathetic. He hadn't attached this much importance to a simple lip-lock since Jenny Vaughn had followed him under the bleachers in fifth grade.

The truth was, he liked women, all shapes, scents, textures, the infinite variety of them. He liked Meg, liked the feel of her mouth warming under his. Loved her body, taut and firm against him, vibrating with energy like a storm. That quick intake of her breath, the way those clear blue eyes darkened as he coaxed her to respond . . . Yeah, he liked that a lot.

But it was the kiss today, that brief, almost innocent peck at the abandoned job site, that had hit him upside the head like a two-by-four.

They'd been talking about her family, he remembered. Meg had said something about coming home because her mother needed her. She'd turned those eyes on him, passionate as always, dependable as ever, nothing standing in *her* way, and he'd kissed her and said . . . He'd said . . .

That's my girl.

Jesus, what a bonehead thing to say. They weren't in high school anymore. She had moved on years ago, moved in with that asshole in New York. Even back when they were kids, Meg hadn't been Sam's girl. Only that one time, when he came home from college, when he was drunk and dumb enough to believe his luck that smart, confident, strong Meggie Fletcher would come to him. Would want him.

She'd regretted it immediately, of course. *Don't tell Matt.*

He never had.

But he'd never been able to forget that feeling, either. Lust? Definitely. Longing? Well, sure. And something else, something deeper, primitive. The feeling he'd had the first time he saw her naked: *Mine.*

Sam headed for the stairs. He needed a hot shower and a cold beer. Or a cold shower, maybe.

"What the fuck do you think you were doing today?"

The old man's voice struck Sam like a rock between the shoulder blades. His back muscles tightened before he turned. "Building a ramp for Tess Fletcher. I told you."

"You didn't tell me you were going to pinch materials off my job site to do it."

"How the hell do you know about that?"

Carl sneered. "I set up security cameras. You think I'm too stupid to protect myself and my investments?"

Sam's jaw clenched. *No, I think you're a stingy, selfish son of a bitch whose heart was in bad shape even before the surgery.* "You know, if I were you, I'd be worried about more than the loss of a few building supplies out there. I was going to pay you."

Carl dismissed him with a wave. "Forget it. Take what you want. But it wouldn't kill you to show a little gratitude for once."

"Thanks," Sam said shortly. "But I pay my debts." He took out his wallet and slapped a wad of cash on the table in the hall. "There. That should cover it."

Carl's face twitched. He looked at the bills without touching them. "I don't want your money."

Sam regarded his father with frustration. "What do you want?" He'd never known. He never could satisfy his father.

"I was thinking of offering you a trade."

Sam's instincts, honed through childhood, went on alert. The old man was a shrewd negotiator, a veteran of backroom deals in the legislature and hard bargains in the boardroom. "What kind of trade?"

"You're interested in my business. What if I gave you the chance to take more than a load of lumber off my hands?"

"How much more?" Sam asked, soft and sharp.

Carl's eyes gleamed like an angler's with a fish on the

line. "Twenty percent of the profits if you get Dare Plantation off the ground."

"Some offer," Sam scoffed, ignoring the kick of his pulse. Because he wanted this deal. Wanted that property. Wanted to succeed on his own terms and jam his success down his father's throat. "That development's not going anywhere in this economy. Not the way you planned it."

His father flushed an unhealthy shade of red. "And you think you have a better way."

"I know I do."

"Multifamily housing," Carl said with scorn, the way another man might say *rat-infested tenements.* "Son, that dog won't hunt. You couldn't get the zoning past this town board. And if you did, you couldn't get investors."

Meg's voice spoke suddenly in Sam's head, her words like a door opening in a dark room, illuminating a sliver of possibility. *You can talk anyone into anything.*

She believed in him. At least, she believed in his ability to get his way in this.

"What if I could?" Sam asked.

"Why would you want to? The big money's in single-family homes on the waterfront. Not cheap-ass apartments with a park or whatever stupid charity project you have in mind."

"It's not charity. It's good business. There's plenty of demand for moderately priced housing on the island. I can make the development pay. For fifty percent of the profits," Sam said.

Carl snorted. "Big talk. Your plan cuts into my profits, too. Twenty and a house."

A house on Dare Island. Sam sucked in his breath. There were three Grady custom homes, sitting half-finished on half-acre lots facing the sound. Even in a depressed market, the value of the land alone was staggering. It was a powerful incentive. One that would tether Sam here, under the old man's eye. Under his thumb.

"I'd have control," Sam said. "It would be my project."

"It's my company," Carl said.

Sam met his father's gaze, his heart pounding. "My project, or no deal."

"I'll give you six months," Carl said after a pause. "Get it through zoning, show me backers, and we do it your way. If not, you'll work for me building spec houses."

It wasn't enough time, Sam thought. Even if he could use the existing federal and state permits, he'd still need time to get the plans together and approved by the town.

And the wily old shark knew it. He had influence on the board and the North Carolina Division of Coastal Management. Would he pull strings to help Sam? Or to ensure that he failed?

"Thirty percent of profits and a house." Sam pulled out Meggie's bread and laid it on the table, next to the money. "I'll even throw in breakfast to sweeten the deal."

Carl eyed the squashy package with suspicion. Sort of the way Sam was regarding his father's offer. "What's this?"

"You'll like it. It's good for you."

"If it's good for me, I won't like it." Plastic wrap crinkled. Carl tore off a corner of the focaccia, sniffing it before he put it in his mouth. "Not bad. All right. You've got yourself a deal."

He ripped off another piece of bread, chewing slowly, not looking at his son. His hands were gnarled and spotted with age. Watching him, Sam felt his chest constrict. Like he was the one with the heart condition.

He must have wanted you, Meg had said to him this morning.

He wanted to win.

Sam believed that. Still believed it.

"Why are you doing this?" he asked abruptly.

Carl swallowed, taking his time replying. "Angela's on my back. She says I'm working too hard."

"Hell, your doctors have been telling you that for years. Why are you offering me this now?"

But if Sam had hoped for sentiment from his father, he was bound to be disappointed.

Carl met his gaze, his dark eyes bright with challenge or malice. "Maybe I want to see what you're made of before I die."

"You won't die." Sam bared his teeth in a smile. "You're too stubborn."

The old man barked with laughter. "You better hope you take after me, then."

Eight

"TURN OFF HERE," Tess said to Tom.

The drive home from the rehabilitation center in Greenville was like a trip through hell. Tess couldn't get comfortable in the Nissan's passenger seat. Every slight bump in the road jarred her bones. The vibration of the highway churned the painkillers in her stomach.

Tom glanced over from the driver's seat, his faded blue eyes concerned. "You going to be sick again?"

"No," she said and prayed it was true.

The landscape rushed queasily by, tall pines and sandy ditches full of cattails and stagnant water. Every skid mark, every glitter of broken glass on the side of the road, made her palms sweat, mute reminders of past accidents. Her accident? The details of that afternoon blurred together like the fractured lines of the road. She'd tried closing her eyes, but her brain kept replaying scenes like a looped tape against the darkness of her eyelids. The instant's terror, the brutal impact, the snapping, tearing, splintering pain. The pressure on her chest as her lungs collapsed with blood.

She swallowed, willing her stomach to subside. "There's a Bed Bath and Beyond right on 70," she said.

Tom scowled. "So?"

She moistened her lips. "I thought we could pop in and pick up Taylor's comforter."

"Babe." Tom's voice was heavy with patience. "You just got sprung from the hospital. You're not popping anywhere."

He was right. Of course he was right. Her new walker rattled in the back, taunting her with her infirmity.

She shifted on the pillows elevating her seat. "The discharge instructions said I should stop and move around."

"We stopped three times in the last two hours so you could throw up." Tom shot her a sideways glance. "I want to get you home and flat."

He'd said those words to her before, she remembered, after a long deployment or driving home after a dance, always with a smile and the promise of sex. Never before because she was too frail to sit, too weak to stand.

Tears of frustration stung her eyes. She was tired of being patronized, sick of being coddled. "I promised Taylor."

Tom reached over and covered her hands, clenched in her lap. "She'll understand if you don't come home with a goddamn comforter. You heard Jerome. Just because the insurance company is sending you home doesn't mean you're healed. Nobody expects you to charge around like you used to."

I expect it, she wanted to cry.

She'd fought hard to come home. Her surgeons were delighted with her recovery. Everyone—doctors, nurses, therapists, Tom—praised her progress and her spirit. But her failure to deliver on her promise to her granddaughter chafed at her, one more thing she couldn't do, one more task beyond her power or control.

She looked at Tom's dear, stubborn face, searching for words to explain. Her big, tough Marine had always retreated from any discussion of feelings. She didn't want to burden him or complain. Twenty-two years after his retirement, she still felt like a military wife. She could do anything. Just not everything.

Screw it. She'd order the comforter on-line when they got home.

She turned her head away, concentrating on making it through the next forty minutes without puking.

It was better when they reached the bridge. Tess rolled down her window to feel the moist air on her face, inhaling the familiar smells of the salt marsh. A boat skimmed the blue-and-silver water like a gull. A white crane stood motionless in the sea grass.

Tom patted her thigh. "Almost there."

She nodded, overcome with sentiment and exhaustion.

The hundred-year-old Pirates' Rest overlooked the sound and the sea, its quiet gray trimmed with deep green and white, its generous eaves sheltering the wraparound porch. Live oaks draped in Spanish moss gave dignity to the grounds. Clumps of coneflowers and black-eyed Susans added color and whimsy around the gate. The beautiful old Craftsman had been her home for twenty years. Her dream for even longer than that.

Despite her exhaustion, anticipation thrummed through her. After weeks of hospital smells and noise, she longed for her own bed with a physical ache, for the cool stillness of the room she shared with Tom, for the smell of sun-dried sheets and the tick of the grandfather clock in the hall.

Home.

Oyster shells crunched under their tires as Tom pulled into the drive. A collection of vehicles parked behind the inn. *Not guests.* Tess smiled. *Her welcoming committee.*

Tom opened her door. She eased her feet out of the car, taking care not to twist, as he pulled her walker from the back.

His gaze searched hers. "Ready?"

She took a deep breath. Nodded.

After the high-tech rollator at the rehab facility, her walker felt like trading down from a Mercedes to a shopping cart. The uneven surface challenged her footing. With Tom at her elbow, she pushed and lifted, pushed and stepped across the strip of grass, through the gate, and past Matt's rental cottage.

"Looks like they're expecting you," Tom said.

She gripped the walker and raised her head, anticipating a gauntlet of concerned faces and watching eyes.

She blinked. There was a ramp.

A very professional, permanent-looking ramp doubling back from the footpath to the apron of the deck, its supports planted in what was obviously a new rose bed. The bushes wilted slightly in the heat, releasing fragrance into the air. A big red bow that looked as if it had been plucked from a Christmas wreath decorated the rail of the ramp.

Easy tears started to her eyes, a cloudburst of relief, fatigue, and gratitude.

Fezzik barked from inside the house. She heard Meg—*"They're here!"*—before the screen door banged open and they all burst out, Josh with his tawny mop of hair and crooked grin; Meg, quick and energetic; Matt with his quiet eyes and rare, slow smile. The pretty schoolteacher, Allison, came out with her arm around ten-year-old Taylor, who was hanging back and smiling.

Their figures blurred together in a haze of happiness and tears.

"Welcome home, babe," Tom said.

MEG ROLLED A lemon under her palm, bruising the rind, releasing the sharp citrus smell into the kitchen.

"I'm going out," her father said.

Anxiety leapt under her skin. She turned from the two raw chickens sitting in a roasting pan on the counter. "What? Where? Is Mom okay?"

"She's fine." Tom scratched his jaw. "She just wants to be alone for a little while. I thought I'd go down to the quay and give Matt a hand."

Meg smiled. That figured. Dad had been cooped up in the hospital for weeks. He could use a little guy time. But all she said was, "Dinner at seven."

"Sounds good." He brushed a whiskered kiss against her cheek, surprising her. Dad had never been what you'd call demonstrative. He sniffed. "Smells good, too."

"That's the rosemary. I'm making Mom's roast chicken."

According to the schedule Matt had created, it was her brother's night to cook. But Meg had noticed he didn't object to coming home to find dinner already started. None of them did. So she'd taken over the family meal prep along with the baking and management of the B and B.

Besides, Matt had already taken half the day off to welcome Mom home, turning his charter over to a hired captain. Meg knew what it cost him to lose a fishing trip this late in the season.

"You sure you don't mind?" he'd asked Meg before leaving.

"Go." She'd waved him away. Maybe she wasn't in

VIRGINIA KANTRA

command of her department anymore, but she had dinner under control. "Meet your boat. Book another client. I've got this."

Why not? She was stuck here all day anyway.

She grabbed a meat skewer and stabbed at the lemon, its rind exploding in little bursts of juice. *Jab, jab, jab.*

Tom stopped in the doorway. "You'll check on your mother."

"Of course," Meg said. "Go do manly things with Matt. Grab a beer or something. You've earned it."

She stuffed the lemons and rosemary into the chicken cavities and trussed the legs lightly together. She rarely cooked for Derek. The few times she'd purchased food, planning a meal, he worked late, or she did, and dinner was either ruined sitting on the stove or spoiled sitting in the refrigerator. It was easier to go out.

She ground pepper over the chickens, her gaze sliding away from the silver laptop sitting idle on the table. At least her family appreciated her cooking. There was something rewarding about rolling up her sleeves and getting the job done, about following directions and getting tangible results.

Too bad her job search didn't work that way.

When the birds were in the oven, she washed her hands and tapped lightly on her parents' bedroom door.

No answer.

Meg eased the door open, hoping Tess was asleep, trying not to wake her. She'd looked so gaunt, so gray, getting out of the car. Not as bad as in the hospital, but her appearance had still shocked Meg. Despite Tess's salt-and-pepper hair, she'd always seemed younger than her fifty-nine years, trim and energetic.

Now she looked frail. Old.

One more shift in the foundation of Meg's world.

Tess turned her head on the pillow, her eyes dark and unfocused.

"Hi, Mom," Meg said softly. "How are you feeling? Do you need anything?"

"I'm fine."

Meg smiled wryly. "Yeah, that's probably what you said to the paramedics when they were cutting you out of the wreck."

Great. Remind her about the accident. That will make her feel better.

"Well." Meg hovered, awkward at this reversal in their roles. How many times had her mother stood by her bedside, dispensing hugs after a bad dream or ginger ale for an upset stomach? "I should let you rest. Dad said you wanted to be alone."

"I said that to get him out of my hair. The poor man's been stuck shuttling between the motel and hospital for the past three weeks. He needs a break." The corners of Tess's eyes crinkled. "We both do."

Meg smiled back. "That's sort of what I said." *Her mother's daughter, after all.* Oddly, the thought didn't bother her as much as it used to. "Sure I can't get you anything?"

"You could keep me company." Tess patted the bed beside her.

Meg sat cautiously on the very edge of the mattress, mindful of the potatoes waiting to be peeled, wary of disturbing her mother's healing bones.

Tess's eyes searched her face. "How are *you* doing, sweetheart?"

"Fine."

"Ah."

Meg flushed. It was true. True enough. Getting fired wasn't in the same class at all as getting hit by a truck. *You should tell your family*, Sam had said, and she would. Eventually. Later, when they'd both had a chance to recover.

"Sam's sister's getting married," she said, seizing on a topic she thought would interest her mother.

"I heard. To a Navy man. A doctor," Tess said brightly.

Meg rolled her eyes. "You want me to marry a doctor, Ma?"

"No," Tess said, surprising her. "You need someone who will put you first, not his schedule or his patients."

Derek puts me first, Meg wanted to say.

But he didn't. So she couldn't. Sam's voice taunted her. *He doesn't have your back, sugar.*

"I can take care of myself," she said.

"Of course you can," her mother agreed.

"Anyway, you married a Marine," Meg pointed out. "That's worse than a doctor."

"My sacrifice was always less than your father's," Tess said simply. "I had the life I wanted with the man I love. How many women are lucky enough to say that?"

Meg thought of pointing out that Tess could hardly have lived her own dream, leaving her large, extended Italian family in Chicago to follow Tom from base to base. Raising three children alone during deployments. Settling after Tom's retirement on Dare Island, where the Fletchers had lived for generations.

But she couldn't argue with her mother's wish. *The life I wanted with the man I love.*

That was what Meg wanted, too. That was what she'd thought she had in New York with Derek.

Tess patted her hand on the covers. "So how is Sam?"

Sam? Meg narrowed her eyes.

Tess smiled. "Hey, don't blame me. You brought him up."

And her mother had always had a soft spot for Matt's friend, even before he'd built her a ramp in the backyard.

Meg sighed. Ignoring Tess's question would only make Sam seem more important than he was. Or should be.

"He's . . ." Meg stopped herself from saying, *Fine*. "He hasn't changed."

Although that wasn't really fair, she thought. Or true. Sam seemed deeper, more caring, than the boy she remembered. Maybe he'd grown up. Or was it only her perception of him that was changing?

"I don't think he has, at heart," Tess said thoughtfully. "Of course, he's more confident now."

Meg gaped at her mother. "Confident? Oh, please. If Sam were any more confident, he'd need a wheelbarrow to cart his ego around. He was the most popular guy in school."

"Who said popularity had anything to do with confidence? Look at you."

"Me? I was never popular. I was too busy."

Tess smiled at Meg as if she'd said something insightful. "Exactly."

Meg's cell phone rang. "Sorry," she said and reached to silence it.

"Do you need to get that?" Tess asked.

"No." Derek never called during work hours. Usually Meg called him at night. And who else had her number? Only the career coach.

"It could be work," Tess said.

No, it couldn't. But Meg glanced at the display just in case. Her heart beat faster as she registered the familiar 917 cell phone area code. *Manhattan*. "Actually, Mom, I should probably . . ."

Tess nodded. "You go ahead."

She took a deep breath and punched the green connect button. "Meg Fletcher."

"Meg, it's Bruce." The head of financial client services

at the outside PR firm she'd worked with for the past twelve years.

"Bruce." Genuine pleasure warmed her voice. "How did you—"

"Kelly gave me your number. We were all really sorry to hear you were gone."

Meg cupped her phone, praying her mother couldn't hear. "Thank you." She edged toward the door. Why was he calling? It wasn't as if she could do anything for him anymore. "I appreciate that."

"Well, we appreciate all the business you sent our way over the years. The partners want to know if we can offer you more than moral support."

Meg closed the bedroom door, swallowing the lump that rose to her throat. No matter how touched she was by this unexpected morale boost, getting weepy would not help her professional image. "Not unless you have a job for me," she joked.

"You don't want to work for us, trust me. It's different on the agency side."

"You mean, at the beck and call of a bunch of corporate divas who expect you to work miracles at a moment's notice?" she asked dryly.

Bruce chuckled. "I didn't say that."

"You didn't have to. I had an internship at an agency when I was in college."

"Did you, now." A pause, while her hopes rose and her fingers curled tightly around the phone. "You know I can't use you in my division," he said at last. "It wouldn't look good, having you in our financial services practice. Franklin is still our client."

She swallowed another lump, of disappointment this time. "I understand."

Maybe the worst part was, she did. She'd hired Bruce in

part because of his integrity. The same integrity that wouldn't let him hire her now.

She opened her lips to ask for names. Contacts. *Network, network*, the career coach had urged. But she wasn't used to pleading for favors. The words stuck in her throat.

"We miss you, though," Bruce added.

She fought to keep a positive spin on things, to keep the bitterness from her voice. "I'm sure Nicole is doing a great job." *My job.*

Bruce made a noncommittal hum. "Let's just say we're still learning to work together."

Industry code for, *She's incompetent and I don't like her.* Meg stifled a stab of pleasure. "Everybody has their own way of doing things," she said soothingly. "I'm sure you'll work things out."

"We're trying," Bruce said. "Derek took us all out to dinner to smooth things over, but . . ."

"Derek?" The word escaped before she could snatch it back. "Why would Derek be involved?"

"Nicole doesn't get most of the financial details around the acquisition. We needed to bring Derek into the loop to back her up. She seems to need a lot of . . ." Bruce paused. "Hand-holding," he said.

Hand-holding?

What did that mean? And who exactly was holding Nicole's hand? Meg's mind spun like the circle of doom on a frozen computer screen. Was Derek . . . ? Would Derek . . . ?

No. She was not questioning her relationship with her boyfriend because of some casual comment from a colleague.

Bruce was still talking. Meg pulled herself together. "What? I mean, beg pardon?"

"I asked if you would be open to working on projects outside of financial services. A change of pace."

"Actually, I . . ." She took a deep breath. "I'd be very open to it."

"Good, good. I'll talk to some of the other heads and give you a call tomorrow. There are a couple projects in the hopper you might be interested in. We've got to get you back to New York."

Before it's too late.

"My thoughts exactly," Meg said.

She ended the call and went to check on her mother.

"I HAD AN interesting call from Bruce today," Meg said to Derek's voice mail.

She hesitated, sitting alone on the edge of her mattress. It was one thing to go straight to Derek with her suspicions, to give him an opportunity to explain. Something else entirely to leave an accusing message on his phone. Derek always said he admired her because she wasn't needy. She didn't cling. The last thing she wanted was for him to see her as one of those insecure females they both despised.

Sam's caustic drawl echoed in her head. *What you deserve is a guy who will be there for you all the time, not just when it's convenient for him.*

But she and Derek had a history together. They had a condo. Six *years* of sharing late nights at the office and lazy Sunday mornings in bed. She'd been so certain she knew where they were going. So sure of herself.

And of him.

She wasn't sure of anything anymore.

Meg stared at the pictures hanging on her bedroom wall, the bold, flat eyes of the pirate Mary Read, the confident smile in her Harvard graduation photo.

"Anyway, call me," she said. Another pause. "I miss you."

I miss our life together.

She ended the call and sat a moment longer, clutching the phone as if she could hold on to her former life, as if she were touching him. Her insides churned. Slowly, by default, her mind returned to the things she could control, the list of tasks she'd inherited from her mother. Dinner dishes, done. Breakfast service, set. Lightbulb in the William Kidd Room, replaced. She needed to refile the movie DVDs, call Bill at the bike shop to confirm this weekend's rental bikes, play homework cop with Taylor.

"Meg!" Her father's voice carried up the stairs, loud, urgent. "Get down here!"

Mom.

Adrenaline propelled Meg off the bed and down the stairs.

The door to the master suite stood open. She crossed the kitchen with quick, decisive steps, faltering on the threshold of her parents' room.

Tess was propped up in bed, all smiles.

Meg stopped in the doorway, weak-kneed with relief.

Matt was there, his arm around Allison, who looked as fresh and pink as the roses in her arms. A welcome home bouquet? But Taylor held a bunch of daisies, too, gingerly, at arm's length, as if they might give her cooties or a rash.

And there, sitting by her mother's bed, looking lean and dark in the crowded room, was Sam.

He was so obviously not one of them—not blond, not a Fletcher—and just as clearly comfortable making himself at home.

He looked . . . good, Meg acknowledged. He'd obviously come from work. A meeting? His tie was loosened and pulled down, his Brooks Brothers shirt was rolled at the sleeves, revealing the column of his throat, his strong, square wrists, his forearms, dusted with hair. His tan glowed against the crisp cotton. His teeth looked very white.

Meg looked away, annoyed by the quick tattoo of her heart, stirred by the memory of his slow, hot, melting kiss. He'd been around for most of her adolescence, she reminded herself. His presence here didn't mean anything.

And neither did his kisses.

Tom was pouring one of the bottles of champagne they kept on hand for the Romance Package into a row of flutes on the dresser. At Meg's entrance, he glanced up, his weathered face cracking in a grin. "There you are. Grab yourself a glass, girl. Your brother's getting married."

Not a crisis, then, Meg thought. A celebration. Matt must have made his announcement.

She glanced again at Sam. *Matt loves Allison. And she loves him. Can't you just be happy for him?*

Her smile felt almost natural. "I heard."

"Come on, shorty." Josh nudged Taylor toward the door. "I'll get you a soda."

Meg flattened herself against the doorway to let them pass. Fezzik's tail thumped her legs as the dog followed them from the room.

Tess was struggling to sit up, another, larger bouquet—sunflowers, red and orange roses, blue delphiniums—lying across her lap.

Meg started forward. "Here, Mom, let me get that."

Tess beamed at her. "Sam brought me flowers."

"Brought all of us flowers," Allison said.

Taylor, too, Meg thought, remembering the daisies. *Slick.* Part of her appreciated his generous gesture, his innate good manners, his charm. The problem came when you took those gestures personally, when you mistook his knee-jerk courtesy for caring.

Sam met her gaze, a corner of his mouth quirking as if he could read her thoughts. "It'll take a while for those rosebushes out back to recover from being transplanted. You all should have something to enjoy until they do."

"So you bought out the flower shop."

His grin flashed. "Just doing my part to support the local economy." He reached down to the floor and then across the bed. "These are for you."

A bold burst of deep-throated lilies, coral, crimson, fuchsia, gold, spilled their fragrance in the room. A wave of pleasure took her by the throat. The vivid colors, the creamy textures, invited her to touch. To smell. She squashed the urge to bury her face in them.

Derek bought her flowers, she thought defensively. For her birthday and Valentine's Day, two dozen stiff red roses with a scattering of baby's breath, the prescribed bouquet of florists and boyfriends everywhere. She wasn't going to lose her head just because Sam had thought to buy her something different.

She sniffed, unable to resist the lilies' perfume. "Pretty. Thanks. I hope Rowan gave you a discount."

Meg had met the owner of The Secret Garden last week when she'd placed an order for the inn. Rowan Whitlock was single, successful, and earthily sexy. Sam's gesture couldn't buy Meg's approval. But his extravagance would certainly have made an impression on the florist.

Sam's eyes laughed at her. "She did. Let me help you get those in water."

Meg jerked one shoulder in dismissal. "I've got it, thanks."

She wasn't trying to be rude. Okay, maybe she was, a little. She needed to establish some space. Distance. Perspective. Somehow Sam's effortless courtesy to every female in the room made Derek's lack of attention even more glaring. And painful.

Twelve bouquets in six years, she thought. Unvarying, interchangeable.

Not that she needed flowers to validate her relationship with her boyfriend.

But she needed . . . something. A phone call.

"I'll just grab another wineglass," she said and escaped.

In the kitchen, she checked her messages again. Nothing.

She stood on tiptoe to get two vases down from the cupboard.

Josh came up behind her, reaching over her head. "Here you go, Aunt Meg."

She sighed. "Thanks, big guy. Taylor, do you want to get your flowers? We should put them in water."

Taylor hitched a shoulder. "I don't care. I don't see why he gave me flowers. I'm just a kid."

"Didn't anybody ever bring you a present for no reason before?" Meg asked lightly.

Taylor's face shuttered. "No."

Something prickled at the back of Meg's neck. She didn't mind that her niece wasn't bowled over by Sam's charm. But surely the child's reaction was a little unusual? Meg remembered the thrill of getting her first bouquet from her father, her first corsage in college. Maybe Taylor associated flowers with her mother's funeral?

Maybe they should both stop looking for problems and picking at motives and just enjoy.

"Sam's just being nice," Meg said.

Taylor gave her a disbelieving look. Dawn had been a single mother, Meg recalled. Taylor barely knew her father, was just beginning to trust Matt. Her experience of nice guys and male attention was probably limited.

"Why don't you get them while I take care of Grandma's flowers?" Meg said.

She arranged the bouquet in a creamy Lenox vase and found a blue pitcher for Taylor's daisies. Conversation drifted from the other room, the rumble of male voices, murmurs from Tess and Allison. Resisting the urge to linger over her lilies, Meg grabbed a glass and a handful of napkins. With brisk, businesslike movements, she assembled a plate from this evening's leftover wine and cheese and the fruit she'd cut up for tomorrow's breakfast buffet. Everything nicely arranged, everything under control.

"Here." She thrust the plate at Josh. "Pass this around."

". . . in my dresser," Tess was saying as they trooped back into the bedroom.

Tom stood like a spar, stiff and motionless, as if he didn't know or couldn't find whatever she was talking about.

"I'll get it, Ma," Meg intervened. She set the flowers in front of the mirror. "What do you need?"

"My old jewelry box. In the bottom drawer," Tess said.

Oh, crap. Meg froze, suddenly comprehending her father's reluctance. But it was too late to back out now. She glanced at Matt as she got the box and laid it on the bed. Her brother's face was set like stone.

Tess's hands trembled slightly as she opened a blue velvet box. "This was my mother's ring," she said to Allison.

The ring that Kimberly had never worn, Meg recalled. *Had never wanted.*

Shit.

Allison looked stunned. The diamond winked in its basket setting, delicate, classic, lovely.

Small. Meg winced.

"Of course, it's a little old-fashioned," Tess said into the silence. "You might want to change the setting. Or the stone. It's not very big. But it's—"

"It's perfect," Allison breathed. Her fingers gripped Matt's arm. A flush rose to her cheeks. You would have thought Tess was offering her the Koh-I-Noor, at least. "Isn't it perfect?" she asked Matt.

Tess's face relaxed into smiles. "She wanted it to go to my oldest son."

Allison held Matt's gaze, her cheeks rosy with hope. "So it's yours?"

He shook his head, looking deep in her eyes, raw emotion in his face. "Yours," he said simply. "If you'll have it. If you'll have me."

Her eyes were dazed with wonder and shining with tears. "You know I will," she whispered.

He kissed her, bruising the roses between them.

They might as well have been alone, Meg thought, despite the room full of family. There was no one else for either of them in that moment.

No one else, ever.

She turned away, swiping under her eyes with her fingertips. "Crap. Now you've made me cry."

"Have some champagne," Sam said with a smile.

She took the glass he offered and gulped. The fizzy liquid eased the tightness in her throat, but not the ache in her chest.

Matt and Allison's embrace dissolved into happy chaos. Matt beamed as he ruffled Josh's hair, as he ducked his punch. Allison was laughing, crying, her joy contagious. She rose on her toes to kiss Tom's cheek, was hugged and thumped by Josh and Taylor, bent over the bed to receive Tess's kiss and her blessing.

She belonged, Meg realized, laying the ghost of Kimberly to rest forever. With Matt. With all of them.

"You must be used to this," Tom said to Sam.

His brows drew together.

"He means because your sister just got engaged," Meg

said hastily. *Not because your father's been married four times.*

"To a Navy man," Tom said.

"Yes, sir. Chelsea's following Ryan out to San Diego after the wedding."

"Good for her."

Of course her father would think so. Mom had traipsed after him for twenty years.

Tess looked up from admiring the ring on Allison's finger. "That's not what you said when we were first married."

Meg had never heard that before. "What? Why not?"

"He was on his way to Cambodia," Tess said.

" 'First in, last out,' " Matt quoted the Marine slogan softly, his gaze on his father.

"Well, obviously you couldn't go with him overseas," Meg said.

"He didn't want me living on base, either," Tess said.

"I thought your mother should be near her family. In case." Tom cleared his throat. "It's different for the squids."

Sam's brows rose. "You have a problem with the Navy?"

Tom grinned. "Nah. The Marines are a Department in the Navy." He paused again for effect. "The Men's Department."

Josh snickered at the old joke.

"Why have you never married, Sam?" Tess asked.

Meg's eyes met his with a jolt. What had he said to her a week ago? *I'm a little old to be blaming Daddy because I haven't found the woman I want to spend the rest of my life with.*

He answered Tess slowly, his gaze on Meg. "If I could find a woman who bakes cookies like you, Mrs. Fletcher, I'd marry her in a minute."

It was a gracious, even flirtatious, answer, made to the woman who had mothered him through his teenage years.

Tess laughed, pleased.

But he was looking at Meg.

That night as she lay in bed waiting for Derek to call, Meg caught herself dwelling on that look, reliving it, deciphering it like an adolescent girl with a high school crush.

If I could find a woman who bakes cookies like you . . .

I'll bake you some cookies . . .

They're made with love . . .

She flopped on to her stomach, punching the pillow in frustration. The mirror above her bureau reflected the lilies back into the room, their colors muted by night.

This was ridiculous. She had outgrown her juvenile fixation on Sam a million years ago. She'd moved on. They'd both moved on.

I'd marry her in a minute.

The scent of lilies drifted through the dark and followed her into sleep.

Nine

MEG PROPPED THE scarecrow against the inn's front rail. Above her, she could hear scrapes and thumps as Tom lashed a life-sized crow's nest to the roof of the porch.

The Pirates' Rest always had gone overboard on Halloween.

"Mom, I've got this," Meg said, tugging on the scarecrow's velvet Blackbeard coat. "You should go inside and rest."

Tess adjusted the eye patch on a stuffed parrot. "I want to help. There's so much to do."

There certainly was. Meg eyed the pile of pirate-themed decorations. "Have you and Dad ever considered cutting back on the whole ghost ship thing?"

"We have. We did. We're not doing the Davy Jones's Locker display this year."

"Was that the one where the pool sprang a leak and flooded the front yard?" Meg asked dryly.

Tess laughed. "That was the Graveyard of the Atlantic. I talked him out of that one several years ago."

"Right." Meg plopped a plumed hat atop the straw pirate's wig. "Seriously, Mom, no one expects you to keep up with everything this year. You were in a car accident."

"Which didn't kill me. It only slowed me down." Tess's jaw set. "I'm sick of feeling that I can't do things. It's Taylor's first Halloween with us. I want it to be special."

"Because nothing says 'home for the holidays' like a skull with flashing eyeballs singing, *Yo ho ho and a bottle of rum*."

Tess smiled and shook her head. "You know what I mean. It *is* a holiday, the first one of the off-season with all the tourists gone. It's time to celebrate and reconnect as a community. Maybe it's different in New York, but—"

"Hey, we have tourists in New York," Meg protested. "And holidays. You should see Halloween in the Village!"

"I'm sure it's wonderful. But it's not the same."

You could say that again.

More than miles separated Dare Island from the mainland. Its centuries-old isolation couldn't be spanned by the bridge or eliminated by a ferry. It was bred in the bone. It lingered in the brogue, in the islanders' fierce independence and their equal willingness to help their neighbors in times of trouble. Living in New York, Meg sometimes forgot how far she had come.

And how much she had left behind.

"Yeah, because you leave the decorations up for weeks," she teased.

"We have two families coming this weekend with children," Tess said placidly. "They'll enjoy the decorations."

"I thought you were looking forward to a Halloween without guests."

"I'm happy to take time for just family, of course," Tess

answered promptly. "But we need our visitors to survive—not just the Pirates' Rest, but the whole island. Besides, I like watching people check in all clutched up or stressed out, knowing our hospitality can help them relax and feel better."

"Of course they're relaxed. They get a holiday, and you do all the work."

Tess's gaze rested thoughtfully on her only daughter. "Is that what you remember about the holidays?"

Yes. Meg flushed. "No."

She didn't want to criticize her mother or her choices.

There were always guests. There was always work. But her parents had been careful to preserve family time, too, rare vacations and regular Sunday dinners. Her father's time in the Corps had made them flexible about scheduling celebrations. Meg remembered one year their Christmas tree had stood decorated in the family room until past Groundhog's Day when Daddy came home from Lebanon. And on Halloween . . .

"We used to make the best popcorn balls." A memory surfaced of forming an assembly line at the kitchen table, Luke's sticky hands and Matt's earnest face and the smell of caramel and vanilla thick in the air. "And caramel apples."

Tess smiled and then sighed. "I'm afraid I won't be able to manage popcorn balls this year."

Of course not. Her mother had to hold on to the kitchen counter for support. There was no way she should be handling pans of hot candy.

"I could do it," Meg heard herself say.

"Oh, honey. I can't ask you to take on another responsibility."

Meg shrugged. "So I'll get the kids to help." She watched the hope bloom in her mother's eyes and added, "You can supervise. It'll be fun."

You need a little fun, Sam's voice whispered wickedly in her head.

Not that this was the kind of fun he had in mind. But at least she couldn't get into trouble making popcorn balls.

WHEN TAYLOR AND Josh came up the back walk after school, Aunt Meg was waiting for them with milk and cookies and a list.

Living with Aunt Meg was like living with one of those birds that ran along the water's edge. Always moving, always poking their beaks into everything. *Yellowlegs*, Uncle Matt said they were called.

It wasn't enough for her to be busy, Taylor thought. She liked to find stuff for you to do, too, like homework or setting the table. Taylor envied Josh, who could get out of things by slipping away to the cottage he shared with Uncle Matt.

But not today.

"Halloween is *tomorrow*," Aunt Meg announced like it was a big deal.

Which it wasn't. Taylor had mostly avoided even thinking about Halloween this year. Mom had always made the holiday fun. Maybe because she was younger than the other moms, maybe because it was always just the two of them, but sometimes it was like they were kids together. Mom never bought little candy bars. *What's fun about fun size?* she'd ask, and Taylor would giggle. Last year Mom took Taylor and her best friend Ashley to Goodwill to find some really cool stuff to dress up as hippies, and then Ashley's dad took them around the neighborhood. But Taylor didn't have a costume this year.

Her throat felt tight. Or a mom. It would never be just the two of them again.

Taylor dunked her cookie in her milk to soften it.

She had a father now, except she didn't *know* him. She never knew what to say when he called. *Please don't die*? That would be dumb.

When they Skyped, it was both better and worse. Better, because she could see for herself that he was safe. Worse, because there was no way to hide that they had nothing to say to each other. When he asked about school and if she was making friends yet, she lied and said yes. When she asked if he was okay, *he* said yes. Maybe he lied, too.

Things weren't all bad. She had Grandma Tess and Grandpa Tom and Aunt Meg, when they were here. Which mostly they hadn't been, since Grandma's accident.

She had Uncle Matt and Josh and Allison. Rachel Wilson said that now that Uncle Matt and Allison were getting married, they would be their own family and they wouldn't want Taylor around anymore.

Taylor bit her lip, watching the cookie crumbs settle to the bottom of the glass. That was not what Uncle Matt said. Uncle Matt said Taylor was staying, and she believed Uncle Matt. Anyway, Rachel was a butt.

But it was true Taylor didn't have anybody to go trick-or-treating with this year.

Virginia Dare Island School was small. It wasn't like her old school, with different groups, the girls who liked horses or Barbies or dodgeball and the ones who were already into boys. Here everybody hung out with everybody else. Which meant if you weren't part of the whole group, you were really on your own, because there was nobody else to make friends with. Ever since Taylor had punched Rachel Wilson's big brother, Ethan, in the stomach, she was out of the group. Nobody messed with her, because of Josh, but nobody liked her, either.

She shoved a cookie in her mouth so she wouldn't have to think about it.

Aunt Meg ran her finger down the list by the phone. "You need to call your Grandma Jolene," she said to Taylor.

Taylor's heart slammed into her ribs. "Why?" she said around a mouthful of crumbs.

"Because she called you."

Taylor swallowed hard to relieve the tightness in her throat. "I'm having a snack now."

"After the snack, then." Aunt Meg dug a big yellow bowl out from under the sink, muttering, "Popcorn. Popsicle sticks. Caramel. Candles."

Josh waggled his eyebrows at Taylor. "It's like watching Martha Stewart on crack."

She smiled weakly, grateful for the change of subject.

Aunt Meg's lips curved, but she pointed a finger at him like a gun. "You."

"What?" he asked, all innocence.

"I need you to go to the organic farm for apples. And we need pumpkins for the sideboard and the hall. We'll all help carve when you get back."

Taylor slid a glance toward Josh. Pumpkins sounded kind of fun. And maybe if they were busy, Aunt Meg would forget all about phone calls for a while. "Can I carve my own?" she asked.

Aunt Meg pursed her lips. "Use a knife, you mean?"

Taylor nodded, her heart picking up speed. "I think Luke would let me." She didn't know. But maybe.

"Your dad," Aunt Meg said.

Taylor nodded.

"We'll see," Aunt Meg said, which usually meant no, but maybe Taylor could talk to Uncle Matt. Uncle Matt let her work on his motorcycle. He might say yes.

"You want me to go to the Hamiltons' farm?" Josh asked.

"You can take the truck."

"Sweet." Josh didn't get a chance to drive Uncle Matt's pickup very often. But he didn't sound happy.

Aunt Meg narrowed her eyes. "Problem?"

"Not exactly."

Taylor stared at her milk. She knew why Josh didn't want to go to the Hamiltons'. It was because of the Hamiltons' daughter, Thalia, who used to come over sometimes to eat pizza and do newspaper stuff with Josh. Taylor liked Thalia. She had big black glasses that made her look smart, and she talked to Taylor like an actual person with a brain instead of treating her like a baby.

Taylor thought Josh liked Thalia, too. Anyway, she was pretty sure she'd seen them kissing. Okay, not kissing, exactly, but they'd jumped apart on the sofa when Taylor came into the room like Uncle Matt and Allison did sometimes.

But after that, Josh and Thalia had some kind of fight.

Now Thalia didn't come over anymore. No more pizza dates. No more other girl in the house to make Taylor feel a little bit less like a freak.

Taylor had tried talking to Josh. *You could invite her over sometimes when you're watching me. I don't mind.*

But he just got this weird look on his face and changed the subject. It was like he was *avoiding* Thalia. And that wasn't right, because Thalia was nice.

"All right, then." Aunt Meg gave Josh some money. "Off you go."

He stuffed the bills in his pocket and grabbed the last cookie. "Come on, shorty. You can help pick out the pumpkins."

"I thought Taylor could come to the store with me." Aunt Meg looked at Taylor and smiled almost shyly. "Unless you'd rather go with Josh," she added, like Taylor actually had a choice.

Taylor was torn. Part of her wanted to tag along with Josh. Finding a cousin was like having the big brother she'd always dreamed of, tall and cool and carelessly kind. And picking pumpkins sounded like a lot more fun than shopping with Aunt Meg. Maybe if she went, she could say something, do something, to get Josh and Thalia to make up.

Except she knew in her heart that *that* wasn't going to happen. Having a little kid along was not going to fix things.

But having some time alone together might.

"No," she said nobly. "I'd rather come with you."

Aunt Meg looked surprised and then smiled. "Okay."

Taylor swallowed a little lump of guilt at lying to her aunt. It wasn't *that* big a fib. Not compared to the other lies she'd told.

"NUTS OR NO nuts for the caramel apples?" Meg asked, holding up a bag of pecans.

Taylor hitched a shoulder. "I dunno." Her tone said, *I don't care.*

Meg suppressed a sigh. Okay, so the Island Market wasn't Bloomingdale's. It wasn't even the mall. Meg wasn't winning any Aunt of the Year Award by bringing her niece grocery shopping. But at least Meg was trying. Couldn't Taylor pretend to be interested?

"Nuts," Meg said, tossing them into the basket. "Then we can make some with and some without."

Taylor nodded without enthusiasm.

"Meg?" asked a female voice. "Meg Fletcher?"

Meg turned. A dark-haired young woman with a mermaid tattoo on her arm smiled at her from behind a shopping cart.

Meg's mind went blank.

"It's Cynthie," the woman said. "Cynthia Lodge?"

"Cynthie. *Hi.*"

A genuine rush of nostalgia and affection caught Meg like a ripple at the water's edge. She and Cynthie were in the same grade in school. Cynthie smoked, she drank, she was always cutting classes. Once Meg started taking honors and AP courses, they'd only had gym together. But Meg would never forget how kind the other girl had been when Meg first moved to the island.

They hugged. Cynthie even smelled the same, like cloves and cigarettes. "It's been forever, right?" Cynthie said. "It's like homecoming week around here. You know Sam Grady's back on the island now, too."

"I . . . Yes." Meg had gotten used to the anonymity of New York, where no one noticed you were gone or remarked when you came back. Here, the web of connections tangled you up. "Matt told me you gave him a hand at the inn while Mom was in the hospital. Thank you."

Cynthie waved her thanks away. "What are neighbors for? It was just a part-time thing anyway, helping out on the weekends. Hey, Taylor."

Taylor bobbed her head.

There were two little girls with Cynthie, one Taylor's age, the other a few years younger with a puff of hair like a seeding dandelion.

Meg smiled at them. "Are these your . . ." Her mind stuttered again. *Daughters?* She and Cynthie weren't that old, were they?

"These are my girls," Cynthie said proudly. "Madison's in Taylor's class. And this is my baby, Hannah."

"Hi," Meg said. "So how's . . ." She tried to remember the name of Cynthie's high school boyfriend. *Donald? Dennis?* "Douglas?"

"I guess he's fine." Cynthie's pleasant voice turned flat. "He lives in Charlotte now. We're divorced."

"Oh, I'm sorry."

Meg's own life plan had never included the get-married-out-of-high-school-and-have-babies scenario. She wanted to go somewhere, do something, be somebody, before she had to live her life for the convenience of other people. Okay, so her career-first strategy hadn't saved her from disappointment. But at least she didn't have to worry about kids.

"Don't be. I was kind of tired of him sitting on my couch and using my credit cards anyway." Cynthie smoothed a hand over her younger daughter's hair. "How about you? You married that New York guy yet?"

The island grapevine, Meg thought, wincing. Everybody knew everybody else, and even years later, they thought they knew you, too. No question was too personal, no topic off-limits.

"I'm not in any rush." Which was what she always told herself and anyone else who asked. In college, she had chosen to study, work, and date unfettered by a serious boyfriend. It was only in the past few years, with Derek, that she'd started to long for a deeper connection, a more conventional commitment. "We're waiting for the right time."

"Or you're waiting for the right guy." Cynthie grinned ruefully. "You always were smarter than me."

Meg's mind flashed back to New Year's eighteen years ago. To Sam. "Not always. So . . ." She glanced into Cynthie's cart, seeking a way to change the subject. "Are you shopping for Halloween?"

"Yep. We've got the candy. Not so sure about the costumes," Cynthie confided. "Madison's at that awkward age."

Madison looked mortified. "Mo-om."

"Too old for trick-or-treating?" Meg asked. That would explain Taylor's lack of enthusiasm.

"You're never too old for free candy. But she's too old to be a princess, like this one, and I won't let her dress up like a hoochie mama, so . . ." Cynthie shrugged. "Here we are. Too bad I don't have time to take them to the mainland. Everything on the shelves is Batman and Jason."

Meg looked from Madison's sulky face to Taylor's carefully disinterested one, an idea slowly forming in her mind. In the week that she'd been home, she'd never seen another child come over to play. Taylor needed friends her own age, a companion other than a big shepherd-Lab mix.

"You know, I just left my parents in a pile of pirate swords and eye patches. Lots of costume options there."

"Pirates are boys," Madison said.

"Not all of them," Meg said.

Cynthie nodded. "That's right. Remember the rooms at the inn, Maddie? Anne Bonney and . . . What's the other one?"

"Mary Read," Meg said. "That's my room, actually."

"There's a picture of her." Taylor looked at Madison. "With an ax."

Madison's eyes widened.

"Well." Meg took a deep breath. She could coordinate a major PR campaign for a Fortune 500 company. Surely she could finesse a simple play date between two ten-year-olds. "Maybe Madison would like to come over and look through costumes. If that's all right with you."

Madison's gaze fell to her shoes. Taylor scowled.

Meg's stomach sank.

"I want to come," Hannah said.

"You're too young," her sister said.

"I'm not. I'm eight. Mom, tell her I can come, too."

"Well, I don't know . . ." Cynthie looked at Meg.

"Let her come," Taylor said unexpectedly. "We got lots of stuff."

Meg smiled. "And we're making popcorn balls. Plenty of work for another pair of hands."

"Your mama always had the best treats," Cynthie said. "When I was little, the inn was my favorite place to go trick-or-treating."

"We're making caramel apples, too," Taylor said to no one in particular.

Madison nodded. "Nuts or no nuts?"

"Both," Taylor said proudly.

"Why don't you all come?" Meg invited recklessly. Taylor wasn't the only one who needed friends her own age.

Cynthie sighed. "I'd love to. But I'm working at the Fish House, four to eight. Soon as we're done here, I'm dropping the girls off at Mama's." She watched the two girls, her expression almost wistful. "Sorry."

It couldn't be easy, Meg thought, juggling shifts at the Fish House with parenthood. "Why don't you leave them with me for the afternoon," she suggested. "I'll bring them to your mother's in time for dinner."

Cynthie hesitated. "I don't want to impose."

"Please, Mom?"

"We-ell . . ."

"What are neighbors for?" Meg said, and at the echo of her own question, Cynthie's face relaxed.

"That'd be great," she said. "Thanks."

It *was* great, Meg thought as she loaded the girls and the groceries into the car. *She* was great. She could be a great aunt.

At least until she went back to New York.

Ten

"YOU LOOK GREAT," Tess said to Meg the following night.

Meg laughed and fingered the ruffle on her shirt as she came down the stairs. Carefully, in her best black stiletto-heeled boots, but inside she was dancing. Big gold hoops dangled from her ears, and she'd tied a bandanna rakishly over her hair. "What the well-dressed pirate is wearing."

"It's not your costume. Though I think it's wonderful that you dressed up to take the girls trick-or-treating. It's you. You look . . ." Tess tilted her head to one side as she considered. "Happy."

Meg grinned. "I am."

Tess raised her brows. "Good phone call?"

Meg's smile dried out at the edges. The problem with feeling good was that it never lasted. What should she say? She still hadn't told her parents about getting canned at work. She needed to tell them . . . Something. Soon. But not now, when she was on her way out the door. "Yeah, it was, thanks."

Tess made that hum, the one that expressed polite disbelief while keeping the lines of communication open. *It must be a mom thing.* "Everything all right with Derek?"

How did she *do* that?

Meg had finally gotten hold of Derek last night. The phone call had not gone well. Their conversation had been brief and unsatisfying, with too many failed connections and awkward pauses. It wasn't so much that Derek had dissed her day's accomplishments—finding a friend for Taylor, making practically perfect popcorn balls. He was simply profoundly uninterested. Kids and cooking had never been part of their daily vocabulary. And when Meg had tried to move the discussion to work, Derek had been almost abrupt.

But all that would change now, she told herself. Now that she really had something important to share.

She shook her head, making the gold hoops swing. "That wasn't Derek. It was Bruce. You remember, from work?"

"What did he want?"

Some of the good feeling came back. Bruce wanted to consult with Meg about a project. It was contract work, not a job offer. But it would get her back on the radar, back in the game.

"He wants to see me."

"And who wouldn't," Tess said.

Meg rolled her eyes. "It's business, Mom."

"I know that. I'm just saying it's nice to be needed. Will you have to go back to New York?"

"Just for a day."

At least initially. Bruce wanted her to meet with the management team on Friday. And the client. An author. *You did say you'd be open to projects outside of financial services*, he'd reminded her. *A change of pace.*

A challenge. Meg almost bounced in excitement.

He was e-mailing her the author's background information, so she could prepare. She wanted to do her own client assessment. She needed to make airline reservations, Meg thought, her mind skipping ahead. At moments like this, she really missed her oh-so-capable assistant, Kelly.

She pulled her thoughts back to focus on her mother. "Are you going to be all right home alone? Tonight, I mean?"

Tess smiled. "Hardly alone. I have your father and a hundred or so trick-or-treaters to keep me company."

"Speaking of trick-or-treaters . . ." Meg glanced toward the kitchen. "Where's my pirate crew?"

Yesterday, the girls' initial stiffness with each other had dissolved during the sweet and sticky process of making popcorn balls. After washing their hands, they had dived into the inn's pirate store. Taylor and Madison were now fully tricked out as fierce female pirates. Even eight-year-old Hannah had insisted on adding a cutlass to her princess finery.

"They're waiting out front with your dad." Tess's smile spread. "He's showing off his special effects."

"Yo ho ho," Meg said and went out to join them.

The light from the hall cut across the porch. She closed the front door quickly behind her so she didn't ruin the scene for the three girls staring wide-eyed from the front walk. Red spotlights bathed the figure of Blackbeard at a giant ship's wheel and the Jolly Roger hanging from the inn sign. The air was full of prerecorded sounds, creaking ropes, and the wash of waves. A deep voice intoned, " 'There will be no survivors. All your worst nightmares are about to come true.' "

Meg grinned as she recognized the movie line from *The Princess Bride*. The little girls gasped and giggled.

A tall, spare figure in a long hooded cape stood beside a control board hidden in a fake barrel of rum.

Standing on tiptoe, Meg kissed her father's cheek. "The Dread Pirate Roberts, I presume?"

Tom pushed back his cowl and winked. "Retired now. You girls heading out?"

Meg nodded. "I'm taking them through the neighborhood down to the quay. Cynthie gets off her shift at the Fish House at eight. I figured we'd meet up with her there and then hit the shops along the waterfront."

"Don't forget your flashlights," Tom said. "And watch out for cars."

He talked to her as if she were still Taylor's age, Meg thought, with amused affection. "I will," she promised. She saw the first trick-or-treaters shuffling up the walk, a butterfly clutching a plastic pumpkin and a very short Spiderman holding his father's hand. "Have fun."

"You, too, babe."

Meg walked the "plank" that led from the porch to the front yard. Behind her, the Dread Pirate Roberts boomed, " 'My men are *here*! I am *here*! But soon *YOU* will not be *here*!' "

Right. Meg squashed a squiggle of discomfort as she joined the girls. Because she was going to New York.

"WELL, I DON'T know, Sam." Walt Rogers, head of the town zoning board, frowned thoughtfully into his beer. While other barrier islands fell to the tides of tourism and development, the Town of Dare had taken the unusual step of incorporating. They had their own police department now and the zoning board, both intended to protect the island's residents against outsiders. "Nobody wants to see a big condo development go up on that end of the island."

Sam kept one eye on Walt's glass and one on the noisy dining room. It was still early in the evening, more about free candy at the hostess station than paying customers in the bar. Webs of orange twinkle lights cast amber sparks on bottles and glassware. The sound system vibrated to Michael Jackson's *Thriller*. The servers, all in costume, threaded their way through tables of excited family groups and sun-burned fishermen.

He leaned his elbows on the bar. "Not condos, Walt. A mixed-use, pedestrian-friendly community."

"I don't see the damn difference."

"More green space," Sam answered promptly. "Public beach access. Priority given to folks who hold jobs on the island. Service jobs especially, teachers, firefighters, with a break on property taxes."

Walt set down his mug. "Lower property taxes mean lower revenues for the town."

"We've got plenty of wealthy summer residents paying their share," Sam said. He signaled to Cynthie to refill Walt's mug. He wasn't trying to get him drunk. He just wanted to get him to listen. "What we need to sustain a year-round economy is affordable housing for the people who live here the rest of the year."

He sounded like a damn politician, Sam thought, disgusted with himself. Talking points might work in Raleigh. But they wouldn't impress the Dare zoning board. Experience had taught the islanders a deep distrust of government experts with their studies and theories, regulations and fishing quotas. The only way to win Walt's support was to remind him that Sam was one of them.

"You say 'we' like you live here, son," Walt drawled. "But it's your daddy's property we're talking about. Your daddy's development. And there are some who think we've listened to your daddy too many times."

"His property. My project."

Walt grunted. "Most of us reckoned you'd be working for him eventually."

Sam's shoulders tightened. "Yeah, that's what he reckoned, too. He wasn't happy when I took off to start my own company."

"But he bankrolled you anyway."

"No," Sam said, surprised. "I went outside for the startup money. My business, my risk."

Cynthie, in a shimmering mermaid corset, delivered Walt's beer. Walt took a pull, looking around the restaurant. "That'd be about the time Carl opened this place."

"The year before," Sam said shortly.

It had been the last straw for twenty-six-year-old Sam.

The Fish House used to be an actual fish house, the place where local fishermen brought their catch to be cleaned. But as changing times threatened the fishermen's livelihood, Carl Grady had figured there was more money in feeding tourists than in dealing fish. He'd converted his valuable waterfront property into a restaurant.

And Sam had finally quit, walked out, turned his back on his father's money and ideas of progress.

"Can't stop progress," Walt said in an uncanny echo of Sam's thought. He took another sip of beer. "All we can do is try to slow it down some."

Sam felt a little leap of pulse, like a poker player drawing an inside straight. He needed an ally. Would Walt back him with the zoning board?

"You can't stop progress," he said cautiously, testing. "But you can turn it to your advantage."

Walt lowered his drink. "Your daddy's always been good at that. Can't say the rest of us have always benefited from his projects. A lot of people were hurt when he closed the fish house."

Sam took a deep breath. "Dare Plantation has deep water access. You can let it go to individual homeowners to put up private piers. Or you can rezone the parcel for mixed use and apply for funding, maybe a government grant, to establish a fishermen's co-op. Reopen the fish house in a new location so boats could offload their catch here instead of having to burn fuel all the way to Swans Ferry."

"A new fish house," Walt said. "That in the plans?"

Sam nodded. *All in.* "It will be. I met with the architects on Monday."

Walt's eyes were bright as grommets in his leathered face. "What's in it for you?"

A house, Sam thought.

A place in the community.

A stake in the island's future.

A vision flashed through his brain of Meg, standing on the empty lot against a background of sea and yellow flowers, her blue eyes shining, strands of hair sticking to her forehead, her warm, sure voice encouraging him. Challenging him. *Why don't you do it?*

Sam had always figured he'd be back one day. But he'd wanted to return to the island as his own man, on his own terms. His father's heart scare had forced him to change his timetable.

Six months, the old man cackled in his head. *Get it through zoning, show me backers, and we do it your way. If not, you'll work for me building spec houses.*

If Sam made this work, if he pulled this off, he'd have something to show for himself. Something to offer.

If he pulled this off.

If he couldn't, he'd be stuck working for the old man for

the next three to five years, building expensive boxes on the beach and trying to sell them as "rental investments."

He shuddered.

"I'm still figuring that out," he said truthfully. "But it's a better plan than chopping up the waterfront for more mansions that nobody needs."

Walt sucked thoughtfully on his upper lip. "We've heard promises before. I'd need to see something on paper."

Sam grinned, sharp and quick. "I'll get you an economic proposal and an environmental impact study," he promised. "Along with the plans from the architect."

He glanced toward the hostess station as another party of trick-or-treaters came through the door.

His heart stopped for a breathless beat before it began furiously pumping all his blood south.

It was Meg. But Meg transformed, Fantasy Meg in skin-tight jeans and high black boots and a ruffled blouse with a plunging neckline. Her mouth was red and wet with a wicked tilt, and she'd done something different to her eyes to make them appear bolder, bigger, more exotic.

His mouth went dry. Not that he cared that much about the wrapping on her package. He wasn't as shallow as Meg thought. He liked her loyalty and her humor. He admired her fearlessness and her never-say-die determination and . . .

Her really excellent ass.

So sue him.

She had kids with her, he noticed. Her niece, Taylor, and Cynthie's two little girls, all armed to the teeth and cute as bugs. Cynthie approached the front of the house and the five of them engaged in some complicated female ritual that involved lots of hugging and you-look-amazing type squeals. When Meg leaned over to say good-bye to the little Lodge girl, her tight jeans clung to her rounded butt like paint.

The resulting rush left Sam light-headed.

"She's a pretty thing," Walt said.

Sam stared at him blankly.

"Tom's girl," Walt supplied helpfully. "Heard you'd been driving around together. Nice to see you young folk moving back, settling down."

Sam shook his head, as if he could restore the blood flow to his brain. The island gossips had it all wrong. Meg wasn't coming back. She was leaving, always leaving.

Unless this time he gave her a reason to stay.

His heart spurted again in panic. Where the hell had that come from?

"Walt, I need to go, uh . . ." Christ, he couldn't think. "Go," he finished.

Walt chuckled. "Hope she's prepared to be boarded."

Sam rolled his tongue back into his mouth and sauntered across the bar, reminding himself to breathe. Playing it cool. He stopped for a better view and looked her up and down, deliberately provoking, determined to regain the advantage in whatever game they were playing.

MEG WATCHED AS Cynthie hoisted Hannah in her arms, smiling at the contrast they made, a mermaid with a princess on her hip, Cynthie's glittery showgirl face against her daughter's soft topknot. Taylor and Madison had their heads bent over the candy bowl, debating the merits of M&Ms over Skittles.

The back of her neck tickled. She felt a premonition like a finger drawn along her spine, like a whisper against her skin, and turned.

Sam.

Of course he wasn't in costume. He was too cool for that.

With his black knit shirt tucked into lean black jeans, he looked dark, dangerous, and ready for action, like an Italian movie star or a jewelry thief.

He perused her head to toe before his gleaming eyes returned to her face. A corner of his mouth curled upward in a smile. "Nice boots," he drawled.

The Stuart Weitzman knee-high boots had been her reward to herself after her March bonus. Even on sale, they were an indulgence. After traipsing almost a mile in four-inch heels, her ankles were wobbly and the balls of her feet hurt, but it was totally worth it to put that look in Sam's eyes.

She tossed her head, making her gold hoops sway. She stepped in close and dropped her voice, enjoying his quick intake of breath. "Hey, sailor," she teased, her lips close to his ear. "Is that a belaying pin in your pocket, or are you just happy to see me?"

He expelled his breath on a laugh. "We use cleats now, darling. If you're talking about sailing."

She drew back and grinned. "Actually, I wouldn't know a belaying pin from my . . . elbow. I just thought it sounded pirate-y."

The slashes in his cheeks deepened. "Next time try blunderbuss."

"Hornpipe," she countered.

"Peg leg."

"Jolly Roger," she said triumphantly, and he raised his hands in surrender.

"You win. Let me buy you a drink."

"I'm with the girls."

"They can have sodas."

She rolled her eyes. "Right. Because more sugar and caffeine are just what they need about now. Hey, girls." They all looked over. "Want to stop and get something to drink?"

Madison's face dropped comically. Hannah stared at her like an abused orphan from her mother's arms.

"Are we done trick-or-treating?" Taylor asked, not arguing. More . . . resigned.

Kid, you have been disappointed too often in your life, Meg thought.

"No way," she said firmly. "This is just a pit stop."

"You wait right here with your drinks," Cynthie said, "and I'll clock out and take you the rest of the way. Okay?"

The little girls scooted into a booth.

"Lemonade or orange juice?" Sam asked, standing over them.

Meg glanced up in surprise. She hadn't expected him to take her caffeine remark seriously.

He took their orders and fetched the girls' drinks from the bar, complete with paper umbrellas and maraschino cherries.

"Very slick," she murmured.

His teeth showed in a brief smile. "I aim to please." He set a mug in front of her. "I thought you might like coffee."

"Thanks." She sipped. Milk, no sugar. There was something flattering, something seductive, about his attention to detail.

She curled her hands around the warm mug. *This* was the secret behind Sam's popularity, the reason that women rolled over for him and men liked him. It wasn't all thoughtless, surface charm with him. He was *aware* of other people. He noticed things. He cared. He made an effort to learn what you liked, to give you what you needed, to earn your approval. He looked at you like you were the most fascinating person in the room, the most important person in the world.

Which of course made it even more devastating when you realized that all that focused attention was nothing special. That you were nothing special. He was like that with everybody.

She swallowed to dispel the sudden bitterness in her mouth.

"All set," Cynthie said, bustling back. "Ready to go?"

"Yeah!" Hannah jumped up in her seat.

"She's little," Madison said to Taylor. "She gets excited."

Taylor grinned and grabbed her pillowcase. Meg gulped another mouthful and started to stand.

"Sit," Cynthie said. "I'll take them around. You finish your coffee."

"You don't have to do that," Meg said.

"I want to." Cynthie's smile flickered, surprisingly sweet in her heavily made-up face. "I don't get enough time to play with my girls."

Probably true, Meg thought. Cynthie was probably too busy keeping a roof over all their heads to simply take a night off with her daughters.

"You go enjoy yourselves, then," Meg said. "Maybe Taylor and I will catch up with you later."

Taylor shot Meg a look and then ducked her head.

"Oh, but she has to come with us," Cynthie said.

"Yeah, Mom," Madison said.

Taylor stared at her shoes, her fingers squeezing her pillowcase as if she could choke it to death.

Meg wished briefly she were back in New York. Managing a department of thirty people and an advertising budget of seventy-four million dollars seemed like a piece of cake compared with the responsibility for the happiness of one ten-year-old.

Matt would know what to do for her. What to say. Meg didn't have a clue.

It's Taylor's first Halloween with us, Tess said in her head. *I want it to be special.* But what did Taylor want?

"Taylor?" Meg asked softly.

Taylor jerked one bony shoulder in the universal gesture for *I don't care.*

"Let her go," Sam said.

Meg narrowed her eyes at him. Easy for him to say. He wasn't the responsible one. "Is that what you want?" she asked Taylor. "To go with Madison and Hannah?"

"I guess." Taylor nodded with more vigor. "Yeah."

"I'll bring her home," Cynthie said. "Around nine, nine thirty?"

"That would be great. Have a nice . . ."

And before Meg could do more than give Taylor her flashlight, they were gone.

"Time." Meg sat back against the bench seat, unsure how she felt about losing control of the evening. "Well. I feel superfluous," she said, not entirely joking.

"You should be feeling grateful."

"Why? Because I'm sitting here with you instead of trick-or-treating with my niece?"

"Because Taylor's acting like a normal ten-year-old. Not clinging. Kids are supposed to ditch you for their friends."

"Oh." She thought about it. "You're right."

"You did a good job there." His eyes were warm.

"Thanks." She curled her toes in her boots, ridiculously flattered, one more victim of the Sam Grady charm. "I thought if I invited Madison over to look at costumes, it might break the ice."

"I meant by letting her decide just now. Poor kid hasn't had a lot of choices lately."

"Well, she's ten," Meg said practically.

"Exactly," Sam said. "Her mom died, what, two months ago? Three? From a brain aneurysm, Matt said." Meg nodded. "So, she goes to live with one set of grandparents until your brother shows up. He dumps her on the other set of grandparents, and she's barely settling in there when your mother's in a car accident. Not Tess's fault," Sam said when Meg would have spoken. "But that's a lot of changes for the kid to have to deal with."

Meg frowned. There he went with the empathy thing again. She didn't know another single man in his thirties who would so clearly see Taylor's dilemma, let alone be able to articulate it. Matt, maybe, but Matt was a dad. Sam . . .

"How did you get to be so smart?"

He shrugged. "I was a kid once, too."

She gnawed her lower lip, a new thought poking her like a splinter. Sam was fifteen the summer her family moved to the island. But before that, he'd already lived with one, two, three stepmothers. Maybe it had given him an insight she lacked.

"Did it bother you?" she asked. "Your dad remarrying so much? All the changes growing up?"

His smile flickered. "You get used to it. Once you figure out what everybody expects, how you fit in."

"Like starting a new school," she offered. "We did that a lot, moving around with my dad."

"Sure. But you all had each other. 'Back to back to back,' right?" Sam quoted softly. "I must have heard you and Matt and Luke say it a hundred times. Pretty intimidating."

She stared at him. She'd never considered how the words might sound, how their bond might appear to an outsider. To Sam. "But Taylor's one of us."

He smiled at her. Raised an eyebrow. "You sure she knows that?"

"Of course she does," Meg said. Taylor had to know that. Because the alternative was just too heart-wrenching to contemplate. "Luke's talked to her. Matt's talked to her."

"But you've still got that custody thing coming up next

week, right? Family court. How much does she know about that?"

"That's not going to be a problem," Meg said. "Matt hired a lawyer. Vernon Long. He said we don't have anything to worry about. No court in eastern North Carolina is going to take custody away from an active-duty serviceman without a really good reason. Taylor won't even be called unless the Simpsons' lawyer subpoenas her."

"Great. But from the kid's perspective, it's all still out of her control. Her life is basically being decided for her by a bunch of grown-ups."

Meg stared at him, stricken.

Sam frowned. "What?"

She shook her head. "Nothing."

Her own situation wasn't anything like Taylor's. Meg wasn't ten. She was thirty-four, totally in control of herself and her choices. She had a plan. She had Derek.

Taylor had nobody.

Correction. She had a father and grandparents who wanted her. She had Matt and Josh and Allison, who cared about her. And now she had Meg, too.

"That's why you said it was good for her to go with Cynthie and the girls," Meg said slowly. "Because it gave her a choice. It gave her control."

"Yeah. And she went, which was great. It shows she's confident."

"You never had any problems with confidence."

He smiled without saying anything.

"Or with making friends," she prodded.

She didn't know what she wanted from him. Maybe she wanted him to reassure her about Taylor. Maybe she was just trying to reconcile this sensitive Sam with the boy she remembered. Because if he wasn't that boy anymore . . .

Maybe he never had been that boy.

Which meant . . . Oh, hell, she didn't know what it meant, except that maybe her mother had been right about him all along.

"Sure." He plucked a trio of sugar packets from the bowl on the table, assembling them into a neat A-frame. "Never would have made it through high school without Matt."

"Not just Matt. You had lots of friends. You were cocaptain of the basketball team. You were prom king."

"I was friendly with a lot of people." The A-frame acquired an addition. "Nobody else I told stuff to."

Okay. She had brothers. She knew guys did not sit around sharing their feelings. But . . .

"How much did you tell him?"

"Not everything." He looked up briefly, his eyes gleaming between thick black lashes. "So that's two things I know about you that your family doesn't."

She watched his strong, clever builder's hands move among the sugar packets, assembling, discarding. *Two?*

Right. She came to herself with a little start. *The job.*

She moistened her lips. "I have something to tell you. To ask you, actually."

"Save it."

"Excuse me?"

He swept the house of sugar packets down with one hand. "You're finished, right?"

She stared, fighting an unreasonable feeling of disappointment. He didn't want to talk, fine. She didn't need a confidant. She didn't want . . .

"Your coffee," he said patiently. "Are you done?"

"Oh." She collected herself. "Yes."

"Come on, then. I'll walk you."

She wasn't ten, like Taylor. She didn't need to be escorted like a trick-or-treater out past her bedtime. She lived in New

York, for crying out loud. "I don't need you to walk me home. I'm perfectly safe on my own."

His eyes, that brilliant bottle green, met hers. His mouth kicked up in a smile. She felt a little flutter like the beat of her pulse low in her belly.

"Who wants to be safe?" Sam said.

Eleven

MEG STOLE A glance at Sam's profile as they left the bobbing lights of the waterfront behind. He looked good in moonlight, strong cheekbones, straight nose, sculpted lips, chiseled chin. And then there were those not-quite-dimples, the promise of humor, the flashes of empathy. Any woman could be forgiven for losing her head a little over Sam.

It wasn't just his good looks and his money and his charm. Okay, those things didn't hurt. But the real appeal was his willingness to put himself out, the way he'd driven to the airport to pick her up or built that ramp for her mother, without looking for payback, without figuring the angles or calculating the cost. She liked that about him. She liked him a lot.

He had always been a friend of Matt's, a friend of the family. There was no reason after all these years that Meg couldn't count him as her friend, too. Her good, close friend.

But nothing more.

The clouds against the blue velvet sky were the colors of an oyster shell, purple, gray, and milky white. The last time she had been alone in the dark with Sam, he'd kissed her senseless. If he tried anything this time, she was ready. She would just say no.

But despite his words in the restaurant, he was being a perfect gentleman.

She shivered a little from the breeze and disappointment.

He slanted a look at her. "Cold?"

She wasn't stupid. She recognized a line when she heard one. "Is this where you offer to put your arm around me to keep me warm?"

"No." He slid out of his jacket. "This is where I give you my jacket to keep you warm." He put it around her shoulders, smiling down at her, making her feel safe and warm and cared for. His jacket smelled like him, masculine with a hint of expensive soap. "Then I put my arm around you," he said, suiting the action to the words.

Meg smothered a laugh. "Where did you learn this move, high school?"

He grinned back, not smug, just . . . Sam. "Why not stick with what works?"

Everything he did had worked for her back then. She'd had the worst crush on him for years. She'd be on her way to the library and see Sam with some girl—always a different girl, always a pretty one—backed up against the lockers. Or glimpse him from an upstairs window shooting hoops in the driveway with Matt as she stripped dirty sheets from the guest room beds. Every cutting comment she'd made had been an attempt to get him to notice her. She was desperate for him to see her as someone other than Matt's annoying little sister, with her nose in a book and a toilet wand in her hand.

And so when she'd found him momentarily alone on New

Year's Eve, his defenses down and Matt nowhere in sight, she'd set out deliberately to seduce him.

It hadn't been all bad, she remembered. Even though he was drunk, even though she had no idea what she was doing, making out with Sam had been exciting. She had drowned in his kisses, exploring his body in a blur of lust and wonder, touching him in places and ways she'd never touched a boy before, letting him touch her. Her breasts. Her belly. Between her legs, where she was hot and damp.

Meg drew an uneven breath. She could even look back now on the inevitable fumbling, painful outcome with a certain nostalgia. At least when Sam was laboring inside her—*Oh, God, Meggie, you're so tight*—she'd felt like a necessary part of the process. When he kissed her neck, when he exhaled into her hair, she'd stroked his back and felt part of him. His. Despite her discomfort, she'd felt a bond, a closeness with Sam that wasn't entirely the result of a girlish crush. She'd had worse sex since. In college, for example. Even recently with Derek . . .

She pressed her lips together, her heart thumping. These were not "friend" thoughts. Not safe thoughts.

The half-moon rode a billow of cloud like a pirate ship in full sail, fleeing before the wind.

Who wants to be safe? Sam whispered wickedly in her head.

She did.

It should have been awkward, walking together. They weren't matched physically. He was too tall, his legs much longer than hers, and her high-heeled boots only shortened her stride. But Sam adjusted his steps, his arm easy on her shoulders, his hip bumping hers companionably from time to time.

"We took the wrong turn," she said suddenly. "The inn is that way."

"And the beach is right here." He steered her gently, inexorably, toward the access.

Their feet crunched on gravel and oyster shells before the boardwalk loomed, ghostly in the twilight.

She shivered again. It was one thing to accept his escort home. Something else to walk open-eyed into a situation that blurred the lines of friendship. Yes, Sam was attractive, confident, and sexy. But she would *not* cheat on Derek. She was not a cheater. "Sam . . . where are we going?"

"Why don't we walk and find out?"

She bit her lip against temptation. "I have to get back."

"Why?"

Her mind blanked momentarily. "I was planning on getting some work done tonight." The new client, she remembered. She was going to research the author, Lauren Somebody.

"You ever just take a night off, sugar?" Sam asked in his midnight and bourbon drawl. "No work, no plans, just . . . be?"

"No. It's important to set objectives. You can't achieve your goals without planning and hard work."

"Planning for what?"

Wasn't it obvious? Everyone she knew on Wall Street, anyone who worked with investments, annuities, life insurance, knew the answer. "The future." What else?

"If you're too busy living for the future, sugar, you're missing what you could have right now. Watch your step."

"What?"

Somehow they had reached the end of the boardwalk already. The salt breeze rippled over the crests of the dunes. Shadowed drifts of sea grass gave way to a long, flat stretch of gray sand and silver ocean. Long pale ribbons of foam unspooled lazily toward shore. Their rushing filled her ears.

Yearning caught her by the throat. "I don't think this is a good idea."

Sam turned back to look at her. "Why not?"

Because I want you. I want this.

She would never say those words to him again. "Because I'm wearing my good boots."

His grin flashed like a knife in the dark. "Some pirate you are."

It was a challenge, she'd never been able to back down from a challenge, and Sam *knew* that. He knew her, damn him.

She jumped down, stumbling as her heels sank into the soft sand, tumbling against him. He steadied her, his arms warm and strong.

She pushed against his chest. "I suppose you're going to tell me real pirates don't lose their balance."

"I'm guessing real pirates don't buy their boots at Bloomingdale's. Not that I'm complaining. I have fantasies about you in black leather." He sank on his haunches in front of her. "Give me your foot."

"No. This is silly." She was breathless. *Fantasies?* Surely not.

"We're not taking off our clothes to go skinny-dipping. Just your shoes. Anybody would think you'd never been barefoot on the beach before."

"I haven't. Well, not since I got back."

Sam looked up, that lock of dark hair falling across his forehead. "You're kidding."

"I've been busy," she said defensively.

He shook his head. "All work and no play, sugar. Give me your foot."

He thought she was *dull*? Wasn't that the rest of the verse? *All work and no play makes Jack*—okay, in her case, Jill—*a dull girl.*

I have fantasies about you in black leather.

She stuck out one booted leg, holding on to his shoulder for support.

SAM BRACED HER sole against his thigh and ran a hand up her calf. She had great legs. Not long—she'd always been a little thing—but curvy where it counted. When his hand reached her knee, she wobbled and clutched him tighter. He grinned, working the zipper down her inseam to her ankle, aware of her breasts inches from his face.

If he leaned forward, he would fall into her cleavage. He thought about nuzzling the ruffle aside, breathing in her warmth, finding skin. He would turn his head into the pale curve of her breast, kissing her, licking her, biting her gently.

Yeah, and then she'd snatch her boot from him and beat him over the head with it.

He tugged on the boot, setting it on the sand beside him. "Next foot," he said, his voice hoarse.

Her bare toes touched the cool sand. She hopped a little, finding her balance, making her breasts bounce.

He thought they were fuller, rounder than he remembered. He used to get hard, facing her breasts across the kitchen table. Hell, he was fifteen. Everything made him hard back then. And then Tess would ask him about his day or he'd catch Tom's do-you-want-to-die look from the head of the table, and he'd stare at his plate and think about something else until his erection subsided.

It was back now, though, pressing against his fly, pointing the way to the good stuff right there in front of his face.

Raising her other boot, she planted it near his crotch. "If I step on a ghost crab, I'm going to kill you," she said conversationally.

"I'm trembling all over," he said dryly.

His hands were shaking like a fifteen-year-old's, a fine tremor of lust. All because he was touching her again. He hadn't touched her leg, her ankle, in eighteen years. He hoped to God she didn't notice.

He tugged the boot from her other foot. Peeled off her sock. Her toenails were painted some dark color that looked almost black in the twilight. Her skin felt cool. Her feet looked pale and very naked. He ran his thumb along the delicate arch, and she shivered.

"Can I have my foot back now, please?"

He looked up at Meg, her bright, intelligent eyes, the quirk of smile playing on her mouth, the only woman he'd never been able to snow, and wanted her. Right there in the moonlight, wanted her now and forever.

Sam dropped her foot as if he'd been burned.

He didn't think in terms of the future. He was a live-in-the-moment kind of guy.

Standing, he brushed his hands on his jeans.

"WHAT WERE YOU and Walt talking about?" Meg asked as they strolled down the beach.

Sam was focused on the angles and shadows of her in the twilight, all short dark curls and smooth pale skin, tormenting himself with fantasies of how she would feel, how she would move, under his hands and tongue.

"Sam?"

He pulled himself together. *Walt. Right.* "I'm trying to talk him around on something."

She nodded. "Well, you're good at that."

"Talking?"

"Getting people to do what you want."

"It's a gift," he said modestly. "Want to go back to the truck and make out?"

She laughed, like she thought he was joking. "I didn't mean me. People in general. So, what do you want from Walt?"

"Support with the zoning board."

She looked up at him, her eyes wide. "You're going forward with the development."

"If I can. I've had a couple meetings."

She nodded. "On Monday."

He looked at her, surprised.

"You were wearing a tie when you came to the house," she explained. "I figured you'd come from a meeting."

He caught himself smiling. He had it bad when it made him feel good that she'd noticed the tie and wondered about his day. "Yeah, with Herb Stuart, the architect for the Riverside development outside Wilmington. And after that, I met with the Parker Group. They're responsible for a lot of low-impact development along the coast."

"And?"

"Well . . ." His smile spread. "They liked the tie."

She laughed. "What else?"

"They're both putting in bids on the project. I gave them the site surveys, the basic direction, and asked them to come up with preliminary plans."

She nodded. "For mixed-use housing."

She listened. Maybe because of that, he found himself still talking, confiding hopes that had just begun to shape themselves in his own mind. "I want to see a variety of housing options, you know, for singles, families, retired couples. Mixed with light commercial, so people are working and shopping where they live."

"Won't that compete with the businesses in town?"

"Most of the shops in town cater to tourists. We don't need another gift shop, another ice cream parlor. I want to bring back the fish house."

Her eyes got big. "Sam."

"It won't make that big a difference to the charter fishermen like Matt and your father," Sam felt compelled to point out. "They can get their ice from the tackle shop, and you have Fletcher's Quay to unload."

"During the sport fishing season, yes," Meg said. "But Matt still puts nets out on the old Sea Lady sometimes. He'd save so much in gas and time if he could sell his catch here, if the fish house were back in operation. But can you make it pay?"

"They made it work on Ocracoke. Why not here?"

"I'm impressed."

He shrugged, embarrassed by her praise, uncomfortable with his own enthusiasm. "Don't be. It's all talk at this point. I can provide the slips and the facilities, but the watermen need to organize to make it work. Cut out the middleman, form a nonprofit to run the fish market. There's a lot of PR involved, not just to get a project like this off the ground, but to sustain the funding."

"It's very promising. And exciting. You have a lot riding on this," she observed softly.

More than she knew. More than he wanted to admit, even to himself. "A house."

"Excuse me?"

It was too soon to tell her. Until he had backers, until he had the fishermen and the town behind him, he didn't have anything to offer her or anybody else. Just a growing, gut-clenching recognition that if he failed in this, he failed everybody.

"The old man is giving me a house if I pull this off." He slanted a look at her. As far as he knew, Meg had never accepted a dime from her parents, never asked for anything from anybody. She'd earned her own way through school and on Wall Street. "Still impressed?"

"Why wouldn't I be? It's not a gift. It's compensation. Like a bonus."

"It's a bet," Sam said flatly. "He's counting on me failing. He figures he can't lose."

"He's not going to lose," Meg said.

His shoulder blades tightened. "You think I can't do it."

She gave him this incredibly patient you-are-such-an-idiot look. "No, I believe you can. And that means everybody wins. Your father gets a great development with the Grady name on it. The watermen get a working fish house. The island preserves a piece of its heritage and stops shedding jobs. And you get . . ."

A chance to prove myself, Sam thought. Or fuck up on a large and public scale.

"Real estate," he said.

"A chance to prove your ideas." She stopped him with a hand on his arm, turning to face him in the moonlight. "Your vision."

Her eyes shone like the night sky. When she talked like that, with passion and conviction, he could almost believe her. Almost believe in himself.

Smiling, he shook his head. "Sugar, I don't have visions. I'm just a builder."

"Liar," she said. "You called me a planner before like that was a bad thing. But you're planning for the future of the whole island, Sam. You're building people's dreams."

He stared at her, shaken by her faith in him. "Meggie."

He didn't waste time contemplating the future. But with no effort at all, he could picture the next fifty years or so with her. Not at the edges of his life, but part of it. His.

Now he just had to figure out how to make her see things the same way.

"If you stay," she continued, "it won't be because of anything your father does. Not because of his health or the house, not because you're rebelling or conforming to his expectations. It's because of who you are. Because of what you want."

He wanted her. His heart pounded. "What about you?"

She blinked in genuine bewilderment. "What about me?"

All in, he thought. "Will you stay?"

She gave a half laugh, like he'd surprised her. "I'm leaving for New York."

His throat felt tight and dry. Deliberately, he swallowed. "You don't have to."

Her brows drew together, forming a little double crease above her nose. "I do, actually. I have a thing, a sort of interview, on Friday with a PR firm I used to work with. That's what I wanted to tell you earlier. Ask you." She smiled at him a bit uncertainly, Meggie, who was certain about everything. "I was hoping you could give me a ride to the airport."

"YOU WANT ME to drive you to the airport on Friday," Sam repeated slowly.

"If you have time." He didn't look very enthusiastic about the prospect of chauffeuring her around, Meg thought. Well, he had better things to do with his time. "Look, if you're tied up with this project, don't worry about it. It's not that big a deal."

"It sounds like a big deal to me. When are you leaving?"

She drew back, confused and a little offended by his tone. "I haven't made my airline reservations yet. I figured I'd fly into LaGuardia early Friday morning. Bruce wants me to meet with the management team and then have lunch with the client." Her earlier excitement returned, overriding her disappointment at Sam's attitude. "It's not financial services, and it's contract work, not an actual position within the firm, not yet, but . . ."

"What time are you coming back?"

"I thought I'd stay the weekend."

"Where?"

"At my place." Where else?

"With him. That Derek guy."

Meg narrowed her eyes. Okay, the tone, the attitude were beginning to piss her off. "Of course with Derek. It's his condo, too. Our condo."

"How many bedrooms?"

Her lungs emptied. Was Sam *jealous*? The notion was oddly, darkly thrilling. And ridiculous. "That's none of your business."

"Are you going to sleep with him?"

Her stomach jumped. She ignored for the moment the fact that she wasn't eagerly anticipating having sex with Derek. She still needed to see him. To talk to him. What they did—or didn't do—after that was between the two of them. "I live with him."

Sam's eyes were dark beneath that cowlick lock of hair on his forehead. "What about us?"

She wanted to pretend she didn't know what he was talking about. But of course she did. Guilt sharpened her voice. "There is no 'us,' Sam. Not the way you mean. We're friends. We have a . . . a history, I guess you'd call it. But that's all."

"Bullshit. You want me."

Her jaw dropped. "Excuse me?"

The laughter leaped back into his eyes. "And I want you," he said. "The labels don't matter."

She felt the situation slipping away from her, the conversation spinning out of control. "Of course they matter," she snapped. "Derek is my boyfriend."

"Then why the hell doesn't he act like he is? Why don't you?"

She was furious with him. And with herself, for letting things get this far. "You have no right to talk to me like that." Her voice shook shamefully. "You have no reason—"

"You want reasons?" Sam rapped. "Fine." He grabbed her upper arms and hauled her against him. "Here's your reason," he muttered and crushed his mouth to hers.

Her brain shut down. His kiss was bruising, shattering. He pressed her mouth open, delving inside, blanketing her in sensation, hot, heavy, smothering. Her skin prickled with lust. He tasted of coffee, bitter, strong, and sweet. She sagged against him, responding helplessly to the blatantly suggestive thrust of his tongue, the rough possession of his mouth and hands. His arms banded around her. Her toes curled in the sand. There was something almost desperate in his demand, something almost indecent about her surrender, yielding, liquid, holding nothing back.

Out of control. She fisted her hands against his chest.

He jerked back. Their eyes clashed.

Her heart hammered against her ribs. She'd never imagined she could be this upset. This aroused.

Screw it. She dragged his head back down to hers, meeting his demand with her own. *No surrender.* He used his tongue. She used her teeth, nipping lightly at his lower lip, taking his mouth as he devoured hers. Her fingers twisted in his shirt, pulling him closer before she shoved him away.

He released her instantly. They stared at each other, their breath rasping against the quiet night. This time, her gaze fell first.

"Meggie . . ."

"I don't want to talk about it." She was burning up, her face on fire, her body aflame.

He swore. "You can't kiss me like that and then go back to him."

Her mouth felt bruised. A vicious tic of arousal pulsed low and thick inside her. "I need to go home."

A long pause before he nodded slowly. "All right. I'll drive you back. Taylor should be there by now."

"No, I mean *home*." She straightened her spine. "To New York."

Twelve

HE'D FUCKED UP.

Sam drove Meg home in quivering silence. The night air streaming outside was cool, but inside the cab the atmosphere was a lot warmer, a slow burn of lust and frustration on his side, anger and embarrassment on hers.

She was pressed against the passenger door, her full lips a tight line, resolutely ignoring him. Like if she gave him the slightest sign of encouragement, he would fall on her like a dog with a bone. Which he had. Dumb move.

But then she'd kissed him back.

The streets were almost empty. The truck's headlights caught a couple teenagers drifting home from the party at the gym, flashed off a cop car cruising under the streetlights.

You have no right to talk to me like that.

So yeah, maybe he should have tried to persuade her,

reassure her, share his *feelings* like a girl instead of acting like a possessive asshole.

But he could fix this. He could make her listen to him.

He shot a considering look at her sharp, white profile. If she gave him a chance.

He pulled in front of the Pirates' Rest, all tricked out for Halloween with creaking shrouds and floodlights and a pirate mannequin glowering from the porch. Meg was out of the truck before Sam could come around to open her door.

He caught up with her on the walk. "You still need a ride to the airport?"

She climbed two steps to the porch, so that their heads were on a level—she wouldn't give him the advantage of height, she wasn't giving him anything—and whipped around. "Go to hell," she said, low and clear, and stalked off.

He grinned. "Meg." He strode up the steps after her, yanked at the door before she could slam it in his face. "*Meggie.*"

Everybody turned. The hall was full of light and Fletchers, Tom, Tess, Matt, Allison.

Sam checked on the threshold. *Shit.*

"Hi, honey, did you have a nice . . ." Balanced on her walker, Tess looked from Meg's stormy face to Sam, stopped dead in the doorway. Her eyebrows rose very slightly. "Well."

Allison blushed as if she were the one they were all staring at. Matt cleared his throat.

Tom's eyes narrowed on his daughter's mouth, her full lips rubbed free of lipstick and swollen from kissing. "Where the hell have you been?"

"Walking," Meg said. "Did Taylor get home all right?"

Matt nodded slowly. "Counted her candy bars and went to bed about ten minutes ago."

"Bouncing from the sugar rush," Allison added with a

smile. "She's probably still awake if you want to say good night."

"I'll do that," Meg said. She swooped on her parents like a bird skimming the water, dart and peck, two kisses good night, and went upstairs without a backward glance.

Sam stood on the faded Morris carpet, listening to her boots clack up the stairs.

"Have a popcorn ball," Tess said.

So they weren't going to talk about it. The knot between Sam's shoulders loosened. *Good.* He didn't know what he would say to them. He respected their concern. Envied their bond. But this thing was between him and Meg. Until they figured it out, until she admitted they had something going on, what could he say?

"Thanks." He stepped forward to accept the wrapped treat.

"Talked with your future brother-in-law today," Tom said.

Sam withdrew his hand cautiously from the candy bowl. Not the opening he was expecting. "Ryan?"

"He called to reserve rooms for the wedding party," Tess said.

"Nice kid," Tom said. "Sounds like his dad on the phone."

The two men had served together, Sam remembered. He nodded, still wary. Meg got her directness from her father. Despite the personal connection, he figured Tom wasn't making small talk.

Tom Fletcher had been a career sergeant major in the Marines. At sixty-four, Tom was leaner and grayer than he'd been twenty years ago when he'd first accepted Sam into his household, taught him to set a screw and bait a hook. But if the old man decided he had reason, he could still kick Sam's ass.

"He might be an officer and a squid, but the boy knows what he wants. And he wants your little Chelsea," Tom continued. He fixed Sam with shrewd, faded blue eyes. "Guess that makes you the holdout in your family, marriage-wise."

Marriage?

A popcorn ball–sized lump scraped Sam's throat.

He swallowed. "I'm not holding out against anything," he said, meeting Tom's gaze steadily. "But marriage isn't something you can rush into."

Especially not when one of you was running away to New York. His mouth compressed.

Tom snorted. "Yeah, I've heard that before. From that fellow Meg's living with."

"Tom." Tess laid a hand on her husband's arm.

"Look at us," he said to her. "I talked you into marrying me two weeks after I met you."

"You can help me to bed now."

"Sam and me are having a conversation here," Tom said.

Tess's eyes lit with humor. "It's only a conversation when more than one person is talking, darling. Good night, Sam. Matt, Allison."

Italian-American Tess would never be mistaken for a Southern Steel Magnolia, but her Chicago-bred toughness was every bit as formidable. Slowly, she and Tom made their way down the hall. He held open the kitchen door as she clumped through with her walker, letting it swing shut behind them.

Allison looked from Sam to Matt's impassive face. "I think I'll head back to the cottage."

Sam shoved his hands in his pockets. "Don't rush off on my account. How was movie night?"

Both Matt and Allison were still in costume—if Matt's jeans and black leather jacket could be counted as "costume." Allison wore a little blue dress with a white apron and a black headband. Alice in Wonderland, Sam supposed.

"From the amount of shrieking and squealing going on, I'd say it was a success," Allison said.

"And that was only during the intermission," Matt said dryly.

Allison laughed. "Anyway, Josh seemed to have a good time. He invited some friends back with him to see Tom's Halloween display."

"A Dare Island tradition," Sam informed her.

"So I hear. Anyway, I should go check on them. You never know what teenagers will get up to when your back is turned."

"Sam knows," Matt said.

Their eyes met.

Yeah, he knew. The muscles tightened at the back of Sam's neck, in the pit of his stomach. And Matt . . . guessed.

He waited until the front door had closed behind Allison before he said, "Most of the trouble I got into in high school, you were right in there with me, buddy."

"Most." Matt paused. "Not all."

Sam rocked back on his heels, trying to gauge Matt's mood. "You got something you want to say?"

"Nope. You?"

A vision swam in Sam's memory. Meg's face, a pale oval in the dark. Meg's voice, pleading, *Don't tell Matt.*

"Not really." He took his hands out of his pockets. "You going to take a swing at me?"

"Should I?"

For what I did eighteen years ago, maybe. Not over what happened tonight. "You want to know if I'm putting the moves on your sister, the answer is yes. You want details, you ask her."

Matt nodded once. "You hurt her, you let her down, I'll come after you."

"Right. Anything else?"

"Yeah." A corner of Matt's mouth kicked up. "She hurts you, she lets you down, I'll buy the beer."

Sam's muscles relaxed. "That's big of you."

Matt shrugged. "Meg's old enough take care of herself. Besides . . ."

"You love me like a brother?" Sam suggested.

Matt's rare smile spread. "I like you better than that asshole in New York, that's for sure."

TESS LAY FLAT on her back in their king-size bed, determined to finish her final set of exercises before Tom returned from the bathroom. She could hear water running into the sink and the sound of his razor against the basin, *tap tap tap.*

She pushed out her breath, sliding her right leg as far to the side as she could, feeling the stretch in her thigh, the pull in her groin. *Out.* She tightened her muscles, easing the leg back. *And in.* Another breath. *Out* . . . A twinge in her hip made her catch her breath. *And in.*

For almost forty years, she had lived by The List, breaking down seemingly overwhelming tasks into small, manageable steps. Through moves, deployments, hurricanes, the start of the tourist season, and the beginning of the school year, it all went on The List, moving boxes, boarding windows, fresh paint, new shoes, immunizations, and permission slips, everything cataloged, crossed off, under control.

She slid her leg out again over the wrinkled sheet, stretching, stretching, exhaling through the pain. *Out.* The orthopedic surgeon had explained that healing would be slow. The stem cell flakes they had sprinkled like fairy dust over the pins in her pelvis would take time to set. *And in.*

She had a new list now, of attainable, adjustable goals assigned by her physical therapist. Roll over in bed. Sit up in a chair for thirty minutes, for forty. Walk to the end of the ramp, to the end of the drive, to the end of the street.

And a private list, compiled in her heart. Shave her own legs. Walk on the sand. Make love with Tom.

Her eyes burned. Her hip burned. She pressed her lips together, breathing in through her nose.

Tom padded into the room in his boxers, the light from the bathroom emphasizing his wide, bony shoulders, his lean waist. "Did you take your pills?"

She exhaled. Nodded.

He flipped off the light and slid into bed. His weight created a shift in the mattress, another twinge in her hip. But it felt good to have him beside her. The scent of his aftershave wrapped around her in the dark, spicy and familiar. Once his shaving before bed had been a preliminary to lovemaking. Now . . .

He lifted the covers and wedged a pillow between her legs to protect her hips before he lay down.

Tess sighed.

"You okay, babe?"

He meant physically, of course. Her Tom had never initiated a discussion of feelings. He had always operated under the military's need-to-know mode. Tess was the one who listened to the children while he was away, who reintegrated him into the family routines when he came home, who encouraged and mediated and explained.

"I'm fine," she said.

They lay in the dark, in the silence.

"Don't worry about the kids," Tom rumbled, surprising her. "They're all right."

His reassurance freed her to speak. Matt *was* all right, at least since Allison had come into his life. Meg . . . Well, Tess intended to have her own discussion with Meg. Tess's thoughts went to their younger son, serving in Afghanistan. "Have you spoken to Luke recently?"

"Sunday. Same as you."

"I thought he might call Taylor for Halloween," Tess said.

"Babe, he's in country," Tom said. "He might not be anywhere near a phone."

"I know."

"It was easier back when there wasn't all this technology to keep in touch all the time," Tom said. "At least when you didn't hear from me, you didn't worry."

"Much," Tess said.

Tom chuckled. "Easier on me, then. No distractions."

Tess remembered when an information officer used to control the flow of news from home. Even Dear John letters were opened and vetted and accompanied by a visit from the IO or a chaplain. Now, except when a unit was in "River City"—their systems temporarily shut down to preserve security—communications between deployed Marines and their families were much easier. Better, she thought. Except all that Skyping, SAT phones, and MotoMail meant that Marines could be hit with every problem from home, every leaking toilet and grade school crisis.

"Do you think Luke's worried about the family court hearing next week?" Tess asked.

"No, he's thinking about his men and his mission. He's counting on us to take care of Taylor." Tom turned his head on the pillow. "Like I always counted on you."

Her heart melted. "Oh, Tom."

He rolled to his side and kissed her forehead.

His breath was warm against her eyelids. She closed her eyes and confessed, "That's what I hate the most. I feel like

I'm letting everyone down. If I wasn't in that stupid accident . . ."

"Not your fault, babe."

She ignored his logic. "If I hadn't gotten hurt, the Simpsons wouldn't be able to claim 'changed circumstances' to get custody of Taylor."

"They can claim whatever they want. Luke left Taylor with us."

"She called again tonight. While the girls were out."

"Who called?"

"Jolene Simpson."

"What did she want?"

"To talk to Taylor, she said." Tess moved restlessly. "And to tell me Taylor has one grandmother who can still take care of her."

"Fuck 'em," Tom said. "Look, you can't control what the Simpsons say or do. You can't change what happened. All we can do is play the cards we're dealt."

"As long as the game isn't rigged," she muttered. She rubbed her cheek against his hand. "I wish I were going with you on Tuesday." *Court day.*

He touched her hair, stroking her bangs out of her face with calloused fingers. "You'd be bored. Hell, I'll be bored. That lawyer, Long, said we'll be hanging all day, waiting. Anyway, only one of us needs to be there."

"I just want to help."

"You are helping. You're taking care of yourself. Getting better, right? Getting some sleep."

She smiled at his gruff tone. "Is that a hint?"

"Could be. Unless you want to stay up and fool around."

She huffed, laughter and frustration mixed together. "Yeah, that's not happening."

He gave her a slow, warm kiss. "Not for another four weeks anyway," he agreed.

"That's right, I . . . Wait." Tess drew back to stare into her husband's face. "You asked Dr. Glover when we could have sex?"

Tom grunted, which could have been either yes or no, except he would have said *No* straight out.

"Thirty-eight years we've been married," Tess said, "three kids, and you've never asked one doctor about anything."

His gaze met hers. "You mad?"

"No, I'm . . ." Relieved. Reassured. Flattered. "Grateful," Tess said. She smiled. "And it's three weeks now."

RESIDENTS AND LONGTIME visitors to Dare complained the island wasn't as remote as it used to be. Clearly, they had never tried to book a flight to LaGuardia in time for a lunch meeting in Manhattan.

The earliest flight out of Jacksonville, with a stop in Atlanta, would require Meg to leave the island at three thirty in the morning. Or she could leave two hours later and drive herself three and a half hours to Raleigh-Durham Airport for a nonstop flight to New York. She'd opted for Raleigh.

At least she could work on the plane.

"Mom, do you think it would be okay for me to ask Matt to give me a ride into Morehead City tomorrow?" Meg asked Tess the following morning. "I hate to dump any more work on him, but I need to pick up a rental car."

Soft, gray light penetrated the kitchen windows. Outside, birds tuned up against a chorus of insects. Tom sat at the kitchen table, mopping the last of his breakfast egg with a piece of toast. Tess stood at the counter with Taylor, supervising the packing of her lunch for school.

"What time?" Tess asked.

Meg headed for the coffeepot. "Five thirty?" she said, a note of apology lifting her voice. Matt was on the water some mornings by five. She still hated imposing on him.

"In the morning?" Tess asked.

"Kind of early for you, city girl," Tom remarked.

"One or two?" Taylor asked, digging her hand into her Halloween candy.

"One," Tess said.

"Two," Tom said at the same time.

Meg poured her coffee. "How about one large, one small?"

"Cool." Taylor deliberated, finally choosing a large Milky Way and a small peanut butter cup. "Where are you going?"

"I have a meeting," Meg said. "In New York."

"I'm sure we can get you a ride," Tess said. "It's good that you're getting back to work."

"Yeah." Meg took a deep breath, setting down her coffee cup. "Actually, Mom . . ."

"Are you coming back?" Taylor asked.

It had never been Meg's plan to stay on the island. But something in the child's expression, the closed face, the hopeful eyes, tugged at Meg's heart. What had Sam said last night? *That's a lot of changes for the kid to have to deal with.* Too many people were coming and going in Taylor's life.

"It's just an interview," Meg assured her gently. "I'll see you Sunday."

The back door burst open to admit Josh. "Hey, shorty. Time for school."

Taylor nodded and grabbed her lunch. Fezzik lurched from under the table and followed her to the door, his thick tail sweeping from side to side.

Josh grinned down at her affectionately. "You got candy for me?"

Taylor jammed Luke's Marine cap onto her short blond hair. "Maybe."

"You need another piece, then," Tom said.

"Thanks."

"Yeah, thanks, Grandpa."

And they were gone.

In the quiet they left behind, Tess turned to her daughter and raised her eyebrows. "Did you say an interview?"

Meg blew out her breath. *Here goes.*

"A sort of job interview." She met her mother's gaze, her chest hollowed out. "I was let go. Franklin let me go. Fired me."

"They what?" Tom growled.

"Oh, honey." Tess started forward, banging into her walker.

"Easy, Mom. It's okay. I'm okay." Meg crossed the kitchen, steadying the walker, folding her arms carefully around her mother, trying to give and receive comfort without putting any weight on Tess's slim shoulders.

Trying not to be a burden.

Meg swallowed. *What a laugh.*

"Do you need any help?" Tom asked, his weathered face creased in lines of concern. *Financial help*, he meant.

Meg's heart swelled. Her throat cinched. She made more in bonuses than her parents earned in a year. "Oh, Dad. No, I'm fine. I got six months' severance."

"Is that enough?" Tess asked. "With your mortgage . . ."

"It's fine. And Derek is willing to help out until I find something else."

Tom grunted. "Least he can do. You can stay here, you know. As long as you want."

"We love having you," Tess added.

They were trying to help her, Meg realized. Emotion welled inside her. To take care of her the way they always had. All this time, she had been worried about helping and taking care of *them,* protecting them, and their first thought was for *her.* Their concern made her want to weep. She didn't deserve it.

The kitchen blurred in a rush of love and tears.

"Hey, now," her father said, alarmed.

She sniffled.

"It's okay." He put his arms around her—long, bony arms, comforting and familiar—and she burst into tears.

"It's all right, sweetie," her mother said. The same words, the same tone, that had soothed scrapes and feelings throughout Meg's childhood. "Everything's going to be all right."

"I'm sorry, I'm sorry." Meg wept. "Damn it."

Tom patted her back awkwardly. He smelled of laundry detergent and aftershave, strong, clean smells. "What the hell are you sorry for? You didn't do anything wrong."

"No-o. I thought . . ." Her voice hitched on another sob. "You'd be disappointed in me."

"Disappointed? In you?" The genuine astonishment in her mother's voice nearly set Meg off again.

"That's stupid," Tom said. "We're proud of you, Meggie. Always have been."

"But I lost my *job.*"

"So? You're not the first or the only one in this economy to get fired. You're a smart girl. You'll come about. They're fucking idiots."

She closed her eyes, letting herself go back to a time when her father's arms could protect her from anything. She was awash with embarrassment, floating in relief, filled to the brim with love. Leaving the office in the cab that day, she'd felt as if she'd lost everything. But she'd been wrong, she realized. She'd never lost this. "I love you, Daddy."

He kissed the top of her head. "We love you, too, baby," he said gruffly.

"Why didn't you say anything?" Tess asked.

"I didn't want to worry you," Meg mumbled. "I was afraid to let you down."

"You've never let us down," Tom said. "You were a big help when your mom was in the hospital."

"And here, too," Tess said. "All we want is for you to be happy."

Meg sniffed. "Will you be all right this weekend?"

Tom patted her shoulder. "Of course. You go take care of business."

"What about Derek?" Tess asked. "Was he let go, too?"

"No, Derek was on the transition team. His job's safe."

Meg saw her parents exchange glances.

"What does he say about all this?" Tess asked.

Meg drew a deep breath. "He thinks it's time I came home."

She had called him at bedtime, their regular time, hoping that hearing his cool, considered voice would remind her of all the ways he was perfect for her.

Or maybe she'd hoped he would say something stupid and hurtful to erase her guilt over Sam. He could offer to buy her out of their condo again, for example.

Instead, Derek had surprised her. *Bruce told me they were bringing you up. I think it's great. You know, your job search would be a lot easier if you stayed in New York. It's time for you to come home,* he'd said, as if he wasn't the one who had sent her away in the first place.

What about stepping back to gain perspective? she had reminded him a little bitterly. *What about examining our priorities?*

That's exactly what I've been doing, Derek had responded. A pause. *I miss you, Meg.*

His admission had gratified a small corner of her heart, soothed the bruise to her pride. And left her vaguely uncomfortable. She missed him, too. Of course she did. But . . .

Meg met her mother's eyes. "He said this could be the opportunity we need to figure out where we're going. To assess our priorities."

Tom gave another grunt that could have meant anything.

"Well, I never thought I'd say this, but I agree with him. Maybe this is your chance to think about what you really want." Tess tipped her head to one side. Smiled. "And who you really want, too."

"*Ma*." She wouldn't call it panic, that quick staccato beat of her heart. "I'm looking for a job, not another boyfriend. I hate to disappoint you, but there's no way I'm going to end up living on the island married to . . ." *Sam Grady.* "Anybody," Meg sputtered. "I love what I do. I love New York."

"And Derek? Do you love him, too?"

Meg opened her mouth, feeling the ground shift suddenly beneath her feet. She wasn't used to examining her feelings for Derek. She certainly wasn't used to discussing their relationship in front of her father.

"If you can't say yes, the answer's no," Tom said.

She flushed. "It's not that simple, Dad. Maybe that's what I have to go to New York to figure out. I'm comfortable with Derek. We've been together six years. I can be myself when I'm with him."

"You mean he doesn't challenge you," Tess said.

"Of course he does. We challenge each other. That's why we make such a good team. We both work hard, we're both career oriented. We don't have to make excuses to each other if one of us is stressed out or working late."

"In other words, neither one of you has to carve out time for a relationship. He's convenient."

"What's wrong with that?" Meg asked. "Why should I sacrifice my job or compromise who I am to be with someone?"

"You shouldn't," Tess said. "Unless . . ."

"Unless what?" Meg demanded.

"Unless compromising who you think you are actually helps you become the person you were meant to be."

Thirteen

"You," Meg said when she opened the back door the next morning.

Sam stood in the yellow glow of the porch light in jeans and a blue work shirt with the sleeves pushed back. For one second, before her brain engaged and started flashing little red warning signs, her heart skipped. *You.* Her eyes drank him in, rangy and relaxed and looking way better than anybody had a right to at five twenty-seven in the morning.

Automatically, her hand went to her diamond studs, her Pucci scarf, the line of her skirt, checking, smoothing, taking silent, reassuring inventory. She looked fine, all traces of nerves and her sleepless night carefully concealed with makeup and the right clothes.

Sam leveled that gotta-love-me Grady grin at her, all teeth and charm. "Me," he confirmed. "Heard you needed a lift."

"But . . . But . . ." She was sputtering. She pressed her

lips together. She wouldn't have such a hard time controlling her emotional response to Sam if she didn't find him so physically attractive. Or maybe she wouldn't find him so attractive physically if they didn't have this emotional history. Either way was no excuse for letting him tie her tongue into knots. "Matt said he would drive me to pick up my rental car this morning."

"No, Matt said he'd take care of it. And he did."

"By asking you." She kept her voice down, aware of her parents still asleep in the master suite off the kitchen.

"I asked him, but yeah. Basically." He reached for Meg's red Tumi carry-on. "We should roll. Is this all you've got?"

She resented the casual way he took charge of her schedule and her luggage, friendly, insistent, too used to getting his own way. But what good would it do to object? She needed her car. He was doing her a favor. She could be civil in return. "Thank you. Do you want some coffee before we go?"

"That would be great."

She had already brewed a pot, figuring she would need the caffeine for the long drive to Raleigh. Now she poured coffee into two of the paper travel cups stocked by the inn and offered him one. "Black, one sugar."

Their eyes met. Her stomach did a slow roll as he took the cup, his long fingers brushing hers. "Thanks."

She cleared her throat and grabbed her own cup, her bag, her trench, reaching desperately for a neutral topic of conversation. "When did you see Matt?"

"Yesterday." Sam opened the kitchen door and gestured for her to precede him onto the porch. She locked up and then followed him down the flagstone walk, hurrying to keep pace with his long-limbed, confident stride.

He opened her door, always the gentleman. "I wanted to get his opinion on who to approach about forming a watermen's association." He held her coffee as she settled into her seat, conscious of his eyes on her legs, his warmth, temptingly close. "And I wanted the chance to see you before you go."

She swallowed, wrapping her hands around her cup as he stowed her rollaway in back. She had too little sleep, too much at stake, to deal with him right now. When he slid in beside her, she said, "Look, I appreciate you taking me to pick up my car. But frankly, I said everything I had to say the other night. I have a really long, full day today. I don't need the distraction."

"You don't have to say anything. Just listen."

"Sam . . ."

"Meggie, let me say this. I kept quiet before. We never talked, I never told you how I felt." He met her gaze, his face set in the glow of the dashboard. "I won't make that mistake again."

Her heart hammered. The conversation was going places she had left behind eighteen years ago. She was afraid to go back, reluctant to revisit the girl she'd been back then.

The girl who had loved Sam.

Or been infatuated with him anyway.

"Sam, we don't need to have this discussion. We were kids."

"Yeah, that's what I told myself back then," he said. "I thought if I pretended hard enough, if I ignored what happened long enough, it would be like it never happened."

She ignored the pang his words caused. "It was ages ago. Why drag up the past?"

"Because it's not past. We can't go forward until we go back. I hurt you, Meggie, and I'm sorry."

His words touched a long-healed scar, soothed an almost forgotten ache. But she had spent too many tears on Sam when she was sixteen. She wasn't wasting any more regrets on something that had happened back in high school. "You don't have to apologize because you didn't like me, Sam. It's okay."

He scowled in obvious frustration. "I did like you. That was the damn problem. I liked you all too much. You meant . . . God, your family meant everything to me. And because I was drunk, because you were . . ."

"Available," she said dryly.

He turned his head. Met her eyes. "Irresistible."

Oh, God. Her body flushed. She could feel herself tightening, softening, inside.

"I fucked up," he continued.

She'd blamed him then. She was older now. Old enough to understand and forgive. "We both did. Face it, Sam, I threw myself at you."

His smile gleamed. "And I was grateful. But I put everything that mattered at risk, your parents' trust, Matt's friendship. You. I didn't know how to face them afterward. I didn't have the balls to face you. Christ, you were still in high school."

"And you were a freshman in college. Only a couple years older than Josh." Wow, she was old. And they had both been so very young. "Neither one of us knew what we were doing. Us, together? It was a stupid mistake."

"Maybe it wasn't. Maybe it didn't have to be." His voice was low, urgent. It was absurd how much she loved his voice, the baritone drawl as smooth and seductive as Irish coffee with whipped cream. "I couldn't stop thinking about you, Meggie. About us. I thought, maybe when I came home for the summer, I'd give you a call. Or I'd come over and you'd, you know, just be there."

She remembered that summer, the summer before her senior year. She'd been working two jobs, saving every dime for college, tackling the AP English reading list, determined to apply early decision to Harvard and UNC. Not Duke. She wouldn't have followed Sam to Duke if they'd offered her a full scholarship and courtside seats to every basketball game. What would it have meant, what would she have done, if Sam had come home, if he'd called her then?

"Why didn't you?" she whispered.

"Matt called me."

Her head whipped around. "Oh, God. What did he say?"

"He told me," Sam said with grim deliberation, "that Kimberly was pregnant. Scared the hell out of me. What if it had been me? What if it had been you?"

"But . . . You used a condom." Something else she hadn't fully appreciated at the time.

"So did Matt. Most of the time anyway. I watched him trying to hold it all together after that. I saw what he gave up. I wasn't ready for that. I wasn't ready for you." Another of those sideways looks, dark and intent. "Then."

Her mouth was dry. She sipped her cooling coffee, welcoming the jolt of reality, the acrid flavor. "Don't tell me you've been nursing a crush on me for eighteen years. Because that's a load of crap."

He laughed. "You know that's the guy fantasy, right? The one that got away. Most times the reality doesn't come close. You see her again, ten, twenty years later, and you think, *Thank God. Dodged that bullet.* But when I heard you were coming back to the island, I wanted to see you again. I wanted to find out if you were still the girl I remembered."

"So, now you know. I can't be that girl anymore, Sam. I'm grown up. I have places to go, things to do. I have a *life*."

"You always did. That's part of what attracted me. And intimidated me."

She snorted. "Please. You were never intimidated."

"Was, too. Why do you think I didn't make the first move?"

It was ridiculous how much she wanted to believe him. "Well, it doesn't make any difference now."

"It makes all the difference. The timing was wrong for us. But we . . ." He reached out, taking her hand for emphasis. "We were right."

She looked at his hand covering hers on her lap and felt her breath go. "The timing isn't any better now."

"Because of the interview."

She was grateful for his understanding. This opportunity was important to her. But he still didn't get it. "Because I'm in a relationship."

"So end it."

"I can't do that."

"Why not?"

She glared at him. "You don't just break off a six-year relationship without talking things over. At least, I don't. I have too much respect for Derek, too much respect for myself, to treat him that way."

"What about the way he treats you?"

"There's nothing wrong with the way Derek treats me. Maybe things haven't been perfect lately, but—"

"Does he make you happy?"

She stared at him, stricken. "That's a stupid question."

"So, no," Sam said.

A sound, half laugh, half groan, broke from her throat. "I cannot believe we are having this discussion on my way to the airport."

His gaze fixed on her face before he nodded slowly. "Bad timing."

His words ran through her head. *The timing was wrong for us. But we . . .we were right.*

Her breath backed up in her lungs. "The worst."

She saw his white grin flash, reflected in the dark windshield. "Later for us, then."

Well, that was easy, she thought. She breathed out, torn between relief and regret that he was letting it go. Letting her go.

Again.

TWELVE HOURS LATER, Meg emerged from the subway into the bustle of rush hour, barely refraining from breaking into a victory boogie right there on the sidewalk.

Her firing had shaken her confidence more than she wanted to admit. All her experience was in financial services, almost all of it on the corporate side. Her long professional friendship with Bruce didn't mean that his partners would like her. She had been concerned about how she would be perceived, how she would fit in.

Meg grinned like a fool as her red rollaway bumped over the curb. She had nailed the meetings with the PR management team and the author client. Meg had focused on the need for niche marketing, for appealing to a new audience of readers who might not otherwise think of picking up the book. Over lunch, they'd discussed angles and tangible take-aways, with the result that the writer was now sharpening her talking points . . . and Meg had a job.

She was back, baby.

She was back. The smell of sweat, cement, sewers, and dying leaves rose from the gritty sidewalk. Energy swirled from the street. Meg pressed forward against the blinking light, part of a stream of swarming schoolchildren, office workers rushing home, joggers and pedestrians racing to get in their daily allotment of exercise. She'd always enjoyed the walk home along the railings of Central Park, the elegant architecture on one side of the street, the bright pushcarts and horse-drawn carriages on the other. The city was noisier, dirtier, more frenzied than she remembered, even in the shadow of the fading trees. Taxis blared. Busses billowed exhaust. Snatches of conversation punctuated the air.

". . . had a urinary tract infection . . ."

"Your *face* is ridiculous."

". . . hammer out a restructuring plan."

"So I told her . . ."

"Don't lick your brother."

The rollaway wheels rattled on pavement. The tall limestone façade of Meg's building rose like a refuge across the street, the green awning extending a welcome. The doorman, Luis, was the first person to make eye contact with her in blocks.

A smile broke his broad face. "Miss Fletcher. It's good to have you back."

"Thanks, Luis." She smiled as he opened the door for her, his jacket parting over his barrel-like torso. "Anything exciting happen while I was away?"

"We've been very quiet." Smoothly, Luis relieved her of the rollaway and pressed the button for the elevator. "Except for a little visit from Mr. Chapman's sister."

Sister?

Meg stopped, grasping the handle of her suitcase. "Derek doesn't have a sister."

Luis's face assumed the impervious stone stare common to Aztec gods and New York doormen. "I must have been mistaken," he said.

The elevator dinged. The doors slid open.

"You have a nice evening, Miss Fletcher," Luis said.

"You, too," she said and wondered why his good wishes didn't produce a greater sense of anticipation.

She expected to feel better—she expected to feel *more*—as she unlocked the door to the condo. Relief. Welcome. Homecoming. The mushroom carpet was spotless, the granite and wood surfaces gleamed, but the air smelled faintly stale as if housekeeping hadn't been by in days. Derek must have let things slide in her absence. Well, he was working hard, she thought, struggling to be fair. He was barely home enough to mess the place up anyway. She wasn't expecting to see him tonight until seven at least.

Leaving her bags at the door, she slipped out of her shoes and padded to the kitchen. A glass of wine would help her feel at home. She smiled as she tugged open the refrigerator. And didn't she deserve to toast her own success?

She reached for the open bottle in the fridge. Paused and frowned at the label. *White Zin?* Poor Derek. His standards really *had* slipped while she was out of town. Shrugging, she poured herself a glass. When he got home, they would go out to celebrate. Maybe she would order champagne.

The thought made her oddly uncomfortable. She needed more than wine. She needed . . .

Her phone chirped from her purse by the door, signaling a new text message. She sipped the wine—*awful*—and checked the display.

No salutation. Just an unfamiliar number with a North Carolina area code on the caller ID and below that, *Thinking of you. Sure you did great. Talk to you when you get back.*
Sam.

Heat sizzled in the pit of her stomach like the cascading shoots of a Fourth of July sparkler. Her fingers itched for the Connect button. She curled them tightly around her wineglass. She couldn't call. It wouldn't be fair. Not to Sam and not to Derek. She couldn't hear Sam's voice, couldn't confide her hopes and plans, couldn't hear the details of his day and share the excitement of hers, and then throw herself in Derek's arms when he walked in the door.

Maybe that was what Sam was counting on, the rat.

Restless, she wandered back into the living room. *Later for us, then.* Actually, he had demonstrated a certain consideration, she acknowledged. He hadn't called in the middle of her day. He hadn't put any pressure on her to respond in any way.

Thinking of you.

She took another unsatisfactory gulp of wine. Sneaky bastard.

As she set the wineglass on an end table, she heard a key in the lock.

She turned, a flush of wine or guilt climbing her cheeks. "You're here early."

Derek came forward, smiling. "I wanted to welcome you home."

He looked the same, blond and well tailored. He smelled the same, of starch and cologne. He moved in to kiss her, the way he had a thousand times, the standard punctuation at the end of the day or the beginning of sex. But instead of leaning into him, she flinched. It felt weird. Wrong on some basic, instinctive, molecular level, like French-kissing her brother or swallowing a bug.

Derek didn't notice her involuntary recoil. Or if he did, it didn't stop him. Meg forced herself to stand still, ignoring the aversion tightening her chest like panic as his moist, warm mouth covered hers. But when he pulled her closer, stabbing at her lips with his tongue, she turned her head.

He noticed that. He raised his head, lifting an eyebrow. "What's up?"

They had been together six years. How could she explain her prickling repugnance now?

She stepped back, clearing her throat. "Nothing. I . . . It's been a long day."

"How did the interview go?"

She felt a spasm of irritation. "My flight was fine. My mom is doing much better. Thanks for asking."

His well-bred face shuttered. "I was only trying to express some interest in the purpose of your trip."

She flushed. "Sorry." She regrouped. "I met all the partners. And I really liked the client. I've never done book promotion, but—"

"Marketing's marketing, right?" Derek interrupted.

"Well," Meg said cautiously, "in terms of identifying a target audience . . ."

He crossed to the dry bar. "Did they offer you a contract?"

She smothered a spark of resentment. It was natural for Derek to focus on the bottom line. He was in finance. "Yes. Yes, they did. I won't be making what I did at Franklin, obviously, but I'm excited about—"

"I'm not surprised. Bruce always was a fan of yours." Derek poured himself a Scotch. Laphroaig, two fingers.

"I like him, too," Meg said. "But I wouldn't have gotten the job if I hadn't demonstrated I could do it."

Derek looked surprised. "I wasn't questioning your competence, Meg."

"Sorry," she muttered. Even to her own ears, she sounded testy.

"In fact, several people lately have pointed out what a good job you did for us at Franklin."

"Not good enough, apparently." Her joke, if it was a joke, fell flat.

"I never recognized how much you did to cultivate relationships outside the company," Derek continued. "Now that you're moving to the agency side, you have a real opportunity to branch out."

She had to talk to him, Meg realized. And not about work. "Derek . . ."

"It's made me realize," he continued, smiling at her, "what a good team we've always been."

Guilt squeezed her throat. "Things change."

He nodded. "I know it was a shock for you, leaving Franklin. But I told you that would work out for the best. In this economy, it's good for us to have two independent sources of income. It's like we're diversifying our portfolio."

A huff, half laughter, half indignation, escaped her. "Oh, that's romantic."

He frowned slightly. "You've never required a lot of hearts and flowers, Meg. That's one of the things I've always admired about you. You take the long view. You're practical."

Two men, she thought, staring at him. One prized her for her contacts and praised her for her practicality. The other . . .

If you're too busy living for the future, sugar, you're missing what you could have right now.

Her mind churned. She couldn't think. She couldn't breathe. What was wrong with her?

"Would you excuse me a minute?" she asked Derek politely, as if they were strangers.

Maybe they were. Did he really see her?

I have fantasies about you in black leather.

"Of course." Derek smiled with the indulgent look of a man who thinks he's about to get laid. "You go get comfortable."

She had seldom felt more uncomfortable in her life. She hadn't come to New York to break up with Derek.

But she didn't want to sleep with him.

Alone in their bedroom, she faced herself in the mirror. She'd come to New York to resume her rightful place in her old life. And now she was back in her condo with her boyfriend and everything felt wrong. Different. Shaken, she met her gaze in the mirror. Her face was flushed, her eyes fever bright. She bit her lip. Something was ending, something beginning, and she wasn't prepared for either one.

She stripped off and folded her scarf—an admitted delaying tactic—and opened a drawer to put it away. Nestled among the socks and scarves was a framed photograph that usually sat on her dresser, a picture of her and Derek taken on that long-ago team-building exercise in Arizona. What was it doing out of sight in a drawer?

She lifted it out, a sunlit shot of the two of them standing on a mountaintop, the world at their feet. Only now did she notice that they weren't touching, all their attention reserved for the person behind the camera, more focused on their image than each other.

She sighed and set the frame gently in its accustomed place. Her reflection watched solemnly from the mirror. She knew she and Derek had to talk. She just wished she knew what she was going to say.

This relationship isn't going anywhere?

It's not you, it's me?

We don't make each other happy. We haven't in a long time.

Yeah, that would go over well. She fiddled with her earring, still stalling. Was she really prepared to throw six years of her life away? Relationships took work. Look at her parents. If two people really loved each other . . .

Her fingers fumbled with the earring. Did she *love* Derek?

The diamond stud slipped from her grasp, bouncing off the edge of the open drawer and under the dresser. *Crap.*

Her father's voice played in her head. *If you can't say yes, the answer's no.*

Oh, hell, Meg thought. I *have* to break up with him now.

She dropped to all fours, cautiously extending her hand

into the shadows under the dresser. Relief washed over her as something pricked her searching fingers. There was her earring. She stuffed it in a pocket. And there . . .

She caught the other object between two fingers and dragged it out. Frowning, she sank back on her heels, staring at the black elastic hair band in her hand. A black elastic hair band with . . . She sucked in her breath. A long, blond hair attached.

Her hand closed into a fist. Pushing to her feet, she picked up the photo from the dresser and carried both items into the living room.

Silently, she set them on the table.

Derek looked from the table to her face, his expression wary. "What's this?"

"I was hoping you could tell me."

"Isn't it yours?"

His dissembling angered her. Maybe she hadn't been completely honest with him, but she hadn't lied. "My hair is short. And dark. Someone else has been in this apartment." *In our bedroom. In our bed?*

Derek's eyes flickered. "I could have done some entertaining while you were away," he said at last.

Her world tipped slightly on its axis. She fought to keep her balance.

"You could have," she said steadily. "Did you?"

"It's possible someone might have left their jacket or . . . a few things in the bedroom."

He was deflecting, using hypothetical, conditional statements. She'd heard him use the technique in boardrooms a hundred times. But this wasn't a board meeting. This was their life.

Had been her life, she corrected silently.

She wasn't going to shriek at him. She wasn't that big a hypocrite. But she had to know. "Did that someone also shove our picture in a drawer? Or, I don't know, buy white Zinfandel for our refrigerator?"

A muscle twitched by his eye. "Don't you think you're being a little unreasonable? You've been gone almost a month."

"A month." The words thumped into her stomach, robbing her of breath. "Wow."

"Your sarcasm is hardly helping the situation."

Screaming and throwing things wouldn't help the situation, you bastard. You're lucky all I'm hitting you with is sarcasm.

"I'm just trying to understand." She'd been wrong about him. She'd been wrong about everything, it seemed. "What's the timetable on infidelity, Derek? Did you wait the whole four weeks, or . . ."

His brows snapped together in annoyance. "Don't be naïve, Meg. You can't tell me that in six years you've never strayed. That you've never been tempted."

She sucked in her breath. "No," she said slowly. "I can't tell you I haven't been tempted. But I've never cheated on you, Derek. I wouldn't do that to you. To us."

"Meg, it was a temporary thing. Nothing for you to worry about. It's over now."

Her brain was numb. Her face felt frozen. "Who was it? Did you pick someone up in a bar, or . . ."

"It was Nicole."

"Nicole Hayden? My replacement? Wow. That's just . . ." There were no words.

A faint red stained his cheekbones. "She's not your replacement. Not in the way you mean. She isn't you, Meg. I've learned that now. Really, this whole . . . episode was for the best. It taught me how much you have to offer."

She stared at him in stunned disbelief. "You're kidding. I win the girlfriend sweepstakes, so you're my prize?"

Derek frowned. "What do you want me to say? I've admitted I may have made an error in judgment. But I've moved past it."

He hadn't admitted a damn thing. Not really. And he hadn't apologized. She thought how different he was from Sam. *We can't go forward until we go back. I hurt you, Meggie, and I'm sorry.*

"You don't get past something like this, Derek. You don't audition somebody else to be your girlfriend, and then decide, whoops, sorry, made a mistake. You should have talked to me. You should have told me you were unhappy."

"I haven't been unhappy. And I didn't say anything because I knew you would blow everything out of proportion."

Her heart throbbed in her chest. "How do you blow something like this out of proportion? You *cheated* on me. And then you lied."

"I didn't lie. Maybe I wasn't completely forthcoming, but that was out of respect for your feelings. We've never been one of those couples who have to tell each other every little thing."

She opened her mouth to deny it. But the words would not come. He was right. Their conversation, like their lives, had always revolved around work. Derek had no interest in her fears and weaknesses, in the secrets of her heart, in the details of her family history. She had enjoyed the reflection of herself that she'd seen in his eyes, polished, professional Meg, sprung into existence as a full-blown adult like the goddess Athena.

Except that wasn't her.

She hadn't been honest with him, either.

"You're right," she said, picking her words carefully. She wasn't going to put all the blame for the failures of their relationship on him. "I'm sorry, Derek. There are things I should have told you, too."

He thawed slightly. "It's understandable. You've been under a lot of stress. Now that you're back, we can—"

"I've met someone, too," she said, plowing ahead. "While I was home. Or rather, I've reconnected with someone I used to know."

"Is this your idea of a joke?"

She'd never felt less like laughing in her life. "I don't find cheating very funny." She took a deep breath, forcing down her feelings, trying to be fair. "What I'm trying to say is, you're right. Maybe this is an opportunity for both of us to acknowledge we're not getting what we need from this relationship."

"Then it's revenge." Derek shook his head. "Really, Meg, I thought you were better than that."

She stared at him, speechless. She needed a drink. She really did. She picked up her wine.

"But I'm willing to put all this behind us," Derek continued smoothly. "We have too much invested in this relationship to let a simple misunderstanding get in our way."

"Derek, you had another *woman* in our *apartment*. I just told you I'm involved with somebody else. That's not a misunderstanding."

"You don't need to overdramatize this, Meg. Obviously in any long-term relationship both parties are going to fail from time to time."

"What do you mean, *fail*? Are you saying it's acceptable to sleep around? Derek." Her stomach dropped. "Have you cheated on me before?"

He poured himself another drink. "I don't much like your tone, Meg."

She watched the back of his head, the defensive set of

his shoulders, remembering all those late nights at the office. All those times he'd turned away from her in bed, too tired or distracted for sex. "Just answer me."

He drew himself up. "I don't choose to dignify your accusations with a response. We've always been good together."

"That's it? We're good together?" A slow-burning rage ignited in her gut. "What about love? What about loyalty? What about simple respect?"

"I've always tried to give you what you need," Derek said stiffly.

Her hand tightened on her glass. "You don't get to decide what I need based on what you're willing to give me, you son of a bitch."

She threw the glass of wine in his face and walked out.

Fourteen

CARL DRUMMED HIS fingers on the arm of his leather arm-chair, *The Wall Street Journal* disregarded on his lap. The evening market wrap-up flickered silently on the giant plasma screen at one end of the room. "What's the matter with you, boy, you got ants in your pants? You're giving me whiplash stalking around."

Sam leveled a look at the old man. Carl was frustrated by the doctors' restrictions, testy over his prolonged convalescence. Fine. That didn't give him the right to jab at Sam for entertainment like a kid with a stick poking a jellyfish on the beach.

Sam continued to pace, fourteen strides along the wall of windows overlooking the darkening sea, fourteen strides back. Because if he stopped moving, if he stopped counting, he would start to think. And none of the thoughts beating at his brain were good.

Seven o'clock, and Meg hadn't returned his text.

She couldn't still be in meetings. Didn't everyone in New York knock off early on Fridays, split for Connecticut or the Hamptons or something?

She was probably back in her condo. Or out to dinner. He hoped to hell she was out to dinner.

Because even the mental image of her squeezed into a booth with that faceless fuck Derek, giving him her attention and her smiles, was better than the idea of her being home— in bed—with the son of a bitch. They'd been together six years. Chapman would know all her favorite places. Where to take her. Where to touch her.

Maybe she hadn't returned Sam's text because she was so fucking happy with Derek. *Derek is my boyfriend.*

Maybe she was better off with Derek. *He's perfect for me.*

Sam shoved his hands into his pockets, pacing. Brooding. Maybe Derek should die.

"Can I get you a drink?"

The question broke the rhythm of his pacing at his thoughts. He looked over his shoulder at Angela.

His stepmother smiled almost apologetically. "When your father gets like this, I fix him a bourbon and branch."

He was not like his father, making life miserable for everyone around him. He took his hands out of his pockets, dredged up a smile. "No, thanks, Angela."

He should find Matt, get a beer. Matt owed him one anyway. *She hurts you, she lets you down, I'll buy the beer.*

Except Matt knew Sam had driven Meg to the airport. He would know Sam had let her go.

What a pussy.

He should have said something to stop her, Sam thought, resuming his track of the carpet. Not from going to New York, but from going back to *him.*

Oh, he'd talked a good game. All that stuff about telling

her how he felt, about not making the same mistake twice. Bullshit. When he got to the line, he'd choked. *Later for us, then.*

He could talk about his feelings from eighteen years ago, the mess of teenage lust, panic, and regret he'd been back then.

But he'd totally dropped the ball on telling her how he felt now. Because everything he felt, everything he'd wanted to say to her, made him sound like a crazy stalker or a whiny loser or both.

I don't want him touching you.

Don't leave me.

"Heard from Walt Rogers today," Carl remarked.

Sam's shoulders tightened. Maybe the old man had the right idea after all. Right now Sam would welcome anything that would distract him from the thought of Meg with Derek, in their apartment, of Derek pulling Meg close, putting his hands all over her smooth soft skin . . . Maybe a fight with Carl would take his mind off his troubles.

He glared at his father. "So?"

"He wanted to know if you were serious about this crazy scheme of yours."

"If you're talking about the fish house, I've already met with the architects."

Carl nodded. "Herb Stuart gave me a call."

Well, that figured. There wasn't anything that happened on the island, anything connected with the industry, that wouldn't get reported to his father eventually. "I spoke with Ed Parker, too."

"Parker's got some good ideas," Carl said. "But he over-promises. Stuart delivers."

Privately, Sam agreed with Carl's assessment of the two architects. But . . . "The Parker Group has more experience with low-impact development," he pointed out.

"A man can adapt his plans. He can't change his character."

Sam nodded slowly. "Fair enough."

"Walt says you're taking preliminary drafts to the zoning board." Carl sent him a sharp look. "Not letting any grass grow under your feet, are you?"

"I don't see any reason to wait," Sam said. Not with his father's six-month deadline hanging over his head. "I want the town's cooperation. And I want input from the watermen."

"Well, they'll give you an earful." Carl drummed again on his chair. "Let me know if you need to set up a preapplication meeting with the Division of Coastal Management."

Sam glanced at him, surprised. For forty years, Carl Grady had played politics, worked deals, and finessed regulations, forever altering the local landscape. With a few choice words, a couple of well-placed phone calls, he could smooth Sam's way. Or completely undercut his efforts.

"I thought you were sitting this one out," Sam said.

"I can still work the damn phones."

Angela looked at Sam in silent appeal, her eyes wide with Botox and concern. Sam felt a twinge of affection for his stepmother. She really did care about the old goat.

Don't upset him, the doctors said.

"I'm not questioning your connections," Sam said. "I'm just curious about your motivation. Why would you help me?"

"Why wouldn't I? It's still my name on the project. Unless you've changed that, too," Carl grumbled.

"All the paperwork says Grady Realty and Development. But if you're not careful, you'll be giving me control of the company and a house."

"Might be the best bet I ever lost," Carl said.

Everybody wins, Meg had said. *Your father gets a great development with the Grady name on it. The watermen get a working fish house. The island preserves a piece of its heritage and stops shedding jobs. And you get . . .*

A chance, Sam thought.

"It's good to see you finally giving a damn about the company," Carl continued. "Committing for the long haul. Showing some fire. A man's got to go after what he wants."

The satisfaction in Carl's voice set Sam's teeth on edge. He'd experienced firsthand the cost of his father's hard-assed, hard-charging approach to business and to life. Three failed marriages. Four failed heart valves. That wasn't Sam's style. It was easier, better, to play it cool. A lifetime of dealing with his father's rigid standards and high expectations had taught Sam to play down his own ambitions and emotions. Less hurt, less disappointment that way for everybody.

But this time he cared. It unnerved him, how much this project mattered. How badly and publicly he could fail.

His phone vibrated. His pulse jumped as he looked at the display. Meg.

Flying into RDU 2nite 10:30, the text read. *Can u meet me in Morehead around 1:30? Will call.*

She was coming back early. She was coming home tonight. She wanted him to meet her.

And if she was flying back tonight—Sam took his first deep breath in what felt like hours—*then she couldn't be sleeping with Derek.*

"Sorry, Dad." He slid his phone into his pocket, already doing the math, calculating minutes and miles. Meg was expecting him to pick her up where he'd left her this morning, at the car rental lot in Morehead City. But if he left now—right this minute—he could drive the extra three hours to Raleigh and meet her flight. "Something's come up."

"Where the hell are you going?"

"Where you said." Sam flashed his teeth in a grin. "I'm going after what I want."

SHE NEVER SHOULD have texted Sam, Meg thought as she wheeled her rollaway from the gate past the closed shops and shuttered eateries of the Raleigh-Durham Airport. Her staccato heel taps echoed in the bright, empty corridor.

She shivered a little, tired to the bone. She still had her trench, but she'd left her scarf back at the condo, along with six years of her life. She wondered what Derek would do with it. With all her things.

Don't think about that now. Put it on the list for tomorrow.

She nodded to the lone security guard as she passed through the checkpoint on her way to the terminal. She had dropped off her car at the rental agency lot here at RDU. The smart thing—really, the only thing—to do was to rent another car and drive straight to Dare Island. She and her family could sort out the vehicle situation tomorrow.

Exhaustion welled up, threatened to spill over. Her head felt stuffy, her sinuses congested from air travel and tension.

The problem was that in the aftermath of that nasty little scene with Derek, she hadn't been thinking clearly. Her only instinct had been to get out, to get home. But now she had to tell Sam that she didn't need him. There was absolutely no reason he should have to leave Dare Island after midnight and drive almost an hour to Morehead City so that she could drop off her rental car tonight. She had to text him and tell him . . . No, she had to *call* him to explain . . .

She emerged from the corridor into the brightly lit cavern of the new terminal. And saw . . .

Her feet froze. Her throat swelled with emotion.

"Sam?" she whispered.

Tall, dark, and broad-shouldered, waiting at the corner by the deserted Starbucks. He smiled crookedly, and something inside her that had been stiff and cold and solid for hours began to thaw. "Welcome home, Meggie."

Her eyes burned. She blinked furiously. "I'm not crying."

"Course not." He put a friendly arm around her shoulders, relieved her of her suitcase with his other hand.

She wanted to turn her face into his chest and bawl her eyes out in gratitude. She gulped. "I can't believe you're here. At the airport."

"Of course I am. You said you needed a ride." He slanted a look down at her. "Well, I'm your designated driver."

"I was going to rent a car."

He shook his head as he steered her past the baggage claim. "You've had a long day. Why would you want to tack a long drive on the end of it?"

"Your day's been every bit as long as mine."

He flashed his teasing grin. "Yeah, but I'm a guy."

An answering smile worked its way from deep inside to tug the corner of her mouth. "That is so sexist."

"We can argue about it on the way home."

"I should have called a friend," she fretted as they stepped onto the moving walkway to the parking garage. She felt light-headed, almost giddy with relief and hunger.

Sam steadied her, one hand at the small of her back. "I'm a friend."

"I mean somebody in New York." Fatigue made her babble. Her blood buzzed with adrenaline. "I could have slept on someone's couch. Or gone to a hotel. But all I wanted was to get home. The only thing I could think of was you." Hot color stormed her face as she realized what she'd said. "I didn't mean that the way it sounded."

Those creases in his cheeks appeared. "I liked the way it sounded."

She watched him pay for parking at the automated kiosk, realizing too late she should have reached for her wallet. "Did I say thank you?"

He pocketed the ticket. "Sugar, you don't have to thank me."

"Yes," she insisted. "I do."

In the world she inhabited with Derek, a subconscious points system ruled, everything tallied to preserve parity in their relationship—picked-up checks, favors, infractions, omissions. She realized with a sense of shock that she didn't live there anymore. The thought was oddly liberating. She didn't have to keep score anymore.

"Have you had dinner?" Sam asked as he started the truck.

Her stomach clenched. "Peanut butter crackers at the airport."

He shot her an assessing look. "Right. Let's get you something to eat, then."

"I'm fine. It's after ten thirty." She smiled, attempting a joke. "We're not exactly in the city that never sleeps."

And her churning system was in no shape to handle the all-night drive-through at Taco Bell.

"I know a place," Sam said.

She could have argued. The longer they delayed, the longer they would be on the road. But there was an almost unspeakable relief in letting someone else take charge for a while.

She leaned her head back against the cushioned leather, staring out at the Carolina pines black-etched against the midnight blue sky, drinking in the quiet. *No effort, no explanations.* Less than ten minutes later the truck slowed at an intersection. Meg caught a glimpse of a spotlit modern sculpture before the truck turned onto a winding, wooded road.

She roused enough to sit up. "Where are we?"

"The Umstead." They pulled under a well-lit arch over a drive of paver stones. Sam handed the keys to a valet while another attendant helped Meg from the car. She paused a moment, trying to get her bearings, and then Sam escorted her past the smiling doorman into another world.

The walls of the entrance glistened like a jeweled cave, rich, muted, glowing. A massive granite table held a small forest of potted orchids, pink and cream. She glimpsed a concierge desk for the hotel to the right, a discreet sign for the formal dining room to their left. The view through the bar extended through a wall of glass to an outdoor terrace overlooking a naturally landscaped garden. Everything was low and soft and welcoming—the lighting, the seating, the voices of the staff, the piano playing one room over.

"Holy crap," Meg muttered. "This is nice."

Sam grinned. "You looked like you could use a drink."

The hostess, young and smiling, asked if they would like to sit on the patio outside or in the lounge.

Meg glanced from the artfully lit trees on the terrace to the cozy private corner inside and then at Sam, trying to read his preference.

"Whatever you want," he said.

Lights gleamed on the flatware, spotlighting the single scarlet orchid reflected in the polished stone table. "Inside, I think."

The next ten minutes passed in a blur of choices between something good or something better, all offered with easy smiles and the comforting accents of home. Flat or sparkling water? Wine or a cocktail? The seared red snapper with succotash or the macaroni and cheese with lobster?

Meg was used to high-powered business dinners and

high-profile restaurants, but not to pampering on this level. She melted into her chair, sinking into comfort, letting the muted noises of the bar—women's voices rising over the men's, the rattle of the bar shaker—wash over her.

She was braced for questions, but they didn't speak beyond commenting on the menu and the music.

Gradually, she relaxed, cocking her head to listen to the melody from the next room. " 'Piano Man'? Seriously? Isn't that a little clichéd?"

Sam smiled. "He can't help himself. It's in the Lounge Performers' Contract or something."

Plates began to arrive, heaped and studded with color like the treasures of Aladdin's cave glowing in the lamplight, delicate greens and rich, acidic tomatoes, sharp olives and melting cheese, succulent seafood and fragrant bread.

Sometime during the procession of food, Meg looked up and flushed, a little embarrassed by her appetite. "I can't believe I'm eating so much."

"It's your recovery meal."

"My what?"

"Fueling after an event." He signaled to their server, gestured toward Meg's glass.

"You mean, like Josh eating a banana after a game?" Meg asked, amused.

Sam's smile creased his cheeks. "Something like that."

"I remember you and Matt coming home after practice. You used to eat standing in front of the refrigerator."

"Only until your mom made us sit down for dinner."

Meg chuckled. Whatever else existed between them, she and Sam shared a history, a mine of memories and emotions that went deep to the heart. He *knew* her.

With a sigh of contentment, she eased away from the table. The setting was as sophisticated as any in New York, but the buzz, the pulse, the pace of the city was missing.

The pressure was off. A weight she hadn't acknowledged even to herself rolled from her shoulders. A handful of business travelers congregated at the bar. A couple in their midthirties sat close together on a couch facing the windows, celebrating . . . What? Meg wondered. A birthday? Anniversary? They looked happy, his arm around her shoulders, her hand on his knee.

She felt a wriggle of envy and looked away.

Right into Sam's eyes. A jolt of sexual awareness tightened her stomach. A trick of the light made his green eyes gleam, cast the planes and angles of his face in sharp relief. He needed a shave, she noticed. She wanted to rub her fingers over his rough cheek, to test the texture with her thumb. Her breath went.

Attraction spun between them, fine and inescapable as a spiderweb, wrapping them in a silken cocoon. She moistened her lips, watched his gaze drop to her mouth.

Their server appeared to whisk away Meg's empty glass and replace it with another. Meg inhaled, ignoring the little twist of disappointment at the interruption.

Later for us, then.

"Thanks," she said to the server. She toyed with the fresh flower petals under her glass, a pink martini made with watermelon and rose water. She never ordered girlie drinks when she went out after work. It was too important to look like one of the guys. But with Sam, she could indulge herself.

The thought made something inside her loosen and then pull tight. "Aren't you having another beer?" she asked him.

He shook his head with a slight smile. "Driving, remember?" He settled back in his chair, at ease in his body. "I wasn't expecting you until Sunday. How'd things go in New York?"

A question. *The* question, couched in the same easy tone

with which he'd made small talk through dinner. Only the utter stillness of Sam's hands, the sharp focus of his eyes, betrayed that he had anything more than a casual interest in her reply.

I broke up with Derek, she almost blurted out.

But once she said the words, there was no going back.

She dropped her gaze to her drink, feeling herself unravel, slowly unwinding with gin and fatigue. Was she ready to tell him? Was she ready for Sam?

She'd been so determined not to cheat on Derek, so focused on her boyfriend as the barrier to any possible relationship with Sam, that she hadn't considered the other reasons why they shouldn't get involved.

She and Sam were . . . connected, she supposed. He knew her family. He was friends with her brother. That closeness, that familiarity, was part of his appeal. But all those connections could turn into complications if they took things to the next level. *I put everything that mattered at risk*, he'd said, *your parents' trust, Matt's friendship*.

She bit her lip. Was any relationship between them worth that risk?

"Hey," Sam said softly. She looked up as he reached across the table and gently brushed his thumb across her lower lip, releasing it from the grip of her teeth. "It's okay. We don't have to talk now."

She held his gaze, her heart pounding.

What if there was no later? What if all they had was now?

Greatly daring, she touched her tongue to the pad of his thumb.

He inhaled sharply.

She sank back in her chair, savoring the salt of him on the tip of her tongue, the unfamiliar hum of power.

Sam's eyes were dark. "We should get going." He signaled for the check. "Anything else you need? Anything I can get you?"

They weren't kids any longer, Meg told herself. They could handle complications.

"Yes." She smiled across the table at him. "Get us a room. Take me upstairs, Sam."

Fifteen

SAM WATCHED MEG cross to the windows overlooking the lake, wobbling slightly as her heels sank into the deep plush carpet, cautious as a cat exploring new surroundings.

Any fantasies he'd entertained about fucking her against the wall the minute the suite door closed behind them died a swift, painless death.

Meggie would let herself be taken, but not rushed.

Fine by him. He wanted to prove to her, to both of them, that he could do better than twenty minutes on musty canvas in a cold, deserted boathouse. He wanted . . . to take care of her, he supposed. To impress her, maybe.

She turned from inspecting the bathroom, her cheeks pink, her eyes glowing, more perfect than any fantasy. "This is great."

He strolled forward, hands in his pockets. *See? Harmless.* "Glad you like it."

She held her ground. "Thank you for dinner. And for coming to get me. And for . . . everything."

"Sugar, I'm just getting started."

"No, really," she insisted. "You didn't have to do all this."

He wondered when the last time was that somebody did something nice for her. When she had let them. Meggie was the take-charge one, self-confident, self-reliant, protective of herself and her family. He liked and admired that about her. But it must occasionally be exhausting. She deserved a change.

She'd discovered the guest bag he'd been given at check-in and was poking inside. "Look at all this," she exclaimed with delight, pulling out little girlie bottles.

Her pleasure made him feel good inside. "There's a spa attached to the hotel. That's their stuff."

Humor warmed her eyes. She held up a handful of foil packets. "These, too?"

Busted. But the hotel store was closed. "I asked the concierge for those when I checked us in," Sam admitted.

"You don't carry one in your wallet?"

Something in her tone made him lift his eyebrows. Something there, he thought. He came up behind her, running his hands up and down her bare arms. The smell of her hair, citrus and spice, worked its way inside him. "Not usually." *Not anymore.* He'd cleaned up his act in the last five years. When he took a woman to bed these days, it was something he planned for, not a quick score. "I wasn't counting on this."

"This." A hint of a question.

"Us." He kissed the join of her neck. "You."

Her head fell back against his shoulder. His hard-on lodged, heavy, ready, just above the rise of her bottom, below the small of her back.

"You haven't asked about Derek," she said.

He skimmed his hands from her upper arms to under her breasts, cupping them. Cradling them. "I don't need to."

Her swift inhale raised her breasts. "Pretty sure of yourself, aren't you?" She sounded more breathless than annoyed.

He smiled against her neck, letting his fingers trace the taut outline of her nipples against her blouse. "Sure of you."

She stiffened even as her back arched, pushing her breasts more fully into his hands, her buttocks more firmly against his aching cock.

Sam turned her in his arms, meeting those incredible eyes full on. "Because I know you. If you were still involved with him, you wouldn't be with me."

Her lips parted, a round, irresistible O.

"And right now I don't give a fuck about Derek," he said and kissed her.

SAM'S LIPS WERE warm and firm, taking hers in sweet, hungry bites. His mouth eased over hers, pursuing, exploring. She closed her eyes and opened to him as he deepened the kiss, as his fingers threaded through her hair, making tiny circles against her scalp. He kissed her until her nerve endings tingled to life, her lips swollen and sensitive, her skin awake and softly clamoring.

I wasn't counting on this. He hadn't taken sex with her for granted. It was a choice.

Her choice, she reminded herself.

Sliding her arms around his waist, she kissed him back, enjoying the feel of him hard and solid against her front. The thick ridge of his erection jutted against her stomach. Even to her more experienced perceptions, he was . . . big. She wriggled, seeking a better fit between their bodies, and he made a sound of encouragement in his throat and widened his stance. His big hands spanned her rib cage. She felt the pop of a button before her waistband eased and her skirt slithered down her legs, leaving her standing in her underwear, blouse, and high heels.

Determined to reciprocate, she tugged at the back of his shirt, pulling it free from his jeans. The skin at his waist was smooth and hot. Sam kissed her again, backing her a step toward the bed, then two. She stumbled out of her shoes, leaving them tangled in her skirt on the floor. She trembled, exposed and off balance. There was something undeniably erotic about Sam undressing her, divesting her of her armor piece by piece while he was still fully clothed. But it wasn't enough.

She wanted him *with* her. Naked.

She reached for his belt buckle, her fingers clumsy with desire. Sam helped her with one hand while his other slid under her blouse to the back catch of her bra. She was shaking, coming apart as he undid the buttons of her blouse one by one, his knuckles brushing the inner curve of her breasts. She caught her breath. *Touch me.*

He slid the blouse from her shoulders, the bra straps from her arms, his face intent. His hand skimmed gently over her, his teasing fingers flirting, sliding, making her hips jerk convulsively toward him.

"God, you're beautiful," he said.

She was embarrassed, burning up, suffused with blushes and lust. "Well, I'm naked. That's enough for most guys."

He smiled, as she intended, but his gaze meeting hers was serious. "You're always beautiful to me."

She swallowed the lump in her throat. "But not always naked."

The creases deepened in his cheeks. "That is a plus."

"You have some catching up to do."

"Eighteen years," he agreed.

Her heart skipped a beat. "No, I meant . . ." She gestured to his clothes.

His grin flashed. He pulled his shirt off over his head and toed out of his shoes, stroking her constantly, her arm, her hair, her hip, as if he might lose her in the dimly lit room. He stroked beneath the stretchy band of her underwear, easing it over the curve of her butt.

Obeying the urging of his hands, she sat on the edge of the bed. He kissed her, his mouth warm and urgent, and then pressed her back until she was lying across the mattress, her feet not quite touching the floor. She went willingly, opening her arms to him.

But instead of falling on top of her, Sam straightened, standing between her legs, looking down. "Look at you." His voice was thick with satisfaction. "All spread out like some virgin sacrifice."

Her stomach quivered low inside. Her nipples were tight, puckered with anticipation. She could feel herself falling, succumbing to the seduction of his hands and voice, sinking into the temptation to lie back and let him do . . .

Anything he wanted. Anything at all.

The realization terrified her. She wasn't used to being vulnerable, in or out of bed.

She moistened her lips, working to inject a dry note in her voice. Ridiculous, when she was already wet for him, her skin damp and blooming. "Hardly a virgin," she pointed out. "Or a sacrifice, either."

This time.

She didn't say the words out loud. She wasn't expecting even to think them. But the past was suddenly in the room with them, smothering and inescapable.

Sam's lashes lifted. His eyes met hers. "I have a lot to make up to you for."

She resisted the urge to squirm. "Don't be silly. I take responsibility for my choices. For my actions."

He continued to hold her gaze, his expression thoughtful. "You don't have to be responsible all the time. How about we agree that for tonight I'm in charge?"

She almost lost her breath.

Sex was another area where she and Derek had kept careful score, neither of them yielding control, both of them stinting what they would give and what they would allow. *You do this for me, and I'll do this for you.* With Derek, she was always conscious of her boundaries. And his. She was comfortable with that.

Her heart pounded. And now Sam was suggesting . . . Sam was proposing . . .

No responsibility. The temptation was staggering.

"Designated driver, Meggie," he whispered wickedly. "I'll get you where you need to go."

She was sure he could. But did she want him to? Did she trust him that much?

She started to speak, but whatever she'd been about to say was lost in a wordless rush, buried in fascination as Sam reached for the front of his pants. He shucked his jeans and underwear, freeing himself to her gaze. Her insides clenched involuntarily. He was undeniably naked. And alarmingly large.

"You're thinking again," he observed. "Don't."

He went to the bag to retrieve a condom before kneeling on the floor between her legs. Running his hands from her knees to her hips, he pressed a kiss to her inner thigh. She hitched helplessly toward him.

Meg cleared her throat. "Maybe we should have a, I don't know, like, a safe word?" she suggested.

Sam raised his head. His smile gleamed. "You won't

remember it," he said. "When I'm done with you, you won't remember your name."

Leaning forward, he pressed his mouth to her in a warm, searching kiss, his tongue stroking straight to her center. Her mind blanked. Her moan shook them both. She grabbed fistfuls of the cover as he harrowed her with teeth and lips, his breath searing against her wet flesh. Her eyes closed. Her head moved restlessly back and forth as he ate at her softly, probing for her response. Sensation shot to her brain. He penetrated her with one finger, then two, driving her higher, taking her deeper, making her pant and groan.

"God. Sam. I can't . . ."

"You will," he promised.

He kept at her, his tongue silky, insinuating, insistent, his hands demanding. The tension twisted inside her, tighter and tighter. He did something else with his mouth and with his hands, and her ravaged system exploded. She saw stars. He licked into her again, making her quiver, before he crawled over her. His chest brushed hers as he reached for the nightstand. She heard the crinkle of the condom wrapper and then he was there at her entrance, blunt and seeking, heavy and warm.

She struggled to lift her arms. "Sam."

"That's right," he said, his voice raw. He thrust inside her. Hard. Deep.

She convulsed with pleasure. It was too much. He was too much. She wasn't in control. The tremors started again, quickening low in her womb. He held her wrists and pinned them to the mattress as he plunged into her again and again. Her muscles contracted helplessly around him as she yielded to brutal delight. Until her spasms caught his and he groaned and jerked and came inside her.

She lay stunned under him, her breathing ragged.

"Meggie." He kissed her, his lips cruising over the arch of her brow, the hot curve of her cheek.

A corner of her mouth twitched. "Who's Meggie?" she slurred, and was rewarded when he laughed.

Sealed together with sweat and sex, they slept.

Sixteen

COFFEE.

The scent sank into Meg's consciousness, sliding through layers of sleep, and gave a little tug. She stretched and sighed between the sheets, floating on a wave of well-being. Every cell in her body felt pampered, replete. Every inch of her skin still hummed with pleasure. Because of Sam.

Warmth rippled through her. Warmth and unease. She opened her eyes, already aroused and wanting him.

No Sam.

Sunlight edged the heavy amber drapes. The large room glowed like a jewel box in shades of topaz, citrine, and gold. Oh, God, it must be late.

She sat up, her head beginning to throb.

"Good morning." Sam stood in the doorway wearing a pair of jeans and nothing else, holding a steaming cup of coffee, looking like every woman's perfect rebound fantasy.

Her system jangled with craving. Warning. Fantasies didn't last. And neither did rebounds. She sat up cautiously, pulling the sheets up over her naked breasts. Breasts Sam had kissed and licked and sucked and . . . A blush spread over her chest. "What time is it?"

He strolled forward, easy in his skin, looking rumpled and morning delicious, wearing a smile and a hint of stubble. A lock of hair had fallen over his forehead. Her fingers itched to push it back.

He offered her a mug. "Just nine."

"Nine?" Another uncomfortable little jolt. "I never sleep that late." She never did all kinds of things she'd done last night.

Sam's smile warmed his eyes.

Her heart performed a complicated maneuver in her chest. *Oh, no.*

"Thanks." She took the coffee, holding it in front of her like a shield. "What time is checkout?"

He sat on the edge of the bed, threatening her grasp on the sheet and her composure. "Relax. I told the desk we wanted a late checkout. Or . . ." His green eyes watched her face, gauging her reaction. "We could keep the room for another night."

A spurt of panic accelerated her heartbeat. *Fight or flight?*

"I can't *stay*," she said.

"I don't see why not," Sam said. He stood. "Are you ready for breakfast?"

"What?"

"I didn't know if you'd be hungry when you woke up, so I ordered a fruit plate and some pastry things from room service. But if you want something hot . . ." He trailed off suggestively.

She flushed.

He grinned. "They do great omelets here. Or waffles."

He sauntered out. Meg stared after him, distracted by all those long, smooth, golden muscles, that lovely indentation along his spine, the red, parallel scratches down his back . . . Her jaw sagged. Dear God, sometime during the night, she'd scratched him. She didn't know whether to feel appalled or smug.

"Fruit is fine." She frowned. Fruit was perfect.

And that, she admitted to herself, was part of the problem. Sam's constant anticipation of her needs, his attention to her preferences, made her nervy and unsettled. She was used to taking care of herself.

She wasn't sure of her moves anymore.

Or of his.

Jumping out of bed, she stuffed her arms into the hotel-provided robe before following him out of the bedroom. "Listen, Sam . . ."

He looked up at her entrance, the devil dancing in his smile. "More coffee?"

She narrowed her eyes. He was laughing at her. Or he was managing her. She wasn't sure which was worse.

She grabbed her dignity with both hands, belting herself firmly into the thick, plush robe. Not the best armor, but at least she wasn't naked anymore. "Thanks." She glanced at the breakfast tray. "This looks wonderful. Last night . . ."

"Was wonderful," Sam said quietly. She met his gaze, all laughter stilled.

And her irritation melted away.

Maybe she was a little out of sorts this morning, overwhelmed by the Grady charm, uncomfortable with her lack of control—over herself, over Sam, over the situation. But she couldn't fault Sam for her feelings. He'd done everything he could last night and this morning to take care of her, to make her feel better. She admired his attention to detail.

She appreciated his genuine kindness. She didn't want to hurt his feelings.

She didn't want to hurt him.

The realization shivered through her. She wasn't used to considering that sexy, teasing, impervious Sam could be hurt. That he had that depth of feeling, that she had that degree of influence. And she *would* hurt him eventually if she made this out to be anything more than what it was, a temporary escape from the rest of their lives.

"It was wonderful," she said. "But we have to get back." Back to Dare Island. Back to reality.

Sam pulled the cloche off the fruit plate, mangos, strawberries, kiwi, pineapple, glowing like a stained glass window. Almost without thinking, Meg sat.

"I'm in no hurry," Sam said. "And your family's not expecting you until tomorrow."

Something Meg was trying not to think about. Why on earth had she called Sam last night and not her brother? "I need to let them know where I am."

"You're thirty-five."

"Thirty-four." She grabbed a sweet roll, annoyed with herself for that quick, defensive retort.

Sam smiled. "A consenting adult. Tell them you're with me."

"That will thrill my mother. Dad, on the other hand . . ."

"Let's leave your parents out of this for a minute," Sam suggested. Under the charm and good humor, she heard steel. "Tell me what's going on. What did I do to screw up?"

"You didn't." She swallowed. "It was perfect."

"Past tense? That sounds like a brush-off."

"It isn't meant to."

He raised his brows.

She sighed. He knew her too well, saw through her too easily. "Look, Sam, I really appreciate you coming to my rescue yesterday. I was upset and you were . . . Well, you gave me exactly what I needed. A real night off. But I don't know what we're doing here."

"Based on last night, I'd say we're recovering from a night of great sex," Sam drawled.

She was crushing her napkin. She relaxed her grip, smoothing the linen square over her lap. "I should say, I don't know what I'm doing." Looking up, she met his gaze. "I just left a long-term relationship. Two, actually. Six years with Derek, and—*poof!*—we're through. Twelve years with the company and—*boom!*—I'm gone. I'm facing a huge learning curve with a new client, and . . ."

"You got the job?"

"I got the contract." Despite her current worries, she couldn't keep the satisfaction from her voice. "A book promotion."

"Congratulations." He sounded warm. Sincere.

"Thanks." Under the pleasure, nerves vibrated. She set down her coffee. "I'm pumped about working on something besides quarterly earnings reports and bullshit class action suits. But I've never done anything like this before. This is the author's first book. It could be big. Really big. There's a lot of media interest in her story already. But I have to figure out how to spin it so she's not a one-book wonder."

"What's her name?"

This was not the conversation she intended to have this morning. But she appreciated Sam's interest. Derek had never asked. Not that it mattered anymore, Meg told herself. "Lauren Patterson."

"The hostage girl," Sam said. "I saw the story on the news. Bank robbery, right? She negotiated to get everybody else out."

Meg nodded. Every time she thought she had Sam figured out, he shifted. Surprised her. "The challenge is that Hostage

Girl doesn't want to be known forever as Hostage Girl. She's so much more than that—she's got a master's in psychology. She has a great message that goes beyond the headlines. It's my job to help her get it out to a wider audience."

"Well, you're good at finding out what people are interested in. What they're passionate about." Sam squeezed her leg where the terrycloth robe had parted. "You'll do great."

His palm was warm and sure on her knee. Meg gnawed the inside of her lip, letting her uncertainty show. "Do you really think so?"

"Sure." His smile spread warmth through her midsection. "Look at the way you hooked me into the Dare Plantation project. You got me working with my father again. Convincing people to buy a book should be a piece of cake."

He'd done it again, she realized, dismayed. Fed her, focused on her, making her relax. Making her open up to him. She took a breath, shoring up her defenses. "My point is I'm dealing with a lot of changes. I don't think we should rush into things."

"I wouldn't call eighteen years of foreplay rushing."

She squelched a quick bubble of laughter, a flash of heat. "You know what I mean. You're launching a major island development that could tie you there for years. I don't even know where I'm going to be three months from now. Neither one of us has the time or energy to devote to a serious relationship right now."

Their gazes held, his expression inscrutable.

"Who says we're serious?" Sam asked evenly.

MEG'S MOUTH DROPPED open.

Sam swallowed a grin. Her reaction went a little way toward easing the slap to his ego, the sting to his heart.

Damn it, they were already *in* a relationship. Had been

for years. They were bound with ties of affection, a thousand threads of memory and feeling. Hell, he was so tangled up in her he couldn't see straight. Couldn't breathe. He didn't want to even think about her going back to New York. But he knew Meggie. Pushing her for a commitment now would only spook her into full, panicked retreat.

He shoved down his own frustration and spoke mildly. "You're overthinking this. Last night was good, right?"

"Are you looking for a grade?"

He laughed and shook his head. "I'll leave that to you. You were the straight-A student. I'm just saying I had a good time."

"Me, too," she admitted. Her blue eyes were soft.

He breathed in relief. "So why not let things be what they are? We can see each other without pinning a label on it."

That double pleat appeared between her brows. "You mean, like an open relationship?"

Hell, no. The very idea revolted him. He watched her carefully. "Is that what you want?"

"No." She pressed her lips together. "Apparently that's what I had before. With Derek. I just didn't know it."

"Son of a bitch." Even though the bastard's actions had sent Meg flying home and into Sam's arms, Sam still wanted to beat the shit out of him.

"Thank you." She curled her hands around her coffee cup as if to warm them.

"The guy's a fucking idiot to dump you."

"Oh, he didn't dump me." Her tone was bitter, her smile wry. "He said the whole thing was a misunderstanding. He said that in any long-term relationship both parties are bound to fail from time to time. He expected me to take him back."

What an asshole. "I hope you told him to go to hell."

"I threw a glass of wine in his face."

"You should have tossed him out a window, but okay."

Her smile flashed. Faded. "You know what really gets me? It's not that Derek deceived me. Okay, actually that really bothers me. But I deceived myself."

"Sorry, sugar, you don't get the blame on this one. He's the one who cheated. He's a dick."

"But I didn't see that, didn't let myself see that. I was so focused on my personal checklist that I ignored my own feelings. My values. I let him diminish me. I diminished myself to be with him. And that was a bigger betrayal than anything he did."

"Well, see, that's one problem we won't have. You already know me. You know my faults. And I know you. I want you. We don't have to pretend with each other."

She studied him, still with that furrow between her brows. "And that's enough for you."

It would have to be. Sam grinned. "It was last night."

"What about tomorrow? Or next week?"

"We both have some experience of living with other people's expectations," Sam said. "Or not living up to them. Why don't we take this thing one day at a time and see where it goes. You in?"

"No promises, no pretending," she murmured.

"No pressure," he said. "But I'll promise you this: I'm here for you, Meggie. I'll try to make you happy. And as long as we're together, there's nobody else for me."

"Okay." She met his gaze, direct as ever. "I'm in. I'm here for you. I'll be honest with you and faithful to you."

"And . . ." he prompted.

She blinked at him.

"And you'll bake me cookies," he said.

Her laugh bubbled up. "I will—occasionally—bake you cookies. And if you cheat on me, I'll throw you out the window."

"Shit, sugar, you won't have to. Your daddy will." He waited a beat, gauging her reaction. "And then Matt will run over me with his truck."

Her smile blinded him. She looked like a girl again, swallowed by that too-big robe, her hair mussed, her face free of makeup, warmth and humor in her eyes.

His blood pounded in his head. She had no idea what she did to him. What he wanted, craved, to do to her.

"I should, uh . . ." *Play it cool*, he reminded himself desperately. *No pushing. No pressure.* "I brought your bag in from the car," he managed. "If you want to shower."

And imagined her naked, pictured her hot, wet, and glowing, soaping herself all over while the bubbles ran down her lovely breasts and the slope of her belly and between her thighs.

"In a minute," she said, bursting his little fantasy. "I want to finish my coffee."

"I'll go first, then." He needed a shower. A cold one.

"Sam."

He turned back.

"Thank you." Her eyes, blue and direct, met his. "For everything. I like knowing where things are going. It scares me, the not knowing."

He nodded. He knew.

"This whole trusting-in-the-moment deal is hard for me. But I trust you."

Trust was good, Sam told himself as he stepped under the spray of the shower. It wasn't let-me-soap-your-back, steamy sex good, but in the long run, it was better. Meg would not love where she did not trust.

Love?

Long run?

His hands stilled on the soap as his heart turned over in his chest, as a trickle of panic ran down his spine.

Of course he loved Meg on one level. Always had. She was a piece of his past, a part of him, his. But *love* . . .

Steam swirled as the shower door opened. Sam blinked water from his eyes.

Meg stood on the marble tiles, the deep V of her robe exposing the indentation between her breasts. He watched, transfixed, as her hands untied her belt. "You said we had a late checkout," she reminded him.

She shrugged and the robe dropped to the floor, revealing her, all pink and white, smooth and beautiful. His blood hammered. His mind emptied.

Meg's smile curved her lush mouth, danced in her eyes. "We might as well make the most of the time we have," she said and stepped into the shower with him.

Seventeen

"I'VE GOT THIS," Sam said, lifting Meg's bag from the truck.

Her heart skipped a beat. "It's not necessary. I'm a big girl. I can carry my own suitcase."

He held on to it, his green eyes glinting. "I'm coming in with you."

"There will be fewer questions if it's just me," she warned.

"Maybe," Sam said. "But we're not doing 'The Night I Took Your Virginity, Part Two.' If we're together, we're together."

She sighed, tipping her head back to inspect the staring windows at the back of the house. "It feels like coming home the morning after prom." Or what she imagined prom could have been if she'd gone with someone she'd really liked.

"How's that?"

"You know. Glowy. Guilty."

Sam lifted an eyebrow. "I didn't take you to prom."

"Different years. You took Misty Rogers." And, oh, Meg had been jealous.

"And you went with Danny Webber," Sam said, surprising her. He'd gone back to college without a word. She hadn't imagined he'd noticed, hadn't believed he'd paid any attention to her at all after that one disastrous New Year's Eve. "And now I must find him and kill him."

She laughed. "Danny only asked me because Matt fixed us up. He never made it past second base."

"Okay. He can live."

She shot him a mischievous look. "Of course, he might have been the tiniest bit intimidated by Dad cleaning his gun on the kitchen table when he came to pick me up."

Sam winced. "Your parents do know you've had sex before, right?"

"New York Meg has sex. Dare Island Meg, not so much. Not under my parents' roof." In fact, Tom's insistence on separate bedrooms was one of the reasons Derek had rarely accompanied Meg on her visits home. She slid Sam a wry look. "And never with you."

Sam carried her bag down the walk toward the back door of the inn. "Good thing I drove to Raleigh to meet you, then."

"It's not too late to back out."

"I won't sneak around. And we're facing your family together."

She had never felt the need for a buffer against her family. They were on her side, always. *Back to back to back.* The idea that she could have an ally outside her immediate family circle was . . . weird. And not entirely unpleasant.

She shrugged. "Okay. But don't blame me if Matt gives you a hard time."

"I'm not worried about Matt. Your dad's the one with the gun."

She laughed, as she was sure he intended. But neither of them was entirely joking.

With his free hand, Sam opened the back door. Meg straightened her spine and walked into the kitchen. The adults were all sitting around the table, Tom, with his USMC Devil Dog mug; Tess, snapping green beans; Matt. And now Allison, her chair pulled close to Matt's, part of the family circle.

Meg braced. At least she'd get this over with all at once. That was better, maybe. Mostly. Wasn't it?

Tom looked up at their entrance. His bushy gray brows rose. "You're home early."

Meg braced. "I flew in last night."

"I picked her up at the airport," Sam said.

Meg's teeth clenched. Like they couldn't guess.

Everybody looked at him. At them.

Tom scowled. "Where did you spend the—"

Tess cleared her throat. "Did your meetings go well?"

Meg took a few cautious steps forward, her shoulders relaxing with relief. "I got the job."

Tess smiled. "That's wonderful, honey."

"Told you, smart girl," Matt said. He glanced at Sam. "Good for you."

"Congratulations," Allison said.

Tom got up from the table and put an arm around her. "We're proud of you, baby."

She leaned into his familiar, bony embrace, aware he was glaring over her head at Sam. "Thanks, Dad."

And thank God, she thought, for Mom. She'd never expected to get a pass on sleeping with Sam, a ripple of reaction instead of a tsunami.

But as she raised her head, she was aware of a tension in the room that has nothing to do with her or Sam.

For the first time, it occurred to her to wonder what they

were all doing home in the middle of a Saturday afternoon.

"What's the matter?" She took a step back. Her gaze skimmed over their faces before landing on the official-looking letter that lay on the kitchen table like the telegram in a war movie. Her blood froze. Her family's faces blurred. That wasn't how . . . It couldn't be . . .

"Luke," she whispered.

Sam came up behind her. His hand pressed warm against the small of her back.

"No," Tess said instantly. "Luke's fine, sweetie."

Meg breathed again. "Then, what . . ."

"It's a subpoena," Matt said. "Delivered today. The Simpsons have subpoenaed Taylor to appear in family court on Tuesday."

Meg frowned. "I thought our lawyer said she didn't have to go."

"The Simpsons must feel they have a better shot at modifying the custody agreement if Taylor testifies," Allison said.

"But they don't, right?" Meg looked around the table. "I mean, she wants to stay with us."

"She's staying," Matt said flatly. "I promised Luke."

When Matt used that voice, a hurricane couldn't shake him. Meg looked at her parents. "So what's the problem?"

A brief, charged silence filled the air.

"I should go," Sam said. "You all obviously have a lot to talk about."

"Sit," Tess said.

Sam glanced at Tom.

"You heard her," Tom growled. "Stay. Hell, you're practically family anyway."

They found places at the table, Tom and Tess, Matt and Allison, Meg and Sam.

She was aware of him, sitting close, listening with that

polite, focused attention of his. It felt odd to have someone at her side, but not that odd because it was Sam. Sam belonged. He had always belonged.

"You know Jolene and Ernie Simpson are arguing that after my accident, I can't take proper care of Taylor," Tess said to him.

He nodded.

"Well." Tess's lips compressed. "We talked to the lawyer. Apparently they're using some incidents at school to claim our home is not a fit environment."

Meg stared at her mother, stunned. "That's bullshit."

Sam rested his arm on the back of her chair. "What incidents?"

Allison answered him. "Taylor got sent to the vice principal's office her first day of school."

"For what?" Meg demanded. "Chewing gum?"

"Wearing a hat in class."

Rage sliced through Meg. "They're going after us because she wears her father's Marine hat?"

Sam dropped his hand onto her shoulder.

"It's not just the hat," Tess said. "She has nightmares."

"Nobody needs to know about that," Matt said. "Besides, she's over them."

Tess sighed. "And one of the parents complained to the office about Taylor's aggressive behavior."

Meg leaned forward, away from Sam's restraining hand. "Are you fricking kidding me? What aggressive behavior?"

"She got into a fight at school," Allison explained. "A couple of weeks ago."

Over Allison's shoulder, the dining room door moved stealthily inward a bare half inch and stuck. Meg narrowed her eyes.

Sam lifted his brows. "Seems to me a kid who's just lost

her mother is entitled to act out a little. No matter where she's living."

He would know, Meg thought. Sam was eight when his mother moved out. But she didn't say anything, her attention focused on the door. She slipped out of her chair.

"That's what Mr. Long—our lawyer—will say," Tess told Sam. "But Jolene is saying that Taylor didn't have any behavioral problems while she lived with them."

The door remained cracked. Meg walked around the table and yanked it open. Taylor fell into the room. Meg reached for her arm to help her up and the little girl exploded.

"Let me go! Let me go! I didn't do anything!"

Unthinkingly, Meg tightened her hold on Taylor's thin arm. Taylor flailed, a whirlwind of anger and tears. One of her fists connected with Meg's stomach.

"*Oof*," said Meg and let go.

"Taylor." Matt's voice dropped into the furor like a stone.

Taylor turned her scrunched little face in his direction. "I didn't do anything. I just wanted to listen."

"Then you should come in," Matt said.

She flushed and fixed him with accusing blue eyes. "You shouldn't talk about people behind their backs."

Tom snorted. "You're not people. You're our granddaughter. Of course we talk about you behind your back."

Tess laid her hand on his arm. "We were going to talk to you, honey. After we decided what to do."

Allison spoke up. "I think Taylor would feel better if she knew she was part of the decision-making process."

Score one for the teacher, Meg thought.

"Come here," Matt said quietly.

The little girl dragged her feet forward.

He tucked her into the crook of his arm, turning her to face Meg. "Apologize to your aunt."

"That's okay," Meg said hastily. "She doesn't need to . . ."

"Sorry." Taylor hung her head.

"I'm sorry, too." Meg sat, gingerly rubbing her stomach. "I shouldn't have snuck up on you."

Matt smiled at her across the table. "Right," he said. "No sneaking. No secrets. We're all in this together. Now sit down while we figure out what to do next."

Taylor turned her head into his shoulder, the brim of Luke's Marine cap shielding her face.

Meg's throat closed at the picture they made, the big, quiet waterman and the scrawny little girl, her brother and her other brother's child. *All in this together. Back to back to back.* Maybe Meg hadn't built the bond with Taylor that Matt obviously had. But they were her family. Luke was her brother, too.

"I don't want to go," Taylor said, her voice muffled.

Matt's arm tightened around her. His big hand patted her back. "You're not going anywhere."

"But I *heard* you."

"What did you hear, honey?" Tess asked.

"They're going to take me away," Taylor said. "Because I got in trouble."

Meg sucked in her breath.

"No," Tess said. "Your Grandma Jo and Grandpa Ernie want you to live with them because they love you. But we love you, too, and your daddy wants us to take care of you."

"But the letter said I had to go."

"Only to court," Allison said. "To talk to the judge."

"Who's the judge?" Sam asked.

"It doesn't matter," Matt said. "Nobody's taking Taylor from us."

Yes, Meg thought, watching their two heads so close together, Matt's hair the color of oiled oak, Taylor's the color of straw, sticking out from under Luke's camouflage cap. Something grabbed at her heart and pulled hard. Whatever it took, Taylor was one of them now.

But despite Matt's assurances and the lawyer's assertions, nobody really knew what would happen in court on Tuesday. There wouldn't be a permanent custody hearing until Luke returned from Afghanistan, two months from now. What if some judge decided Taylor was better off with the Simpsons until then?

Taylor leaned against Matt's arm, her face shiny with tearstains. "Will you go with me?"

Matt and Allison exchanged glances over the child's head.

"I'll be in court with Grandpa," Matt said carefully. "But Miz Dolan—the lawyer your mom used to work for, remember?—said you can wait in her office until it's time for you to come to the courthouse. And Allison is going to try to get Tuesday off so she can wait with you. Okay?"

Taylor nodded, her blue eyes doubtful.

The child trusted Matt, Meg knew. But she hadn't lived with them long enough to understand. To believe.

Meg looked around the kitchen table. The dining room was for holidays and celebrations, but the kitchen was the place where news was shared and plans were made, the scene of Sunday dinners and family meetings, the go-to spot for homework and cutthroat card games.

Her parents were there as they'd been there all of Meg's life, Tom frowning in fierce concern, Tess with busy hands and worried eyes, a solid unit of love and support. Meg's gaze shifted to Matt, rock steady and constant as the sea, and Allison at his side, pretty and earnest and determined to help. All of them, she thought with a squeeze of heart, ready to do their best for Taylor.

That was what they did. In hard times, family stepped in. Stepped up.

"I'll be there," Meg said. "I'm staying."

Sam closed his hand over hers on the table. Could he know how much she needed, how much she treasured, that light, undemanding touch at that moment?

"Well, that makes things easier," Tess said. "It could be a long day. We don't know when Taylor's case will be called."

"Yeah, fine, but I meant . . . I'm staying here. On Dare Island." Without thinking, Meg turned her hand over, laced her fingers with Sam's. "At least until Christmas."

"Why Christmas?" Matt asked.

She'd been thinking about it, turning over the options, considering the angles. "The Simpsons' motion is based on Taylor's 'changed circumstances,' right? They're saying we can't take care of her. Well, for the next eight weeks, I can. After that, Mom will pretty much be back on her feet again. And Luke will be home."

Tom frowned. "What about your new job?"

She appreciated his concern. "I'm a subcontractor, Dad. The agency hired me to do a job, but I'm not actually their employee. At this point, I can handle everything on-line or by phone while Taylor's in school. Even if that changes in the next eight weeks—if they bring me into the firm or I get another offer—nobody in New York will expect me to start before New Year's."

"What about . . . your condo?" Tess asked.

What about Derek? she did not say.

"I'm selling my share in the condo," Meg said evenly. "It wasn't as good an investment as I hoped it would be."

"Good," Tom said. "I never liked him."

Tess rolled her eyes. "We're aware of that, honey."

"Then you're coming with us on Tuesday?" Matt asked Meg.

She nodded, grateful for his quiet intervention. "That way Allison doesn't have to take a day off." She glanced at her soon-to-be sister-in-law. "If that's okay with you."

"Very okay with me." Allison smiled. "Of course, my students might feel differently."

"Somebody's got to stay with your mother," Tom said.

"I'll be fine," Tess said. "It's only for a few hours."

"We don't know when Taylor's case will be called. We could be gone all damn day."

"So Josh or Allison can check in on me when they get home from school."

"What if you fall?" Tom asked.

A short, charged silence.

"I'll stay with you," Sam said.

They all looked at him.

He shrugged. "Why not? I'm always willing to spend a day with a beautiful woman." He grinned at Tom. "And you said it yourself. I'm practically family."

Eighteen

THE AFTERNOON SUN edged the clouds, playing off riffles in the bright blue waters of the bay. Driving home from the grocery store, Meg noted the white boats at anchor, the scattering of Jeeps and trucks behind Evans Tackle Shop. The working watermen had knocked off for the day.

Among the other vehicles, Sam's pickup stood out like a shiny black swan in a flock of gulls.

Her heart thrummed like the wind over the dunes. Her foot eased off the gas. Like she was fifteen again, inventing excuses to walk by Sam's locker at school, hoping for a glimpse of him. Should she stop? They'd barely had a chance to speak since he'd driven her home on Saturday. And tomorrow she'd be gone all day at the custody hearing.

It wouldn't hurt to drop in for just a minute, she reasoned. To say thank you.

She pulled into the lot behind the long wooden structure and went in. The vacationers' side of the store, with its bright

T-shirts and cheap tourist tackle, was almost empty. But around the coffeepots on the other side, sitting in the mismatched chairs and jammed between the aisles of tools and oil, fishermen clustered in twos and threes and fives. A buzz rose on the air, more animated, more agitated than the standard gossip and jokes, the usual complaints about the weather, or the latest fishing quotas.

Heads turned when Meg walked in. Her step faltered. She certainly wasn't the only woman in the place. She recognized Robin Johnson, a gillnetter like her father, and Hannah Doyle, who had a master mariner's license and a degree in marine sciences from the University of Florida. But Meg was the only woman not wearing waders.

George Evans waved at her from behind the counter. "Hey, Meg. You just missed Matt. Took off right after the meeting."

What meeting? she wondered. "That's okay. I came, um . . ."

To see Sam. She spotted him talking to Walt Rogers, hands in his pockets, leaning forward courteously in that listening way, and for a moment she lost her breath and track of her thoughts.

"Ah . . ." She met George's interested, inquiring eyes. "To pick up a few things," she finished vaguely.

"Sure," George said. "What do you need?"

Her gaze skated over the ranks of unfamiliar fishing equipment, the cans of chewing tobacco and cigarettes behind the case. "Just . . ." She grabbed a pack of gum and then a drink can cozy and slapped them on the counter. "These."

George rang her up with a twinkle. "Always happy to have your business. Sam should be ready for an interruption about now," he added. "Walt's been bending his ear for the last twenty minutes."

Her face heated. "Thanks."

Living in New York, coming home only for the holidays, had distanced Meg from the island rumor mill. But she could imagine the speculation now that Tom Fletcher's daughter was dating Carl Grady's son. Bad blood between the two men since Carl had tried to buy Fletchers' Quay from Tom's father forty years ago. The Fletchers had held out when Carl gobbled up the rest of the waterfront, but no one denied his money or his power. Most islanders probably thought Meg had landed a good catch. In their eyes, nothing she ever accomplished—not Harvard, not an MBA, not even a half-million-dollar salary—would be equal to that.

She tried not to let it bother her.

But the whispers left her with a dilemma. Should she frustrate the gossips or feed them? Walk on by with a friendly greeting? Or wrap her arms around Sam's neck and plant a long, deep, hot one on him?

Which of course would be promptly reported to her parents. She winced. Better to go with the casual greeting.

When she passed Sam, though, he took her arm. Her hand.

"Well, hi." The patented Grady smile appeared, only slightly frayed at the edges.

She studied his face. He looked tired, she thought. Or tense. There were lines dug into his forehead, a subtle stiffness in his shoulders. But he didn't look annoyed to see her.

She smiled back, squeezing his fingers. "Hi, Sam. Mr. Rogers."

"You called me 'Mr. Rogers' when you were twelve, honey. I think you're grown up enough to call me Walt. We missed your daddy today."

The meeting, whatever it was. "He's home with Mom."

"I hear she's doing better."

"Yes, sir." And that, she reflected, was the other side of

the small town grapevine. Your neighbors might all know your business, but they cared about your welfare.

"You be sure to give her my best," Walt said before turning back to Sam. "I hear what you're saying. But none of those agencies are lining up to hand us the money."

Sam glanced at Meg. "I was telling Walt about some of the government initiatives for watermen."

"And I'm not arguing with you," Walt said. "I'm just saying if you're on the water at five in the morning, you don't want to come home and bust your brain writing up grant applications and proposals for a bunch of bureaucrats, trying to convince them you deserve funding more than the next guy. It takes forever, it's a pain in the ass, and I'm telling you—no one around here has the time, the energy, or the know-how. And without those government grants, you're dead in the water."

Write grant proposals? Convince people to come around to your way of thinking?

"I could do it," Meg said.

They both looked at her.

She shrugged. "It's what I do for a living. I'd have to look at the agency guidelines, meet with the fishermen to identify their needs, but the actual grant applications wouldn't take me too much time at all."

"How much is too much?" Walt asked.

Meg smiled. "That depends on how difficult you are."

"Huh." Walt's lips twitched. "You're pretty smart. Guess Tom was right to send you to Harvard after all."

"Thank you," Sam said to Meg as they left the tackle store.

"You're welcome. I take it that was the first meeting of the watermen's cooperative?"

"Yeah." Sam stopped in the sunlit parking lot, taking a deep breath of crisp November air.

"How'd it go?"

"Not bad. Not good"—his grin flashed briefly—"but not bad."

Not just tired, she thought. Discouraged as well. "Meaning?"

He rolled his shoulders. "They're islanders. They're ornery and independent. They don't want to be beholden, and they don't trust the government in Raleigh. They've been screwed before and they've got long memories."

She nodded. She knew her island history. Dare's stubborn independence went beyond its frustration with state regulations to the start of the Civil War. When the rest of North Carolina had seceded from the Union, the inhabitants of Dare and Hatteras had declared their loyalty to the North.

"They'll come around," she said. "They'll see it's a matter of survival, like incorporating the town."

Sam ran his hand through his hair. One lock flopped forward on his forehead. "I hope you're right. They're worried. For the co-op to succeed, we need more than a building or even the dock space. The fishermen need to be able to sell their catch at a fair price. That means increasing the demand for locally caught seafood."

"Sounds like you need a PR person."

The gleam reappeared in his eyes. "You applying for the job, sugar?"

She smiled, hoping to tease him out of his frustration. "You can't afford me. Do you know what my hourly rate is?"

He slid his arms around her. "Maybe I can't afford not to hire you."

"Mm." She pursed her lips, pretending to consider, aware of the press of their lower bodies. He felt so good, warm and hard against her. "I suppose I might be persuaded to give you the friends and family discount."

"Not necessary. I wouldn't want to take advantage." He

nuzzled a sensitive spot below her ear, and she bit back a gasp. "But if you want to work out a trade of professional services . . ."

She struggled to keep her eyes open, her head from dropping back. At any minute, somebody could walk out and see them. "I don't need another ramp."

"Those weren't the services I had in mind."

Take me, she thought. "Big talk," she scoffed.

"I'm prepared to back it up with action. Want to drive out to the job site and neck?"

Yes.

She swallowed temptation. "I can't," she said. "I've got milk in the car."

He raised his head, his gaze warm and considering. "You doing the grocery shopping now, too?"

"Somebody has to. I'm the one who's home all day."

"Running the inn, taking care of your mother, being there for Taylor when she gets home from school. When do you get your own work done?"

"I have Dad to help take care of Mom, and Matt does a lot with Taylor. I get it done."

"It's still a lot. I'll understand if you don't have time for this grant application stuff."

She felt a twist almost like panic. "I want to do it. I like the challenge. I can't clean toilets and bake cookies all day." *All my life.*

"Okay." Sam paused. "I know this is hard for you, putting your life on hold for the next eight weeks because your family needs you. But I admire the hell out of you for it."

She lifted one shoulder, uncomfortable with his praise. "I'm just doing what has to be done. We all are."

"Taylor's lucky to have you."

"She's lucky to have Matt. And Allison. I'm just there to cook. I don't know anything about little girls."

"You were a little girl once."

"A long time ago. I don't know how to talk to her," Meg confessed. "I don't know how she feels. What she needs."

"She just lost her mother," Sam said. "That leaves a hole you never completely recover from. It'll take time for her to adjust."

Her breathing tangled. He would know. He'd lost his mother, too, when his parents divorced.

"You're right," Meg said. "I know you're right. See, even you understand her better than I do. I just . . . Shit." Her throat closed. She blotted at the corners of her eyes with her fingertips. "I don't know why I'm upset."

Sam's eyes were warm and compassionate. "Maybe because you understand her better than you think."

She shook her head, wordless.

"Meg . . ." Sam stroked his hand down her arm. "When Tess was in that accident, it changed things. All of a sudden, you had to accept that she was vulnerable. That you could lose her. And then you lost your job, and then you lost . . . you dumped that jerk you were living with. Maybe you should give yourself time to adjust, too."

She sniffed. "I don't think any period of adjustment is going to turn me into my mother."

He smiled. "I think you're more like Tess than you know."

"Not really. Luke has her generosity. Matt has her heart. I just have . . ." Meg floundered, overwhelmed by a sense of inadequacy. "Her recipes."

"Don't sell yourself short," Sam said. "You're loyal, like your mother. And hardworking. And fierce in defense of the people you love. You're a great example for Taylor."

"She doesn't need an example," Meg said. "She needs a mom. And I'm no good at it."

The thought burned. Meg had always adored her own

mother, loved her, laughed with her, and was sometimes irritated by her. She admired Tess's strength in a crisis, appreciated her calm and cheerful management of her family and the inn. But Meg had always secretly believed her mother could have done better, ought to have done more, with her life.

Until now. Until Taylor, who came with feelings and needs and no instruction manual. The realization of how much Tess had always done without complaint or apparent effort made Meg feel grateful. And the tiniest bit ashamed.

"You're doing fine," Sam said. "You took Taylor trick-or-treating. The other girls, too."

"That was a holiday. Holidays are different. They come with a script, like a checklist. Pumpkins, popcorn balls, trick-or-treating. I can do that. It's the day-to-day stuff I suck at. That whole come-home-from-school, how-was-your-day routine. I can bake her cookies, but she doesn't talk to me."

"Sometimes the cookies are enough. The asking is enough. I never told your mother about my day, but it meant something to me that she cared enough to ask."

Because nobody else ever had, Meg realized.

She cupped his face with her hand. "You know she always liked you," she offered.

He turned his head and kissed her palm. "I'm glad. She's an amazing woman."

"I appreciate what you're doing for her, staying with her tomorrow."

"It's nothing. There's not much I wouldn't do for your family, Meg." His eyes met hers. "Or for you."

Her heart wobbled. She could fall in love with him so easily, she thought. And that would be a mistake for both of them.

Under the easy charm and teasing humor, he was deeply perceptive and almost shockingly sincere. Driven, like her, to succeed. She appreciated his kindness. She was determined to enjoy whatever time they had together. But she didn't kid herself it would be enough. For either of them.

She curled her fingers, holding his kiss inside.

She didn't doubt that Sam wanted her. But he wanted everything, the whole package, Island Meg, with the complete complement of family and community that came with being a Fletcher. And she'd spent her entire adult life leaving all that behind.

She was still New York Meg.

CARL GRADY SCOWLED when Sam walked into the dining room. "When I said you needed to work longer hours, I didn't mean you should be late for dinner."

"Hi, Dad. Hi, Angela. I'll grab something in the kitchen." Sam strolled into the room and handed Angela a bright sheaf of flowers tied with the Secret Garden's distinctive ribbon. "These are for you."

"Well, goodness, Sam, they're lovely."

"What are you giving her flowers for? It's not her birthday."

Sam smiled at his stepmother. "It occurred to me today that I haven't given you flowers—or thanks—nearly enough. It can't have been easy for you, taking on a snotty fifteen-year-old stepson. But you were always there. Figured it was time I told you how much I appreciate that."

"Of course she was here," Carl said. "Where else would she go?"

"Hush, Carl. Let me enjoy my flowers." Her eyes misty, Angela got up from her chair and kissed Sam's cheek. "Thank you, Sam."

"Jesus, woman, don't blubber. I never knew flowers made a woman so emotional."

"They're not birthday flowers, that's why. You think about that, and then you think about whether you maybe should buy them for me more often." She smiled as he sputtered. "I'll just go put these in water."

Carl humphed and waited until she left the room before he pulled out a cigar.

Sam lifted an eyebrow. "Should you be smoking that?"

"If she can have flowers, I can have a damn cigar." Carl glanced after Angela. "Don't tell on me now."

"I don't have to tell," Sam said, amused. "She'll be able to smell it."

"That's why you should have one, too," Carl said, producing another cigar. "Outside."

Sam followed the old man onto the deck. They smoked awhile in silence as the tide rolled in.

Carl studied the lit end of his cigar. "How'd the meeting go?"

Sam didn't ask how his father had found out about this afternoon's meeting with the watermen. "About the way you'd expect."

"Well, you got an old dog like me rolling over," Carl said. "You'll get the rest of them to heel soon enough."

"Thanks," Sam said, surprised by the vote of confidence.

The clouds scudded across the purple sky like whitecaps before the wind.

Sam blew out a stream of smoke. "I need a favor," he said abruptly.

"Thought you might," Carl said with satisfaction. "Which jackass on the board needs his tail twisted?"

Sam's shoulder tightened. He shook his head. "This is personal."

He hadn't asked the old man for anything in eight years. When he'd left home, he'd been determined to succeed or fail by his own efforts. On his own terms. But more was at stake here than pride or business.

Carl shot him a bright, assessing glance. "So which is it? You got a ticket that needs fixing or a body to hide?"

The old rascal. "You're friends with Vernon Long."

"I wouldn't say friends. He's the reason your first stepmother is residing on Martha's Vineyard with a sizable amount of my personal fortune. But seeing as Vernon made out nicely on that settlement, I'd say we're friendly enough."

"He's representing the Fletchers in Taylor's custody hearing tomorrow."

Carl sucked his cigar. "Luke's little girl."

"That's right. His family's taking care of her while Luke's in Afghanistan. But the Simpsons—her mother's people—want her to live with them."

"I heard. What do you think I can do about it?"

"I have no idea," Sam admitted.

"Well." The old man stubbed out his cigar. "Let's find out."

Inside, Sam listened to one half of a phone call, tension ratcheting between his shoulder blades.

"Vernon, it's Carl Grady . . . wanted to ask you who's on the bench tomorrow . . . Really? I went to school with old . . . Well, of course I wouldn't interfere. I know how you all frown on that. I just thought old Skip would want to know how it is with the Fletchers . . . Hell, yeah, my boy practically lived at their house back then . . . I sure can . . . By tomorrow morning? You bet. Much obliged, Vern."

"Well?" Sam demanded.

Carl bared his teeth in a grin. "Get Angela. I need her to notarize something for me."

"Thanks, Dad," Sam said.

"I hope you know what you're doing, getting involved."

"They're good people. Matt's my best friend."

"I meant with the girl. Meg."

Sam's throat was suddenly dry. "We're figuring it out."

"I'm glad to see you finally settling back on the island. I'd hate to see you throw it all away for New York."

Sam swallowed. "I'm not going to New York."

Carl nodded. "You make sure she knows that."

Nineteen

TAYLOR'S HEART POUNDED as she walked to the courthouse between Aunt Meg and Miss Dolan. *Please, please don't let me puke.* She'd been too nervous to eat the breakfast Grandma Tess had cooked, and then she was hungry in the lawyer's office, and there was nothing to do while they were waiting except eat the leftover Halloween candy Miss Dolan kept in the bowl on her desk. And now Taylor's skin felt cold and her face felt hot and her stomach felt like she was going to throw up all over the new shoes Aunt Meg had insisted she wear to court.

"You have to look like we're taking care of you," Aunt Meg had said as she'd laid out colored jeans and a stupid ruffled sweater on the bottom of Taylor's bed this morning. "Image is important."

Taylor hated the clothes, which were stiff and tight and way too bright. She didn't want people looking at her. She didn't want to be there at all. Every time she thought about where they were going and why, she felt sick and dizzy. But she understood what Aunt Meg was trying to say—*Wear this, or they'll take you away*—so she put the clothes on anyway. Besides, Aunt Meg was dressed up, too, in what Uncle Matt called her City Girl clothes. Miss Dolan wore a suit and lots of makeup. Taylor had never seen Miss Dolan without a suit, but everybody in their dark, stiff clothes reminded her of a funeral, Mom's funeral, and thinking about her mom just made things worse, so she stared at the cracks in the sidewalk and tried not to think at all.

She swallowed. At least they let her keep her hat.

Over her head, Miss Dolan was talking to Aunt Meg.

". . . Marines hardly a stable family life," Miss Dolan said. "But it will carry a certain weight with the judge in this case."

"My father's a Marine," Aunt Meg said.

"Yes," Miss Dolan said, short and cool. "So is mine."

Mine, too, Taylor thought, but her . . . but Luke wasn't here, and that made her feel sad and kind of mad, too. She'd never had a dad before. She'd never needed a dad. Mom said that as long as they had each other, they didn't need anybody else. But now Mom was gone and Luke was gone and he *said* he was coming back, but he wasn't here now, was he? Taylor's throat burned. She needed him *now*. If he was here, they wouldn't take her away. And he'd fight them if they tried.

The lines on the sidewalk blurred, and she stumbled in her stupid new shoes.

Aunt Meg grabbed her hand before she fell. "Are you all right?" she asked.

Which was what everybody had been asking her all day until Taylor wanted to scream. What would they do if she said *no*?

But Aunt Meg meant well, so Taylor mumbled, "Fine."

Aunt Meg took a breath and then paused, like maybe she expected Taylor to say something else.

Taylor looked over her shoulder at her mom's boss, at Miss Dolan, standing there waiting. Listening. Taylor's stomach churned. She couldn't say anything to anybody. Not Aunt Meg. Not even Uncle Matt.

She dropped her head, her heart thumping, the Big Scary Bad pushing in at her thoughts, waiting for her like a monster at the end of her bed. She wanted to curl up under the covers with Fezzik to protect her. She wanted to run and run somewhere they'd never find her. But she kept walking, one foot in front of the other, while they talked about her over her head.

"Mistake to bring the child in at all," Miss Dolan said. "Judges don't like these King Solomon decisions. Frankly, I don't think the Simpsons have a snowball's chance in hell."

Snowball. It was too much.

Taylor's eyes burned. Her throat burned. One hot tear welled up and slipped down her nose. Another.

"Oh, sweetie . . ." Aunt Meg sounded shaken.

Taylor squeezed her eyes tight shut, willing the tears away.

"Now what?" Miss Dolan said.

"I think . . . she had a cat named Snowball," Aunt Meg said.

"Oh, for Christ's sake," said Miss Dolan.

There was a rustle, and then someone gripped Taylor's shoulders hard. She jumped—she didn't like people grabbing her—and opened her eyes. Miss Dolan was kneeling on the sidewalk in her suit and high heels, looking Taylor right in the face. Taylor had never been this close to Miss Dolan before. Her hair was red and you could see that she had freckles under her makeup. Freckles and . . . Taylor blinked. A scar. A short, deep gash high on her left cheek.

"You're going to be fine," Miss Dolan said in a voice that said, *or I'm going to kick somebody's ass*. "Both sides have agreed to let you talk to the judge in chambers. Do you know what that means?"

Taylor's head wobbled *yes*. "He's going to ask me questions."

"Right. Nobody else will be there. Just you and Judge Dixon. You can tell him whatever you want. As long as you're honest with him, everything else will work out."

Taylor licked her lips. "What if I say the wrong answer?" she whispered.

"There are no wrong answers," Miss Dolan said. "The judge wants to know how you feel. Feelings are never wrong, they're just feelings. Okay?"

Taylor was pretty sure it was more complicated than that, but she nodded anyway. Maybe she could talk about her feelings without telling . . . without saying everything.

"Good." Miss Dolan squeezed Taylor's shoulders and stood.

Aunt Meg took her hand, and instead of jerking away, Taylor let her fingers curl around her aunt's. "Ready?"

Taylor nodded, more confidently this time.

"Right." Aunt Meg smiled at her, a real smile, and the hot band around Taylor's chest loosened. "Let's get this over with."

"WHAT'S TAKING THEM so long?" Meg whispered to Kate Dolan.

The courtroom looked like something on TV, wood veneer and beige paint and anxiety like a grimy film over everything. Because they'd come in late, Meg and Kate were forced to sit in back. The chairs in front were full of men with thinning hair and sagging faces and women with dull, accepting eyes, victims of broken families, broken bones, broken promises. Meg could barely see the top of her father's gray head where he sat with his elbows on his knees, his hands clasped. Beneath his navy blazer, Matt's shoulders were rigid. Their lawyer was standing, chatting amiably with Jolene Simpson's lawyer. At least, Meg assumed he was their lawyer. He wore a bow tie. And pleated pants.

She curled her nails into her palms.

"This isn't long," Kate said. "The judge is actually speeding things up since it's only a temporary custody hearing. That's why he accepted the affidavit instead of requiring Mr. Grady to appear as a witness."

Meg sat up straighter, distracted by movement at the front. "What?"

"Here they come."

At last. A door behind the judge's bench opened, and Taylor appeared, dwarfed between the black-robed judge and a female deputy.

Meg held her breath. Taylor's face looked thin and pinched and pale. Her gaze darted over the courtroom until it landed on Matt in the front row. She gave him a small, crooked smile.

That was good, wasn't it? Please let it be good.

The deputy—bailiff?—whatever—leaned down to say something. Taylor nodded before she came down the steps toward Matt. Meg so focused on watching them that she missed half of what the judge was saying.

". . . Inappropriate use of the court's time. Motion denied without prejudice to either party."

Meg turned to Kate. "That means we won, right?" Relief stung her eyes and nose. "We won!"

"It's not right!" Jolene's voice rose from the front of the courtroom before she was hushed by her lawyer.

Through a blur of happy tears, Meg saw Tom grinning. Matt had his arm around Taylor. Taylor, usually so reluctant to hold and be held, leaned into his sheltering side.

"Pending resolution of the claim for permanent custody upon Staff Sergeant Fletcher's return," the judge said.

Kate nudged Meg. "We can go out now. This way. They can meet us in the lobby."

Meg swallowed and sidled past legs and stepped over purses on her way to the aisle. "Thank you," she said to Kate when they were outside the courtroom.

"Happy to help." A hint of uncertainty crept into Kate's gaze. She was a stunningly beautiful woman, with a hard polished shell that contrasted oddly with her curling red hair. "I wish I could have done more."

"I don't know what else you could have done," Meg said.

"I meant . . . when Taylor's mother died."

"You contacted my brother," Meg said. "That's good enough for me."

"I'm still not sure that was—"

The courtroom doors opened, cutting her off.

"I never thought I'd be grateful to Carl Grady," Tom was saying as he came out.

"Why?" Meg kissed her father's cheek. "What did he do?" She swooped on Taylor for a brief hug, surprised when Taylor actually hugged her back. "Good job, sweetie."

Matt answered her. "Carl sent a courier to Vernon Long's office this morning with an affidavit testifying to our fitness to be guardians for Taylor."

"*Carl* did?" Meg blinked. "But how did he know?"

"Hell, everybody knows. Raised you and your brothers, didn't we?" Tom said.

"But why would he . . ." *Sam*, she realized. Warmth flooded her veins. Sam must have asked his father. For Taylor's sake. For hers.

There's not much I wouldn't do for your family, Meg. Or for you.

She couldn't wait to get home to thank him.

"I SMELL DINNER," Tom said.

Meg sniffed appreciatively as she came through the kitchen door. The mouthwatering scents of red wine and pancetta rose from the heavy-bottomed pot on the stove.

Tess turned, smiling, from the sink, up to her elbows in soap bubbles. "I made pot roast with Amarone. It just needs to simmer for a couple of hours."

He stooped to give her a brief, hard kiss. "You're working too hard, babe."

"I had to keep busy. Besides, I had Sam to help me."

More hugs, more kisses as Matt and Taylor trooped in. Taylor dashed upstairs to change.

Meg's gaze found Sam standing at the counter, lean and relaxed and deliciously male with a dish towel in his hands. Every woman's fantasy. "You've been helping everybody today."

He met her eyes, his mouth curving, his look as warm and potent as a kiss. *Take me now*, she thought. "You had all the bases covered," he said. "I just asked Dad to have a word with the umpire."

"Much appreciated," Tom said.

"You'll stay to dinner," Tess said. "To celebrate."

He smiled at her. "I'd like that."

"I owe you," Matt said quietly.

"No," Sam said.

Taylor reappeared, dancing from foot to foot. "I'm ready."

"Where are you off to?" Tess asked.

"Uncle Matt's taking me and Josh and Allison for ice cream. Do you want to come?"

"Grandma needs to lie down," Tom said.

Her blue gaze switched to him. "What about you?"

"Grandpa's going to lie down with her," Matt said. "It's you and me, kid."

"And Josh," Taylor said.

"Yeah."

She gave a little bounce. "And Allison."

He smiled down at her. "That's right."

"Can Fezzik come, too?"

"As long as he rides in back."

Meg watched them go, man, child, and dog, and thought with sharp and shocking clarity, *I want that. One day.*

Tom helped Tess to bed. Meg turned back to find Sam regarding her, a smile on his lips and heat in his eyes. Her heart slammed against her ribs.

She cleared her throat. "I guess that leaves just you and me."

"Looks like it."

"Want to go out to your truck and neck?"

He laughed and crossed to her, his hands spanning her hips, bringing her into full, firm contact with his body. "I have a better idea."

Her insides contracted with desire. "We can't go upstairs. My parents . . ."

"I know." He kissed her, long and slow, running his hand up her side to take her breast.

Ten minutes later, her skirt was bunched up and her blouse was undone and she was seriously rethinking her position on having sex in her room with her parents in the house. Hell, in another five, Sam could probably have her on the kitchen table.

He broke their kiss, breathing hard. "Right. Time for my idea."

She grabbed his wrist, bringing his hand back to her breast. "If you stop now, I'll be forced to kill you."

"Sugar, you're killing me already." He kissed her again, his mouth searching, his hands claiming, making her system jangle with lust. "Okay, that's it." He pulled away, his color high, his eyes almost black. "That has to hold us 'til we get there."

"Get where?" Disbelieving, she watched as he tugged her skirt down her thighs. "Sam, I don't want to wait."

He steered her toward the door. "I'll make it up to you, I swear."

"Make it up to me?" she sputtered as he bundled her out to the truck. "I may not let you touch me after this. Hell, I may not even be speaking to you."

His grin flashed. "Don't sulk."

He drove fast, one hand on the wheel and the other on her knee. It wasn't enough. She wanted him naked. She wanted his hands, his mouth, all over her. She was on edge, vibrating with impatience.

The truck slowed as he turned onto the unfinished road of the Dare Plantation development. The track went down, then up, then down, farther than they'd gone before. He parked amid the dunes and blowing grass near a stand of ancient live oaks. A frame house on stilts rose half finished in the sun.

Grabbing a tarp from the back of the truck, Sam opened her door. "Here we go."

"Where?"

"Up there." He guided her up a flight of unfinished stairs,

with daylight showing through the treads, boosting her with a hand on her bottom when the handrail disappeared.

Meg poked her head cautiously through an opening in the floor. Light poured over the platform. The open walls, the oaks all around, gave the unfinished structure the feel of a tree house. "Sam, it's beautiful. But . . ."

"We couldn't make love at your house," he said. His gaze met hers, warm as the sun that flooded the boards around them. She melted inside. "So I brought you to mine."

She turned in a cautious circle, taking in the views from the sound to the sea. "This is your house?"

"It will be. This is the master bedroom. And this"—he spread the tarp—"is the bed."

She laughed and sat, patting the canvas invitingly. "Maybe we should test it out."

"That's my plan." But instead of joining her, he walked to one corner of the platform and reached up behind one of the joists.

She frowned. "What are you doing?"

"Turning off the security camera."

"Oh." Her breath went in a puff of laughter. "Good idea."

Her laughter faded as he stripped off his shirt. She loved looking at him, his smooth, muscled chest, the shadow of coarse hair that ran like an arrow down his abdomen. She shivered in anticipation as he stalked toward her, his skin prickling in the cool air.

Was she actually going to make love outside? In broad daylight? In November?

Yes.

"We're going to freeze," she predicted.

Sam lowered himself beside her. "I'll keep you warm," he said and proceeded to make good on his promise.

His hands were fluid as they flowed over her, lingering in the places that gave her the most pleasure. His mouth was warm and coaxing, taking, giving, taking a little more. He set her blood on fire, set her skin aglow. She closed her eyes, sinking into a molten, golden sea, flooded with sunshine and well-being. He dealt with the condom before he covered her, whispering love words—*like that, sugar, take it, yes*—moving into her, pushing into the heat and the laughter, slowly and deliberately taking her, making her gasp and shudder, making her arch and moan. Making her his. She twined her legs around him, holding him to her and in her with everything she had, making him hers, over and over. Until their pace quickened and raced, until their rhythm crested and broke, until he shuddered and spent inside her and she dissolved in waves of bone-melting heat.

Afterward they drifted.

He kissed her nose.

She touched his jaw. "I like your house," she murmured.

He stretched on top of her, wakening her nerve endings, working the kinks from his back. "It could use a mattress."

She smiled and rubbed the back of her head. "I was thinking some pillows."

"And you," he said. Their eyes caught. Locked. "It needs you."

Her heart rolled over in delight. Her stomach sank in dismay. They had agreed to take things one day at a time, to enjoy the journey. But they were traveling too far, too fast, and she could see the end of the road too clearly.

"Why don't you show me the rest?" she suggested, fighting to keep her voice steady.

She felt the tension in his long body, the masculine resistance before he levered himself off her. But he was too smart to push. Instead, being Sam, he set himself to impress.

To charm. After they were dressed, he showed her the job site from their vantage point on the platform, where the channel allowed the best access for boats, where the fish house and the housing and the greenway would be. His enthusiasm fired her imagination. She could see, so clearly, all his hopes, all his plans taking shape in the island's soil.

She didn't understand all his talk about strategic flows and runoff storage measures, but she felt his passion.

"This isn't a competition with your father anymore," she said. "It's your dream."

He looked back at her steadily, confidence in every line of his body. "It's my future."

She looked away, aware of him waiting for a response she couldn't give.

But during the next two weeks, she felt herself being dragged farther and farther down the road with Sam. She knew they were getting too close, but she couldn't seem to stop herself.

She wanted him. She wanted to be with him.

He ate dinner with her family.

She came to dinner with his, talking with Angela about Chelsea's upcoming wedding, arguing politics with Carl.

"He's proud of you," she said to Sam afterward. "He doesn't like to show it, but he is."

They went out with Matt and Allison to the Fish House one night, shooting pool and drinking beer.

And they made love every chance they got. They had sex in Sam's truck, steaming up the windows like a couple of teenagers, and in the tree house bedroom of the unfinished house so often that Sam finally moved an air mattress and a sleeping bag up to the platform.

Meg's appetite for Sam, for his body, for his conversation, was growing and insatiable.

And he knew it, she thought. He fed it, teasing her with possibilities, seducing her with glimpses of what her life could be.

If only she gave up everything she'd ever worked for.

Twenty

"ALL GOOD AND on schedule," Sam confirmed over the phone. "We'll use the existing elevation drawings, and I've got the surveyors coming back Monday. Yeah, I will. Thanks, Nate."

He ended the call, using his phone to anchor one end of the drawing on his desk. *All good and on schedule*, he repeated to himself, feeling relieved and hopeful and thinking of Meg.

He'd been careful not to push her. Not to rush. *Why don't we take this thing one day at a time and see where it goes.*

But by now even a blind man could see where they were heading. And why not? It wasn't like either of them had anything against marriage as an institution. Look at her parents, still going strong after forty years. Look at . . . Okay, his parents hadn't made it work. But look at the old man and Angela. Meg's brother, Sam's sister were both taking the plunge this year. Given their backgrounds, given their families' history and expectations, it only made sense for Sam to be thinking in terms of, well, the future.

And if *he* was thinking that way, you could bet that *she* was. Planning for the future was her thing.

"Hey." Her voice broke into his thoughts.

He looked up and she was there, smiling at him in the open door of his office. His day, which had been good, got even better. "Hey, yourself."

"I hope I'm not interrupting. Shelley said to come on back."

"Not interrupting," he assured her. "Want some coffee?"

"Thanks, but I can't stay." She dug in her purse. "I'm expecting a call, and . . ."

He took her by the shoulders and kissed her, a soft, glad-to-see-you kind of kiss, drawing it out until he felt her lips warm and yield and his blood begin to pound. And then he let her go.

"Well." She licked her lips, her smile turning mischievous. "Now you've made me really glad I decided to bring the copy by instead of e-mailing it to you."

"Copy?"

"Something I wrote for the watermen's association website." She reached into her bag again and pulled out a folder. "I used a lot of the same points that I put in the grant applications, but I also have some ideas here for spotlighting restaurants and fish markets that serve locally caught seafood."

"You need to start billing for hours."

"I will once they get the grant, believe me."

"Not them. Me."

"I'm not worried about the money. Wait until you hear my idea. The thing is . . ." Her blue eyes sparkled with enthusiasm. "We don't have to wait until the fishermen's website is up to start implementing a marketing plan for local catch."

He was amused. Impressed. She talked about marketing plans the way another woman might talk about shoes or diamonds. "We don't?"

She shook her head. "The biggest market for fresh seafood on the island is vacationers. And the simplest way to reach vacationers is through their rental company. So if you want to encourage restaurants to buy local seafood, you start recommending restaurants that feature local seafood on the Grady Realty website. And in your rental packets."

"Good job, Harvard."

"I know. I'm brilliant."

He moved in. "Have I mentioned that brilliant women really turn me on?"

Her lips curved. "I'm discovering everything really turns you . . ." Her cell phone chirped. "Damn. Sorry. Do you mind if I take this?"

"Go ahead." He retreated to the coffee machine to give her an illusion of privacy.

"Hi, Bruce, can I call you ba—you did?"

Sam stopped, caught by her sudden change of pitch.

Meg cupped her phone, turning her back. "Well, of course I . . . They did?"

A trickle of unease went down Sam's spine. It was probably nothing. It was probably . . .

"I am," Meg said. "Very interested. Yes, I will. I'll have to call you back. Say, in half an hour? Thank you so much, Bruce. Me, too."

His back tensed. He made an effort to speak calmly. "That sounded important."

She turned her glowing face to his. "It was. It is. It's wonderful. That was Bruce Adler from the PR firm. They've had an unexpected opening in Crisis Communications and they want to hire me."

Don't overreact. Play it cool. "I thought you had a job with them already."

She waved a dismissive hand. "Contract work."

Something inside him twisted. "You were pretty excited about it a couple of weeks ago," he said carefully.

"I still am. I love working with Lauren, and it was fun to try something new."

Was fun, he noted dully. Past tense.

"But this is much more in line with my experience," she continued. "And my pay scale."

"You just said you weren't worried about money."

"Sam. This is a salaried position. With benefits. In New York."

Each short sentence plunged into him like a knife. "So, that's it? Just like that, you're taking it?"

She frowned. "Well, no, obviously, I need to review a copy of the offer and the benefits package. And I need to negotiate the start date."

He felt like an idiot. While he had been thinking about the long road, Meg had been taking a little detour in her well-planned life. Taking him for a ride. "But you're going."

"Not until after the holidays."

Anger spurted. He welcomed it. Anger was preferable to pain. "One phone call, and you're running back to Derek."

Red flags flew in her cheeks. "That's a despicable thing to say. This isn't about Derek. It's about me, about what I've worked for all these years."

That what he was afraid of. Terrified by. He stood a chance against Derek. He had no defense against her dreams.

He stared at her dumbly, bereft of words and charm. Like a harpooned animal, bleeding.

As if from a great distance, he heard himself say, "What about us?"

Her face changed, indignation sliding into distress. "This isn't about us, either. Sam, you know I care about you. You've done so much. Given me so much. But this is something you can't do for me. You can't give me everything I want."

She might as well have hit him with a hammer.

Rejection roared in his ears. He wasn't good enough to keep her. Nothing he did would be enough to hold her.

"I guess I hoped that part of what you wanted was me."

Her breath jerked. "You could come to New York."

"My future's here. You're the one who showed me that."

"For God's sake, Sam, this isn't the end. We can still see each other."

He wasn't playing that game. "I have one long-distance relationship in my life already. With my mother. Once-a-year visits and a nice present at Christmas." He shook his head. "Sorry, sugar, not interested."

"I don't know what you expect me to say." Her voice shook between temper and tears. "We've only been seeing each other for a couple of weeks."

"We've known each other for *twenty years*."

"Then you shouldn't be so quick to throw us away."

"I'm not throwing anything away. I'm trying to hold on, damn it. To my life, to my work, to you. I thought you saw that. That I'd have a chance to convince you. How the hell can we have any kind of future together if you're in New York?"

Temper won. "How the hell can you ask me to give up my life? My work?"

"Fine. Take the job if that's what you really want, if that's what's important to you. But you're out of my life."

"I don't have to be. Sam . . ."

"I'm not asking you. I'm telling you." He met her eyes, ignoring the sickness in his gut, the howling of his heart. "If you go, you're out of my life."

HE WAS A jerk.

Meg drove, dashing tears from her eyes, tissues littering her lap. Thank God, she thought with the portion of her brain that was not numb, that the season was over, the vacationers gone. The last thing she needed was to lose control of her car and kill a tourist on a bicycle.

Who did Sam think he was, raining on her parade? Telling her what she could and could not have? Giving her ultimatums.

Breaking her heart.

She went, as she'd always gone, to her mother for comfort.

"Mom?"

She wasn't in the kitchen or lying down in her room.

"In here." Tess stood before the mirror in the master bathroom, wearing plastic gloves and a ratty T-shirt, a disposable squeeze bottle in one hand.

Meg stopped in the doorway. "What are you doing?"

Tess waved the squeeze bottle. "Coloring my hair."

"Why?"

Tess smiled. "Too much time on my hands?"

"But . . ." Her mother had always rocked the salt-and-pepper look. "You looked fine."

You looked like my mother.

"I wanted a change. I want to be in control. I may not be able to run up and down stairs like I used to, but by golly, I can color my hair." Tess's eyes sharpened in the mirror. "Honey, what's wrong?"

Meg's throat closed. Her eyes welled. "It doesn't matter. It can wait."

"Don't be silly." Tess stripped off her gloves, glancing at the clock. "I have thirty-five minutes before I have to rinse. Talk to me."

The invitation loosed a flood of words and grievances, tumbling in a rush to get out. *Sam said . . . I told him . . . He didn't understand . . .*

She raged and wept, pacing the tiles that Sam had helped install nearly twenty years ago, while Tess listened and watched with concerned, not entirely sympathetic eyes.

"I can't be you," Meg said. "I can't give up my dreams to follow some man around."

Tess dropped the empty hair color box into the trash. "Who says I'm not following my dreams?"

Ouch. Meg flushed as she met Tess's eyes in the mirror. Venting was one thing. Disregard for her mother's feelings, her mother's choices, was something else. "I'm sorry, Mom. I didn't mean that the way it sounded. But you can't tell me you enjoyed moving from base to base, living in military housing for twenty years."

"Now you sound like *my* mother," Tess remarked. "If you're asking if I dreamed of becoming a military spouse when I grew up, the answer is no. It's a hard life. You get used to people asking you, 'How do you do it?' But the truth is when you love someone, you don't have a choice other than to do it."

"I respect that, Mom. I do. But Sam's not in the military."

"He's committed to something bigger than himself. Something you have a chance to be a part of."

Meg rubbed her temples. Her head was pounding. Her throat was raw. "I thought you'd sympathize with me. I thought you'd understand."

Tess smiled. "Maybe I understand better than you think. Do you love him?"

Panic jittered in Meg's stomach. "He didn't say he loved me." A fresh pain, another insult.

"I'm not interested in Sam's feelings at the moment." Tess tipped her head, considering. "Okay, that's not true. Let's say I'm more interested in yours. Do you?"

Yes.

"That's not the point," Meg said.

"It's the only point that matters. Sometimes love means taking turns. Finding compromises."

"Except you never got your turn. You were always the one who compromised."

"What do you mean?"

"Even after Dad retired, you did what he wanted. Lived where he wanted. Moved back here."

"Meg . . ." Tess frowned, her familiar features transformed by the darkening cap of hair goo. "I thought you knew. That was my choice. Your father would have gone anywhere. Back to Chicago, if that's what I wanted. My brother Nick would have taken me back into the restaurant. But I fell in love with North Carolina when your dad was stationed at Lejeune. You kids always liked it here. Running a bed-and-breakfast was my idea. The Pirates' Rest is my dream."

"But I always thought . . . I just assumed . . ."

"That I followed your dad around with no ideas or ambitions of my own?" Tess's smile was sharp. "You better start examining some of your assumptions, honey."

She was confused. Hurting. Her mother was supposed to be on *her* side. "Sam said I had to choose between him and my job."

Tess's brows flicked up. "And you're going to let him define your choices for you?" She paused a moment to let that sink in. "I'm disappointed in you, Meg," she added, and the quiet words stung more than a slap. "You can't always be in control of your life. But you can control your choices. Ever since you were a little girl, you've fought for what you wanted. If you want Sam and the job in New York, you need to find a way to make it happen. Figure it out. Fight for them. Don't quit now."

FEZZIK WAS WAITING on the porch with Aunt Meg when Taylor got home from school. He woofed when he saw her, jumping off the steps to greet her on the walk.

Taylor dropped to her heels, throwing her arms around his solid, hairy body, almost knocked on her butt by his doggy happiness. "Hey, Fezzik. Hey, boy. Did you miss me, fella?"

He dashed off, racing in joyous circles around the yard, making her giggle before he returned and dropped, panting, on her feet.

"Yeah, you did," she said, rubbing his head. "Dumb dog."

"Did you walk home alone?" Aunt Meg asked. Her voice sounded strange. Scratchy.

"Nah, I walked with Madison." Taylor said it casually, like it was no big deal to have a friend again to walk home with after school.

Aunt Meg nodded, not moving from the porch. That was weird. Usually she couldn't sit still.

Taylor squinted as she got to the porch. Up close, Aunt Meg's nose was red and her eyes looked funny, like she'd been crying.

"Aunt Meg? Are you all right?"

Taylor winced. The question sounded just as stupid coming out of her mouth as it did from a grown-up. But Aunt Meg didn't seem to mind. She sighed and kind of smiled and shook her head.

Taylor thought about going into the house. But it didn't

seem right to walk past and leave Aunt Meg sitting there. Not when she was sad.

Cautiously, Taylor sat on the porch step beside her, not touching, just, you know, there, and Aunt Meg draped her arm over Taylor's shoulders, like Taylor did sometimes with Fezzik. Like she needed a hug. Because Taylor knew what that felt like, she sat still, not moving away, searching her mind desperately for something else to say.

"Can I get you anything?" That was the one Aunt Meg asked all the time when she looked in on Taylor before she went to bed. "Like a glass of water?"

Aunt Meg smiled. A real smile, this time. "Thanks, sweetie, I'm fine." She said, almost to herself, "I have to figure this one out on my own."

Taylor understood that, too.

"I only wish I knew the right answer," Aunt Meg said softly, not like she expected Taylor to say anything. More like she was talking to the dog.

Taylor thought. "As long as you're honest, everything will work out," she offered.

Aunt Meg looked at her, surprised. "What?"

"That's what Miss Dolan said," Taylor reminded her. "Before I had to talk to the judge? She said there were no right or wrong answers, just feelings, and feelings were never wrong."

"Huh. That Miss Dolan's pretty smart."

Taylor shrugged. "Worked for me."

"You're pretty smart, too," Aunt Meg said.

Taylor grinned and ducked her head, pleased. Aunt Meg went to Harvard. She should know.

"I'M SORRY, SON." Tom almost succeeded in sounding regretful. "She's gone."

"Gone." The word hit Sam's gut like a wrecking ball. He stood on the front porch—he didn't want to test his luck by going to the back door, the family entrance—clutching his sorry bunch of flowers, feeling like an ass. "Where did she go?"

But he knew the answer already. He felt sick.

"She had some business," Tom said. "In New York."

Of course she did. What choice had he given her? *If you go, you're out of my life.*

It hurt, being with her, knowing he wanted a future with her, knowing she didn't feel the same. Not yet.

But it hurt a lot more not being with her.

Panic clawed his throat. "When will she be back?"

Tom shot him a sharp look. "Have you called her?"

Called, texted, e-mailed. He'd lost track of how many times in the past two days. She didn't answer, didn't respond, didn't want anything to do with him.

Under the circumstances, he couldn't blame her. But he was starving for her already, the light in her eyes, the sound of her voice. Her smile. Her energy. He didn't want half a life with her, him here and her in New York. But without her, he had no life at all.

"She doesn't pick up," he said.

Tom rubbed his stubbled jaw. "If she wanted you to know her schedule, I reckon she would have told you."

"Mr. Fletcher . . . Tom . . . Please," Sam said desperately. "I screwed up. I can't fix things if I can't talk to her."

Tom pulled himself up to sergeant major size, six-foot-four and scary as hell. "What makes you think I give a good goddamn whether you fix things or not? You don't deserve her."

Sam broke into a sweat. "No, sir. But I love her. I'd never hurt her."

"You did hurt her. You made her cry." Tom scowled. "Takes a lot to make my girl cry."

Oh, God. "I know. I'm sorry. I was a prick. I won't do it again."

Tom grunted. "I expect you will. You won't mean to, but you're a man. That means you're going to screw up and she's going to cry. What I want to know is, what are you going to do about it?"

"I don't know," Sam said. Charm didn't work. Ultimatums didn't work. "But I'm not walking away."

Tom grunted again. "That's a start."

Sam blew out his breath. "I thought I'd try groveling."

"Groveling's good." Tom eyeballed him. "I guess I can tell you when her flight gets in. Now that you have a plan."

"Thank you," Sam said fervently.

"Just try not to fuck up. And Sam."

Sam braced. "Yes, sir."

Tom's faded blue eyes gleamed. "I didn't deserve her mother, either."

RALEIGH-DURHAM AIRPORT the Tuesday before Thanksgiving was crowded with comings and goings, the usual business travelers almost lost in a sea of students with backpacks and earbuds, soldiers with duffles, young families with strollers. Mothers kissing daughters, fathers hugging sons, old friends and young lovers going into each other's arms, reconnecting with relief and joy.

All going somewhere, Meg thought. Not in control of every step of the journey, but hopeful about their destinations.

Like her.

She wheeled her bag into the terminal, determined to hit Starbucks before she hit the road.

And there he was, in almost the same place. Part of the landscape of her heart, her signpost home.

Sam.

He hadn't seen her. She gave her thirsty heart a moment to drink him in. She'd missed him. They hadn't spoken in three days.

Mostly because until she made this trip, she didn't have a clue what she was going to say to him. And partly because in some small, bruised corner of her heart, she wasn't ready to forgive him.

He looked . . . rough, she decided. Oh, he'd shaved, and his Egyptian cotton shirt was pressed and rolled precisely the right amount to reveal his tanned, muscled forearms. But he looked tired. Tense. As if he wasn't getting enough sleep.

A small part of her was pleased. Why should she be the only miserable one? Then his eyes met hers, and she forgot about being miserable and mad and was simply glad to be home.

But nothing had been said, nothing had been changed between them yet.

He strode through the crowd.

Meg smiled crookedly at his approach. "We've got to stop meeting like this."

His hands brushed along her arms, down, up, finally closing on her shoulders to pull her tight. His body felt so good, so right against hers, she shivered. He kissed her, his mouth sweet and urgent. Tears pricked her eyes.

Raising his head, he said, "Or we could get used to it. Me visiting you. You visiting me."

She swallowed. "Why would we be doing that?"

His face changed, a dark flush rising on his cheekbones. "Meg, I came to tell you I'm sorry. Give me a chance. Tell me it's not too late."

"It's not . . ."

"You were right, okay? I was wrong. I shouldn't have asked you to give up a job that was important to you because I didn't think it fit whatever the hell I thought I needed. What I need is you. I love you. And if I have to fly my ass up to New York City every weekend to prove it, I will."

"Sam . . ." she said, shaken. He wasn't being charming. He was sincere.

"Don't say no. Don't. Let me finish." They were attracting a crowd. Apparently he didn't care. Her heart lodged in her throat. "I love you," he repeated. "I am so in love with you, Meggie. You're my family. You're my future. You're my life. I need you to plan with me and play with me and just be. Be with me, Meg."

"Oh, Sam, I love you, too."

He kissed her again, while soldiers and lovers, husbands and wives, parted and shifted around them. Everyone hurrying home for the holidays.

When he raised his head this time, she was smiling. "Why do you think I went to New York?" she asked.

"To accept the job."

"Yes. And no. I went to pitch the services of my agency to the partners."

"Your agency," he repeated.

"Yes." Her smile broadened. "You were right, too. I *am* excited about the possibility of branching out. I told the partners that I'll take on some of the duties of the crisis communications position, but as a subcontracted agency. My own agency."

"They agreed?"

"They're delighted. I'm highly qualified, I meet their needs, and I'm saving them a lot of money in office space and benefits."

"But then it's not as good a deal for you."

"Actually, given that the cost of living is so much lower on Dare Island, my salary is quite comparable."

"The cost of living . . ."

"On Dare Island," she confirmed.

"What about New York?"

"I'll have to go up there once or twice a month, but—"

"Is that enough?"

Why didn't he stop asking questions and kiss her some more? "The partners seem to think so."

He dragged a hand through his hair. "I meant for you. I thought you wanted the big career in the big city."

"What I want are options. Choices. My agency gives me that. Plus trips to New York when I want them." She smiled at him almost shyly. "Maybe you'd like to come with me sometimes."

"To carry your bags?"

"If that's what you're offering," she said steadily.

"I'm offering everything, Meg. My love, my life, my work, my heart."

"I want everything. And I'm offering you everything I am, everything I can be with you beside me. I love you, Sam."

His arms tightened around her. "Your father was right. I don't deserve you."

"I guess you got lucky." She stood on tiptoe to press her lips to his. "We both did."

"That's the plan."

Her laugh rippled between them. Her heart swelled, too full to contain her joy. "Good plan."

"In fact . . ." Sam smiled into her eyes. "I booked us a room already."

"Pretty sure of yourself, aren't you?"

"Damn straight. Sure that I love you. I was just praying I could convince you that you loved me."

She sighed with contentment. "I always did say you could talk anybody into anything."

"Yeah? How about . . ." He lowered his head to whisper in her ear.

Heat rose in a warm glow from her toes to her cheeks. "Why don't you take me to that hotel and find out?"

Turn the page for a preview of Virginia Kantra's next
Dare Island novel

Carolina Man

Coming soon from Berkley Sensation!

HELMAND PROVINCE, AFGHANISTAN
AUGUST

IN AFGHANISTAN, THE kids threw rocks.

Staff Sergeant Luke Fletcher watched four boys in the street take aim at an oil barrel and counted himself lucky that today, at least, they'd found another target.

He didn't dislike kids. They were sort of cute when they were under the age of five. From a distance. The kids in Iraq used to tag after the Marine patrols hoping for handouts; candy, maybe, or soccer balls or humrats—humanitarian rations.

A stone ricocheted off the metal barrel like a bullet. Twenty-three-year-old Corporal Danny Hill, sweeping the bomb wand at the front of the column, froze.

"Easy," Luke said. "It's just some kids throwing rocks at a . . ."

Shit. At a dog.

He could see it now, slinking in the shadow of the wall, just another stray, abused, malnourished, obviously feral.

Nothing he could do about it. The weak picked on the weaker. Yelling at a couple of ten-year-olds wasn't going to make them respect the dog or the law.

The dog yelped.

"Hey!" The word jerked out of him.

His tone needed no translation. The boys scattered in a flurry of jeers and stones. Nothing Luke could do about that, either.

He and his men were here to provide training and support for the Afghan National Police who would replace them. For two days their joint patrol had hiked from town to town, sweating through the afternoons, freezing through the nights, trying to buy the ANP time and breathing room to hold this desert province once the Marines were gone.

Sergeant Musa Habib, the Afghan team leader, met Luke's eyes. "You know they will be back."

He meant the kids with the rocks. Or he could have been talking about their fathers. Their brothers. The Taliban.

"You do what you can do." Luke glanced at the dun-colored mutt shrinking behind the barrel. He had too many people depending on him already. The last thing he needed was to take responsibility for a dog. "Maybe it will be gone by then."

The mutt didn't move.

Luke dug in his harness for an MRE. He'd eaten the snacks already. Ripping open the leftover meat pouch, he squeezed a chunk on the ground.

Anthony Ortega, an ex-gangbanger from East Los Angeles, grinned. "I wouldn't feed that shit to my dog."

But the mutt wasn't so picky. It poked its head out from behind the barrel. Its ears were cropped, one eye swollen nearly shut.

Nineteen-year-old Private First Class Cody Burrows whistled in sympathy. "They really messed that bastard up."

"Kids didn't do all that," Luke said.

Fresh blood oozed from a gash on its shoulder. But its other scars were older injuries, puckered and scabbed over.

"No," Habib agreed. "This dog has been used for fighting."

The mutt inched forward, quivering.

"No way that's a fighting dog," Ortega said.

"It's big enough." Hill offered his opinion.

"Often the bait dogs, they are cut like that," Habib said. "To rouse the other dogs and make them fight."

Poor mutt. Luke threw another piece of MRE. The dog's eyes rolled toward him as it took the food. Its big, black-rimmed eyes made it look like a bar girl after a bad night.

"Gee, Daddy, can we keep him?" Hill said.

"He's a she, numbnuts," farm boy Burrows said. "Look at her belly. She's gonna have puppies."

They all stood around watching the dog, like feeding some pregnant stray was the best, most entertaining thing to happen to them all day. Which it was.

"We should take her back with us," Hill said. "You saved her life. That makes you responsible for her."

Luke shook his head. "Don't give me that Zen shit."

Rescuing strays was not part of his mission. He put the rest of his MRE on the ground, watching the mutt lap it up almost delicately from the foil.

He liked dogs. His family always had a dog.

He pushed the thought of home away, rolling his shoulders to resettle his pack. "Break time's over." He looked at Habib. "What do you want to do?"

The Afghan sergeant looked momentarily surprised. But the rules had changed in the past few months. Now it was the Afghans who were supposed to step up and take the lead.

Habib cleared his throat. "We should patrol the market."

Luke nodded.

They walked the narrow alleys between residential compounds. Luke watched the doorways and roof lines, braced for sniper fire. Everything in the village was parched and brown, the color of the never-ending dust that hung like fog over the landscape. It was part of him now, engrained in his skin, choking his sinuses.

He missed the blue Carolina sky with a longing that burned the back of his throat.

The squadron emerged into the bazaar. A few stalls were open for business. Motorcycles zipped by like wasps, kicking up clouds of dust. A circle of men—village elders—squatted in the shade, surrounded by a standing ring of boys. Always boys, never girls. They kept their women out of sight. Luke's sister would have had something to say about that.

Habib looked at Luke, seeking guidance.

"Ask them how it's going," Luke said.

The new Afghan police force needed to build rapport with the community, to establish trust in the new government. He stood back, an itch between his shoulders, watching the villagers' faces as Habib and the elders went through the usual bullshit.

No Taliban, the villagers said. They hadn't seen anybody. They just wanted to be left alone.

"Is there anything we can do for them?"

No. Nothing.

"They got kids?" Luke asked.

One of the younger men nodded.

"You tell him he can go to the base if they need medical attention."

More nods, more smiles, more bullshit. It was the same in every village. The patrol moved on.

"Hey, look," Burrows said. "That dog's following us."

"Happens when a bitch gets knocked up," Ortega said.

Laughter rippled up the column, relieving the tension.

Luke looked back. Sure enough, the dog had fallen in behind the last man like a member of the patrol.

She was still with them when they made camp that night on a plateau of hard-packed gravel. They could have sheltered in the last town. But despite Luke's mission to improve community relations, he didn't trust their hosts not to report them to the Taliban while they slept.

As the temperatures plummeted, the dog crept closer, drawn by the need for warmth or food or simple companionship. Luke could sympathize. He tore open another MRE and set it on the rocky ground.

"Why do you feed it?" Habib asked.

"Staff Sergeant's our den mother. He takes care of everybody," Burrows said.

Luke couldn't take care of everybody. But by tagging along, the dog had made herself one of them. Theirs.

After ten years at war, Luke wasn't fighting for freedom and democracy. He was in this for the guys next to him, to keep them safe, to bring them home alive.

The mutt licked the wrapper, her thin tail stirring cautiously.

Out here, it was the little things that mattered. Making the world safe from global terrorism sounded good, but these days Luke measured victory one step, one sunrise, and now one dog at a time.

"You ever have a pet growing up?" he asked Habib.

The Afghan smiled wryly. "We can barely feed our families. We do not think of animals as you do."

The dog sighed and settled her head on her paws, fixing her dark, mascara-ringed eyes on Luke. Like a hooker who'd been knocked around and still hoped this time would be different. Better. *Help me. Save me. Love me.*

He looked away.

"Think she'll make it back to camp with us?" Ortega asked, seeking reassurance.

Luke didn't know. He didn't know if any of them would make it. The weight of responsibility pressed on his shoulders.

No Marine left behind.

Or dog, either.

"Sure," he said. "As long as we keep feeding her."

"She's eating for two now," Hill said.

"More like seven," Burrows said.

"How many puppies you think she's got in there?"

Luke listened to their good-natured speculation, his shoulders gradually relaxing. By the time they reached the forward outpost two days later, the mutt was taking point with Luke at the head of the column, barking to warn of the approach of other dogs or people, and Ortega was making book on the size of her litter.

No way was Luke enforcing the ban on pets on base. His men were denied enough of the comforts of home. No beer, no porn, no barbecue. Only a hard-ass would deny them a dog.

Luke had more important things to worry about.

His report made, he sat on his bunk, turning over the thin stack of MotoMail that had accumulated while he was on patrol. Three letters in five days.

The fine hair stirred on the back of his neck.

He got mail, of course. His mom, trained by twenty years as a Marine wife, sent plenty of care packages, tucking in notes with the eye drops and baby wipes, hard candy and homemade cookies. His dad always had a word during Luke's infrequent phone calls home. *Stay safe. Shoot straight.* But Dad wasn't much for writing, never had been, even when he'd been the one on deployment.

And it wasn't like Luke had a wife and kiddies back

home, sending him love letters and complaints about the toilet and scrawled crayon drawings.

He flipped to the first envelope, glancing at the return address. Katherine M. Dolan, P.L.L.C., Beaufort, North Carolina.

His brows raised. *A lawyer.*

He didn't need a lawyer. He wasn't sixteen anymore, getting pulled over for drunk driving. Anyway, no Beaufort attorney was going to solicit new clients in Afghanistan.

He ripped the envelope open.

Dear Staff Sergeant Fletcher, he read in neat type.

Okay, so this Katherine Dolan wasn't some woman he'd met in a bar during his last leave. That was good.

This office represents the estate of Dawn Marie Simpson.

Dawn. Jesus. That name took him back. All the way to high school. Pretty blond Dawn, with her wide smile and amazing breasts.

His hand tightened on the letter. And now she was . . . ?

I am sorry to tell you that Dawn is deceased as of August 9.

Dead.

Shit. Ten years in the Corps had hardened him to violence. But death came to the battlefield. Not to girls back home.

His gaze dropped back to the letter.

I am writing to inform you that Dawn left behind a minor child, Taylor Simpson, born February 2, 2003. In her will, Dawn identified you as the father of her child . . .

The tent broke around him, a kaleidoscope of shards, as his world, his heart stopped. His vision danced.

. . . and as such, named you as the child's guardian and trustee.

His heart jerked back to uneven motion. His head pounded. He didn't have a child. He couldn't. It was a damn lie. A joke. He hadn't seen Dawn in ten years, since she dumped him at the end of senior year for Bo Meekins. No way was he the father of her baby.

He read the first paragraph again. *February 2, 2003.* Not a baby. It hit him like a kick in the gut.

I understand that you are currently deployed with the U.S. military, the letter continued in crisp, impersonal type. *Pending instructions from you, Taylor is living with her maternal grandparents, Ernest and Jolene Simpson. Please advise me of your intentions for assuming parental responsibilities for your child.*

He dragged in an uneven breath. His responsibilities were here. His life was here. The familiar tent whirled and refocused around him, his surroundings assuming the flat, clear detail of a firefight: boots, locker, green wool blanket, everything coated in a fine layer of grit. Time slowed. The paper trembled slightly in his grasp.

I realize this news must come as a shock. In addition to her will, the deceased left a letter for you, which may address some of your questions and concerns. I will be happy to forward it per your instructions. Dawn was adamant that you were the right person to care for Taylor in the event of her death.

Dawn was out of her fucking mind. That was the only explanation that made sense.

I hope that you will consider your response very carefully in keeping with Taylor's best interests. Your present situation may not be conducive to the raising of a minor child. There are other options that you and I can discuss. I look forward to hearing from you. Sincerely, K. Dolan.

She was going to hear from him, all right, Luke thought grimly. As soon as he could find a damn phone.

* * *

"I WANT A paternity test," Luke said.

It had taken him four days to arrange transportation to the main camp, Leatherneck, so he could make this call. Another eight and a half hours waiting for Eastern standard time to catch up with Afghanistan so that he could talk to this lawyer person, K. Dolan, in her office. His head throbbed. His mouth was dry. His nerves stretched tight with stress and fatigue. This was not a conversation he intended to have via email. Not a conversation he wanted to have at all.

But he was determined to be responsible. Reasonable. He had no proof this kid was even his. Only Dawn's word, and Dawn was dead.

"That's understandable and practical," the lawyer said in a voice that matched her letter, crisp and dry. "If you're not a blood relative of the child, you have no real standing for custody."

Perversely, her attitude made him want to argue.

"Except for Dawn's will," he said.

"The court is not bound by Dawn's decision," the Dolan woman said. "If you want to renounce your claim to the child, her grandparents are very willing to take her."

Grandparents. God. How would his parents react to the news? They'd already rallied once, to help raise his brother's child. He couldn't ask them to . . .

But she wasn't talking about his parents, he realized. She meant Dawn's folks, Ernie and Jolene Simpson. Were they even around anymore? He vaguely recalled his mom saying they'd moved off island when the fish house closed eight years ago.

"That's not what Dawn wanted," he said.

"I don't think Dawn truly anticipated this situation ever arising. Her death was very sudden."

Dawn. Dead. He still couldn't get his mind around it. There had to be something he should say, something he could do. "When's the funeral?"

"August thirteenth."

Two weeks ago. His throat tightened.

"I'm sorry." The lawyer's voice softened slightly.

He swallowed. "Why the hell did it take you so long to contact me?" he asked roughly.

"I took the will to the clerk's office to be probated within a few days of Dawn's death. After which, I had to locate you."

"How'd you find me?" It wasn't like he and Dawn had kept in touch. He didn't even know she had a child. *He* had a child. Hell.

"Your parents still live on the island where Dawn grew up. I looked them up."

"Do they know?"

"Only that you've been named in a will that I'm probating and I needed to get in touch."

"Did you tell them it was Dawn?"

"I didn't see the need," the lawyer said coolly.

So it was up to him to tell them. To explain that while he was overseas, they had suddenly somehow become grand-parents again. "How did she die?"

"An aneurysm. A ruptured blood vessel in the brain," Dolan said, as if using little words would help him under-stand. "The doctors said it was probably the result of a con-genital condition."

"Did she suffer?"

"As I said, her death was very sudden." Did he imagine it, or did her voice shake slightly? "Dawn had a headache, a bad one. I told her to take the afternoon off. And then . . ."

"Wait. She worked for you?"

"Yes."

"Where was the kid?" *The kid*. His kid. He didn't believe it. Dawn would have told him.

Wouldn't she?

"In school," Dolan said.

Yeah, sure, the kid would be school age. Nine? Ten?

Dawn had written to him in boot camp, he remembered suddenly. Once, ten years ago, the summer after high school graduation. But try as he might, he couldn't remember anything beyond some hello-how-are-you kind of bullshit. He'd had other, more important things on his mind than a remorseful ex-girlfriend. He'd been too exhausted, or too pissed off still, to reply.

And when he'd gone home for his ten days of leave before his unit was deployed, Dawn had already left the island with ol' Bo.

Part of him had been disappointed she wasn't around to admire him in his new uniform. Maybe he'd even been hoping for one more fling for old time's sake, a little pre-deployment nookie. But he'd been relieved, too. Dawn had made it clear when she dumped him that she didn't want a boyfriend in the Marines. She was already part of his past, part of the life he was leaving behind.

How the hell was he supposed to know she had been pregnant?

He struggled to organize his thoughts. "You said she left a letter. What did it say?"

"It was sealed."

"But you're her lawyer. You could open it."

"I would have, if there had been no other way to find you. Since I was able to locate you through your parents, that wasn't necessary." The lawyer had this precise, deliberate way of speaking, like an officer covering his ass.

Luke bit back impatience. "Well, can you read it to me?"

"If that's what you want."

His teeth clenched. What he wanted didn't enter into it. This was about what needed to be done. "Yeah."

"One moment. All right. Here we go." He heard her take a breath. "'Dear Luke, I guess you never expected to hear from me again. But Kate says every parent ought to have a will naming a guardian, and I couldn't think of anybody better to raise our baby girl than you.'"

Oh, shit. He cleared his throat. "Who's Kate?"

"Me." The lawyer sounded subdued. "When Dawn came to work for me, I told her that a lot of cases I see . . ."

"Yeah, okay, I get it. Go on."

"Er . . . 'Her name is Taylor. She's wonderful, Luke. The best thing that ever happened to me. I feel bad because you haven't had a chance to see her, how special she is. Maybe you never will. I didn't figure I'd ever have to ask you for anything. We've never needed anybody, Taylor and me. But if you're reading this, then she needs you now. I love her more than anything. I hope you can, too. Take care of her for me. Dawn.'"

No explanations. No excuses. None of the answers Luke craved. Just the faint, remembered rhythm of her speech and the weight of expectations reaching across the years and miles.

His blood pounded in his head. *She needs you.*

"It'll take me a couple days to get there at least," he said.

"Excuse me?"

"I'll get emergency leave. But even with a good connection through Ramstein Air Base, it's thirty hours from Kandahar to Lejeune."

The phone was silent. Then, "I appreciate the thought. And your effort, Staff Sergeant," the lawyer said carefully. "But we need to find a long term solution for Taylor."

"That's why I'm coming home," Luke said. "I can't take care of this over the phone." *Take care of her for me.*

Another measured breath. "I hear what you're saying," the Dolan woman said almost gently. "But we have to think practically. Taylor has no relationship with you. You're a stranger to her."

I feel bad because you haven't had a chance to see her.

"So she'll meet me now," Luke said. "If she is my kid, she's entitled to military benefits. I can take her to the base, get her ID."

"Obviously, it's in Taylor's best interest to have health care," the lawyer said. "I can ask the court to grant you temporary custody, which would allow you to remove her from the Simpsons' home. But the issue of long-term care still has to be addressed. You have options. Dawn's parents . . ."

"We'll talk about it when I get there," Luke said.

After the paternity test. After he'd met her, this daughter.

The daughter he'd left behind.

Meet the Fletchers of Dare Island.

FROM *NEW YORK TIMES* BESTSELLING AUTHOR
VIRGINIA KANTRA

Carolina Home

A DARE ISLAND NOVEL

Home to the Fletcher family for generations, Dare Island is a fishing village rocked by changing times. Single dad and fishing boat captain Matt Fletcher deferred his own dreams to support his innkeeper parents and build a future for his sixteen-year-old son. Matt has learned to weather life's storms by steering a steady emotional course...and keeping a commitment-free approach to love.

Newcomer Allison Carter came to Dare Island to escape the emotional demands of her wealthy family and to make a lasting place for herself. She doesn't want to be another Woman Who Once Dated Matt Fletcher, but something far more.

Then Matt's brother, Luke, makes a sudden return home with a child of his own—and a request that will change all their lives. With a child's welfare at stake, Matt must turn to Allison to teach him to let go of the past, open his eyes...and follow his heart.

virginiakantra.com
facebook.com/VirginiaKantraBooks
facebook.com/LoveAlwaysBooks
penguin.com

M1243T0113

THE FOURTH CHILDREN OF THE SEA NOVEL FROM

VIRGINIA KANTRA

Immortal Sea

When Dr. Elizabeth Rodriguez comes with her children
to World's End, Maine, to take the open position of the
island's doctor, the last person she expects to find there is
her teenage son's father. What she doesn't realize is that
Morgan is finfolk and a leader of his people. Morgan takes
one look at the teenage Zack and realizes that Zack too is
finfolk—and his son. However, Liz and Morgan literally
come from two worlds. The attraction from sixteen years
prior is still there—but is it enough to turn to love and
bridge their differences?

penguin.com